P9-DVQ-477

Praise for *Last Christmas in Paris*

"This joint collaboration between authors Heather Webb and Hazel Gaynor is a gripping epistolary novel in the tradition of *Letters from Skye* and *The Guernsey Literary and Potato Peel Pie Society*. Beginning with heartbreaking gaiety at the start of the First World War, *Last Christmas in Paris* follows a progression of letters between a spirited female journalist, a bookish new-minted soldier, and the various bright young things who make up their band of friends, charting the slow, heartbreaking passage of years as war and disillusion grind away youthful dreams and ideals. Humor, love, tragedy, and hope make for a moving, uplifting read. A winner!"

—Kate Quinn, author of *The Alice Network*

"For fans of *The Guernsey Literary and Potato Peel Society* comes another terrific epistolary historical novel that is simply unputdownable. In a crowded historical fiction market, *Last Christmas in Paris* stands out not just for the beautiful prose, but also for the characters that literally shimmer on the page. WWI comes to life in evocative letters from the Home Front of England and the trenches of the front line, leaving the reader breathless, white-knuckled, and thoroughly engrossed. It's a novel of war and loss, but it's also a story of friendship and love, and the connections of the heart made by solid strokes of pen on paper. Kudos to Ms. Gaynor and Ms. Webb for a seamless transition between characters, and for this remarkable novel that will undoubtedly go on my keeper shelf."

—Karen White, *New York Times* bestselling author of *The Night the Lights Went Out*

"*Last Christmas in Paris* is an extraordinary epistolary novel that explores the history and aftermath of the Great War in a sensitive, memorable, and profoundly moving fashion. A book to savor, to share and discuss with friends, and above all, to cherish."

—Jennifer Robson, internationally bestselling author of *Goodnight from London* and *Somewhere in France*

Praise for *Fall of Poppies*

"With so many established and beloved names included, this title will be easy to suggest to the existing fan base of a particular writer as well as anyone looking for historical fiction with elements of intrigue and romance."

—Library Journal

"Nine internationally acclaimed authors reflect on that mystical day and time in stories of the regret, hope, valor, secrecy, redemption, and mystery that united soldiers and civilians, parents and orphans, lovers and enemies whose lives were forever changed by the Great War. . . . An atmospheric homage to one of history's most emotionally devastating episodes."

—Booklist

Last CHRISTMAS in PARIS

Also by Hazel Gaynor

The Cottingley Secret
The Girl from The Savoy
Fall of Poppies
A Memory of Violets
The Girl Who Came Home

Also by Heather Webb

Fall of Poppies
Rodin's Lover
Becoming Josephine

Last
CHRISTMAS
in PARIS

A Novel of World War I

HAZEL GAYNOR *and*
HEATHER WEBB

WILLIAM MORROW
An Imprint of HarperCollinsPublishers

This book is a work of fiction. References to real people, events, establishments, organizations, or locales are intended only to provide a sense of authenticity, and are used fictitiously. All other characters, and all incidents and dialogue, are drawn from the author's imagination and are not to be construed as real.

P.S.™ is a trademark of HarperCollins Publishers.

LAST CHRISTMAS IN PARIS. Copyright © 2017 by Hazel Gaynor and Heather Webb. All rights reserved. Printed in the United States of America. No part of this book may be used or reproduced in any manner whatsoever without written permission except in the case of brief quotations embodied in critical articles and reviews. For information, address HarperCollins Publishers, 195 Broadway, New York, NY 10007.

HarperCollins books may be purchased for educational, business, or sales promotional use. For information, please email the Special Markets Department at SPsales@harpercollins.com.

FIRST EDITION

Designed by Diahann Sturge
Snowflake background © Natali Zakharova/Shutterstock, Inc.
Eiffel Tower illustration © N-2-s/Shutterstock, Inc.
Bow on title page © pixelliebe/Shutterstock, Inc.
Map by Nick Springer. Map copyright © Springer Cartographics.

Library of Congress Cataloging-in-Publication Data has been applied for.

ISBN 978-0-06-256268-5

17 18 19 20 21 LSC 10 9 8 7

For our agent, Michelle Brower, with gratitude, awe, and love.

"Perhaps some day I shall not shrink in pain
To see the passing of the dying year,
And listen to Christmas songs again,
Although You cannot hear."

—Vera Brittain, extract from "Perhaps"

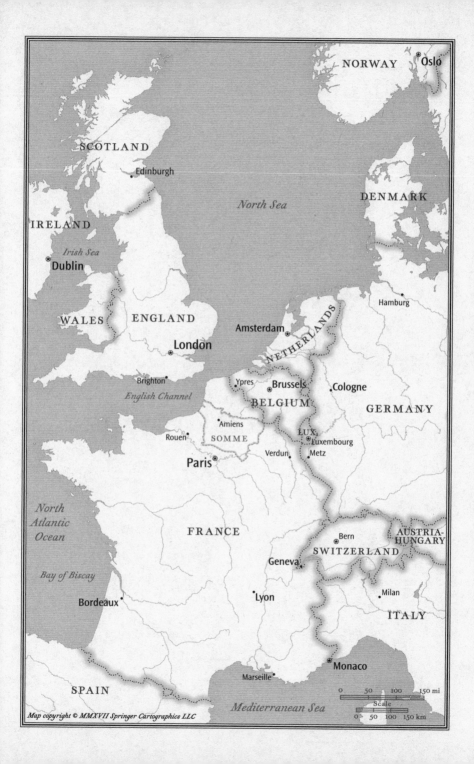

Prologue

Richmond, London
15th December, 1968

Life is forever changed without her; without the sense of her somewhere near. Empty hours wander by as I listen for the soft tread of her footfall on the stair and wait for her laughter to cheer these lifeless rooms. When I close my eyes I can conjure her; the scent of her perfume, the feather-touch of her fingertips against my cheek, those intense blue eyes looking back at me. But it is all illusion. Smoke and mirrors that conceal the truth of her absence.

I push myself up wearily from the chair, clutching my cane like an extra limb as I hobble to the window. Snow sprinkles from a soft grey sky, gathering in pockets along the river, quick to find shelter from the hungry waters of the Thames that flood the inlet behind the house. A skiff bobs to the gentle rhythm of the tide. It reminds me of how I rowed with such vigour as a young man, desperate to impress. I see her there still, sitting on the riverbank, skirt tucked behind her knees, laughing as she launches a stone and watches it sail higher and farther than the others, looping in a great arc and splashing me with its perfectly aimed descent into the water.

I see her everywhere. In everything. How can she not be here?

I feel for the necklace in my pocket, and remember how she loved to quote Miss Brontë's words. *I am no bird; and no net ensnares me: I am a free human being with an independent will.*

What a fool I was.

"Mr. Harding?" Margaret perches in the doorway. Her pristine nurse's uniform takes me back over the years to the noise and smell of field hospitals and clearing stations, and all that once was. "It's time, Thomas. The car is here."

Taking a laboured breath I rest my face against the window, savouring the icy chill of the glass against my skin. My gaze wanders over the neighbouring houses, the moody old Thames, and the view beyond the hill towards London. I, alone, know it is the last time I will look upon these places I hold most dear. The doctors tell me I don't have long. It is a reality I have made my peace with, a reality I hide from those who would only fuss if they knew the full extent of my illness—my nurse included.

"Are my letters packed, Margaret?" I ask.

"They're in your suitcase as you requested."

"All of them? The sealed letter as well?" I can't bring myself to say, "the last one."

"Yes, Thomas. All of them."

I nod. How many were there in the end? Dozens, and more. So much fear and hope captured in our words, so much longing and loss—and love. She always said her war was fought in words; her pen and prose the only weapons she, as a woman, could wield. She felt it was important to keep a record of all the correspondence, curating the memories of those years with as much determination and care as any exhibition at the British Museum. That a fragile bundle of paper sentiments survived the war when so many people were lost has always angered me, but now I am glad of them. Now, I am ready to relive those days, read through our letters one last time in Paris, as was her dying wish. I think about the sealed letter: *To be opened in Paris on Christmas Eve.* I wonder what more she might have to say.

Margaret waits patiently as I make my way across the room. She knows I am a stubborn old fool and that I will only grouse if she offers me her assistance. She glances at the window, and frowns.

"Are you sure Paris is a good idea, Mr. Harding? The snow is really coming down."

I wave her concern away. "Paris is always a good idea," I reply, my breathing heavy as I reach the door. "Especially at Christmas." I falter at my words. Words which were once hers. "And because I promised."

"I've never been." Margaret smiles brightly. "I hope we'll see the Eiffel Tower."

I mutter under my breath that it is difficult to miss and turn to take one final look at the room, moments and memories hidden beneath the dust sheets that have always turned our London home into a temporary mausoleum at this time of year. "If ever a city was made for snow, Paris is it."

She nods and holds out a tentative arm. "To Paris then, Mr. Harding? And don't spare the horses!"

Her youthful enthusiasm reminds me of an old friend and I

smile as I loop my arm through hers. "To Paris," I say. "I hope she is as beautiful as I remember."

Margaret closes the door behind us and I say a silent farewell to all those I have loved and lost, and to all the precious gifts that life has given me. If I have understood things correctly, Paris may yet have one final gift in store.

But first, I must go back to the beginning of our story, back to the beginning of a war none of us wanted, a war they said would be over by Christmas.

I keep the first bundle of letters in my pocket and as the plane taxis down the runway, I untie the red ribbon, and start to read . . .

PART ONE

1914

"They were summoned from the hillside
They were called in from the glen,
And the country found them ready
At the stirring call for men."
—*Ivor Novello, "Keep the Home Fires Burning"*

10th September, 1914

Oxford, England

Dear Father,

I write to you from the Officers' Training Corps at Oxford. I've done it—I've joined the army—so I might serve our country in these great times and prove myself an honourable citizen, just as you did during the South African War. You returned as a hero, and I wish to live up to your legacy, at least in this way. There is a real sense of adventure here, a feeling that enlisting is the right thing to do. So many men have applied for a commission with the old Bugshooters that they've had to speed up the application process. No more aiming at flies on Christ Church Meadow! This is serious business now.

I am troubled by how we left things the last time I saw you. Two grown men, especially family, shouldn't shout at each other to settle things. I know you want me to take the helm at the newspaper, but we are different people, Father. I hope one day you will understand my passion for scholarship. To become a professor at one of the most prestigious universities in the world is nothing to scoff at, though I know you disagree. At least by taking an active role in the war I won't disappoint you. War makes equals of us all. Isn't that what you once said?

Will Elliott signed up as well. In fact, we'll be in the same regiment. I thought you would be glad to see me placed with my closest friend. All believe the war will come to a speedy end, so you might expect me home by Christmas, and we can talk again then. I'm certainly looking forward to a swift victory and yuletide cheer.

Sending good wishes, Father. I will be thinking of you in battle.

Your son,

Thomas

From Evelyn Elliott to Will Elliott

12th September, 1914

Richmond, England

Dearest Will,

Mama told me about your enlisting. I expected nothing less, and wanted to send a few lines to let you know how incredibly proud we all are. The British Army will be lucky to have you. Finally, you'll have a chance to bring back some medals of your own to add to the family collection. Papa is all puffed up with pride, as I'm sure you can imagine, although I'm afraid he doesn't expect you to see much action. He expects it will be over before you've even got to your training camp. While I know you will be eager to do your bit, I hope Papa is right.

I hear Tom Harding also enlisted. You two always were inseparable, and if you must go to war then I am glad to know that your greatest friend will be with you. If this were a battle of wits and intellect, the British Army could not wish for two finer recruits, although I can hardly imagine Tom Harding rushing into battle with a rifle and bayonet. I suspect he would far rather write a thesis about it than participate in it. Keep an eye on him. You know how stubborn he can be at times.

Papa is still livid about the suspension of the last two matches of the County cricket championships, especially with Surrey on course to win again. He says September without cricket is like December without snow—it just doesn't feel right. Poor Papa. I think he feels rather left behind with all the younger men heading off to war.

Write a few lines now and again, would you? You know how Mama fusses.

Your sister,

Evie

X

From Will Elliott to Evelyn Elliott

15th September, 1914

Oxford, England

Dear Evie,

Many thanks for the vote of confidence—Tom and I are bristling with something like excitement, though that isn't quite the word. Josh and Dean are here, too, and Bill Spry; the whole College almost, off to vanquish the enemy. The bloody Krauts won't know what hit them.

Be good to Mama and Papa while I'm away. None of that mischief you're so fond of stirring up, do you hear me? I won't be there to bail you out.

With all good wishes,
Will

From Evelyn Elliott to Thomas Harding

1st October, 1914

Richmond, England

Dear Thomas Archibald Harding,

(I'm sorry—I couldn't resist the opportunity to poke a little more fun at your recently discovered middle name. How on earth did you keep that a secret all these years?)

I am really quite hopeless. You, Will, and the rest of the boys are gone less than an hour and already I find myself bored and restless. So much so that I am at Will's writing desk, penning my first letter to you. After all, I did promise to write soon, and you know how much I hate to break a promise (you may yet regret complaining of having no female relations to write to you). You know I have a dreadful tendency for overenthusiasm and I'm afraid this war may bring out my very worst best intentions. Can you ever forgive me for sending you into the

Cherwell with my overzealous punting? If I catch the post this afternoon, it is entirely possible my letter will arrive at your training camp before you do (and I give you full permission to claim it is from your sweetheart and be the envy of everyone there).

You won't be surprised to know that I envy you and Will, heading off on your grand adventure, just as I envied you when you returned to Oxford after the long vacation. It seems I must always be the one to wave you off and stay behind but I live in hope that one day I'll be the one heading off somewhere exciting. I suppose a girl can dream.

It was a lovely crowd to see you off, wasn't it? Some of the women were inconsolable, but I retained my composure, as did Mama. We are terribly proud of you all and can't wait for you to return as heroes—although, in all honesty, you looked more like a group of nervous bachelors heading to their first tea dance than a troop of soldiers heading to war. No doubt you'll look the part once you have a rifle in your hand. Send a photograph if you can. I should like to see what Thomas *Archibald* Harding looks like as a proper soldier.

Alice says I'll have to find a way to divert myself while you're gone. I have a mind to take up a new hobby. Golf, perhaps. Or maybe I'll dust off Will's bicycle and join the local ladies' bicycling club. In any event, they say the war will be over by Christmas and then all I'll have to worry about is how to survive another weary afternoon of cribbage with Mama and her friends.

If you have time to respond between drills and polishing your boots, it would be nice to know where you are and what you are doing. If I cannot go with you both to France, you will have to transport me there with your words.

Your friend,

Evelyn Maria Constance Elliott

From Evelyn to Will

1st October, 1914

Richmond, England

Dear Will,

I have just written five pages to Tom Harding—four more than I'd intended—and now I am running out of ink and words, so please forgive me if this is rather brief.

I'm sitting at your writing desk, and it wishes to inform you that it is much happier with its new occupant. Far less banging of fists and gnashing of teeth and spilt ink. You're not gone two hours and I must say that I already feel very much at home here in your room. The view over the garden is lovely. How funny that I never really appreciated it before. I can idle here now, you see, absorb the view at leisure with no mean big brother to chase me out. I might even sleep in your bed, Will. I might have a good old rummage through your drawers. I wonder what terrible secrets I might unearth!

I hope your training camp is comfortable, although no doubt a far cry from your London clubs. Don't worry. You'll be dining and dancing at The Savoy again before the year is out. Don't do anything foolish, Will, I know how impetuous you can be, and please send word as soon as you can—if not to me then at least to Mama. Spare me the misery of her inevitable fretting. Please. I will forgive you your most terrible secrets if you can just write a short letter home every now and again.

Do your duty and hurry home.

Wishing you well, and safe onward travels.

Evie

X

From Thomas Harding to Evelyn

5th October, 1914

Surrey, England

Dear Evie,

I laughed when I received your letter, just as we arrived. I suppose the postal service is faster than we think it is. And for your information, yes, I am an Archibald, and I'd happily lob an ice cream at you if you were here. Make fun, Evelyn Maria Constance Elliott, but don't forget the tree house or the horse manure and your little rag doll. I may be a proper soldier now, but I'm not above pranks and retribution!

It looks as if we'll train and learn the drill here at camp in Mytchett for four weeks, then ship off to the Front. The regiment is all enthusiasm and energy; we are all looking forward to seeing the real action. Already I've learned marching orders, basic first aid, and face-to-face combat. Your brother and I decided the training isn't so different from wrestling with Robbie Banks. That bullheaded fellow was always looking for a brawl at the pub. I'm anxious to get to the more interesting bits. Will is brimming with eagerness. You know how he can be.

You asked for a picture of what it's like at camp, so here goes. At reveille the bugle drives us out of bed at the start of the day. I say "day," but it's so early we're up hours before dawn when it's black as pitch. Still, no one grumbles about a lost hour or two of sleep, not when we're headed to war. We dress, eat, and do some variation of training until noon when we break for a short lunch, after which we have more training until four or five in the afternoon. We're free to head into town then if we wish, though not every day. Most often we hang around the billiards hall or play rounds of cards, smoke, etc. Being a lieutenant, I try to avoid getting mixed up in any mischief with the privates. Well, not too often anyway. I spend a lot of time in my bunk alone, in fact. Looking back at Oxford—and this is difficult to admit—I'm thankful for my time in the Officers' Training Corps. (Don't tell Will. He'll give me hell.) Some training, though little, was certainly better than none. Anyway, the privates really are the last rung, poor chaps. They will bear the brunt of the attacks. If I were among them, I would work like the devil so I could move up in the world.

That's all for now. Getting called to the card table.

Sincerely yours,

Lieutenant Thomas *Archibald* Harding

15th October, 1914

Richmond, England

Dear Thomas Archibald,

You replied! How jolly to see your letter among the morning post. It made for a very pleasant change from polite invitations to tea, and the rather less polite rejection of my latest attempt to have a piece published in the *Times*. Perhaps I should submit my next under a male pseudonym. If it's good enough for the lady novelist who writes as George Eliot then it's good enough for me. Evan Elliott has a rather nice ring to it, don't you think?

Joking aside, I do sometimes wish I were a boy so I could see more of the world. Even the prospect of the battlefield is more appealing right now than sitting here waiting for a marriage proposal. "Boys go to college and war. Girls marry well." This, from Papa when I complained of it being unfair earlier today.

Speaking of marriage, Mama checks the casualty lists daily for news of Charlie Gilbert. She clings desperately to the hope of my receiving a proposal from him when he returns, while I, meanwhile, hope he will fall in love with a beautiful French girl and forget all about his infatuation with me (which, as you know, I have always enthusiastically discouraged). Poor, dull Charlie. He's not a bad sort, but you know how he is—and how I am. Marrying Charlie would be rather like marrying a broken carriage clock. How the hours would drag.

Your training sounds much like dorm life at school. Didn't

they wake you with a bugle there, too? Or was it a gong? I forget. I imagine you and Will having great larks with the other
chaps. You certainly sound in very good spirits and ready for
the off. I expect the waiting is terribly frustrating. Like waiting
for Christmas—all the anticipation, and yet still no snow and
still no parcels under the tree.

Talking of Christmas, do you think it silly of me to still
hope we might manage that trip to Paris we all became rather
excited about after a few too many sherries? Papa says the city is
full of refugees and that despite the allied victory at the Marne,
it may still come under German attack again. If we do make
it, Alice Cuthbert will come to make a foursome. She's terrific
fun, and you know how fond she is of Will. (Remind him,
would you. It would make me so happy to see the two of them
together.) They say Paris is impossibly pretty at Christmastime,
and it will be just the tonic after months of fighting for you and
months of boredom for Alice and me. Let's say we'll go if we
can. *Ça va être merveilleux!* All those hours hunched over my
French textbooks may prove to be of use after all.

In quite exciting news, I am now a member of the Richmond
Lady Cyclist's Club. I mostly fall off so far, but the ladies assure
me they all struggled to control their bicycles at first, and that
I must keep practicing. I would far rather ride an unbroken
horse to be honest, but I shall persist and try again tomorrow
(you know how stubborn I can be!). If I ever do master the
art of bicycling, I have plans to ride all the way to Brighton to
visit Alice. I recently read about Tessie Reynolds's exploits in
The Lady and find myself having grand notions about dashing
around the country on two wheels. Don't tell Will.

I hope this reaches you before you head off. Papa says you won't be able to tell us where you are once you leave Mytchett in order to prevent information from falling into enemy hands. He says all letters from the Front will be censored before they reach home, so be careful of spilling any secrets or you'll be court martialed before you've pulled the trigger once.

Is there anything I can send before you ship out? Mama said you would probably be grateful for some decent tobacco. She is convinced you are all living in squalor. I've included the best Virginia I could find, just in case.

Yours in friendship,

Evie

From Will Elliott to Evie

20th October, 1914

Surrey, England

Dear Writing Desk,

Do not be fooled by Evie's charms. She is untidy and presses too hard with her pen. She will have you ruined in weeks. Please pass on my thanks for her letter (albeit half the length of the one she sent to my friend Tom) and reassure everyone at home that I am in the best of health.

Not much to report from training camp, except that we are keen to get to the Front, see an end to this and return home as swiftly as possible to reclaim what is rightfully ours, writing desks included.

Behave, Evelyn.

Yours, in ink,

Will

From Thomas to Evie

25th October, 1914

Surrey, England

Dear Evelyn Elliott,

I assure you, you look much better as a woman than a man. I can see it now, Evan Elliott in heels and skirt, riding a bicycle like a banshee from hell. Gave myself a good laugh over that one. But in all seriousness, you should keep submitting your articles. You're quite the writer. Don't let them make you believe otherwise.

Camp life is going swimmingly. Glad to be here and so proud to march on, even if it means leaving my father's struggling newspaper business behind. More on that another time.

I'm glad of your letters. Though I'm just one of a bunch of chaps playing poker at the moment, and not exactly a heroic representative of our country, I suspect at some point I'll be desperately glad to have news from home. And you're just the girl to deliver it, so thank you.

Speaking of home, are your horses spirited away somewhere?

Will worries about Shylock and Hamlet. We've seen the shipments go out—hundreds of them, or thousands, really. We've been told they're confiscating all the horses and sending them to the Front. Your brother will commit treason if his are taken. You know how he loves them. If they were to go to battle . . . Well, let's not speak of it. Do what you can.

I'm sure you've heard the Allies are holding the lines, keeping Paris relatively safe for now? The government is taking precautions, though, and moved south to Bordeaux. So it would seem, my friend, that Christmas in Paris might still be a fine idea, even without half a bottle of sherry in my stomach. We might have joked when we talked about it at first, but there's no time like the present, I say. Besides, I welcome a diversion at that time of year. Since my mother passed, I've never felt the same about the "jolliest" season, and all that. The last Christmas I spent with her was in Edinburgh when I was twelve. It snowed and we had a grand party with the rest of the family. Father never let me go to Scotland for Christmas again after that. He was so hurt and angry when she left him, and angrier still that I enjoyed spending time with the other half of my family. I suppose I should be grateful I spent so many summers there before she died. I'm planning to visit after this is all over. Scotland has always felt like my other home, you know?

Damn it, Evie. Now isn't the time for such thoughts, is it? I should have nothing but honour on my mind.

For now, I send you a hurrah for the kingdom (!) and a friendly salute (I may have had one stout too many).

Sincerely,

Lieutenant Thomas Archibald Harding

From Evie to Thomas

31st October, 1914

Richmond, England

Dear Lieutenant Thomas Archibald Harding,

(I presume formal address is a requirement now?)

Thank you for your letter. It's curious how a few lines can cheer one so greatly over a cup of tea and a slice of toast. I hope my letters are as eagerly received. It's a wonder they ever find you among so many men there at the camp. And thank you for your kind words about my writing. You are quite right. I must persevere. I suppose there will be plenty to write about with so much going on in the world.

Charlie Gilbert sent a letter last week (I won't trouble you with the romantic details). He is somewhere in France and sounds dreadfully glum, although Charlie always tends to exaggerate so I take his words with a pinch of salt, especially since the newspapers are all talk of victory and the men being in high spirits. He says they are all encouraged by the news about successful recruitment campaigns and they are eager for the latest troops to arrive.

Will sent a short note as well. He complained of the typhoid vaccination, which has left him feeling a bit green around the gills. He also enclosed a photograph of your regiment. I must say you both look terribly smart in your uniforms. The photograph has pride of place on the mantelpiece. We are immensely proud.

You ask what news from home? Not much, I'm afraid, other than to tell you that my bicycling has improved. There's a wonderful freedom in hurtling along the lanes with the wind in my hair. I don't know why I didn't learn to do it sooner. I found a wonderful little volume in Papa's library called *Handbook for Lady Cyclists*. The author, Lillias Campbell Davidson, gives the following advice on appropriate attire for cycling tours: "Wear as few petticoats as possible and have your gown made neatly and plainly of flannel without loose ends or drapery to catch in your bicycle." I'd rather wear a pair of men's trousers, but Mama would never speak to me again.

Other than swotting up on cycling tours, there's an awful fuss among next season's debutantes and their mothers who are worried sick about a lack of eligible escorts for the spring season. Please make sure to send some decent sorts back home. You are in charge, are you not? I will hold you entirely responsible for the dashed hopes of an entire generation of young women and their dressmakers if you fail in your duties.

In other news, the horses. Oh, Tom. It's really quite awful. The army have indeed requisitioned any animal that isn't already lame and Shylock and Hamlet are both gone to serve as war horses. I did my very best to plead their case, insisting they were both ruined by too much love and sugar lumps and not at all cut out for battle, but my protests fell on deaf ears. Papa says we must all do our bit—even the animals. I don't know how to tell Will. He'll be heartbroken. Perhaps you could tell him? It would be far kinder for him to hear it from a friend than in a few rotten words in a letter. Mama has organised a fund-raiser for the Royal Society for the Prevention of Cruelty to Animals

Fund for Sick and Wounded Horses at the Front. I am only too happy to help. At least it is a small way to feel useful.

I imagine you will be heading off soon to join those already fighting. I'm sure with such vast numbers of reinforcements we'll see an end to it all. The recruiting offices are inundated. It makes one extraordinarily proud to see.

Do write whenever you can, and ask Will to do the same.

Your friend,

Evie

P.S. I am sorry to hear that you have been thinking of your mother and Scotland. I suppose the prospect of war is bound to set your thoughts tumbling back to the things you have loved and lost. I've never been to Edinburgh. I hear the castle is rather impressive, but the haggis rather less so.

From Thomas to Evie

1st November, 1914

Surrey, England

Dear Evie,

I don't have much time because we're shoving off! We head to France tomorrow at first light. I'm not sure how long it will take us to get settled on the continent, but the men are in great spirits. Our grand adventure is beginning at last!

Will sends a sharp pinch and a pat on the head. (He's your big brother after all, isn't he.) I suggest you wear glasses when you ride that bicycle of yours. There's nothing worse than an eyeful of dead bugs.

Wish us luck.

Sincerely yours,

Thomas

From Thomas to his father

1st November, 1914

Surrey, England

Dear Father,

Though I haven't received a reply from you, I wanted to let you know we are heading to France tomorrow. We'll disembark at Brest and train in from there. We were warned not to share any specifics of our location since the French intelligence will strike out any information they consider a risk to our security. I'll write again from France. I hope you'll put our differences in the past and support me, Father.

As for training, you know me, I'm bringing cheer to the troops when I can. But I admit—to you, only—I'm worried about what we will face at the Front. It's easy to be swept up in the camaraderie and tales of courage before we've faced loaded artillery and the barrel of a gun. I suppose you know this all too well. At times I still feel like the little boy on your knee, wishing he were all grown up. I suspect I'll do a lot of growing up soon.

Your son,
Thomas

From Evie to Alice Cuthbert

5th November, 1914

Richmond, England

Dear Alice,

A few lines to say hello to my dearest friend and to tell you how miserable I am.

I'm sorry to be glum, but you are the only one I can tell. To everyone else I must be all cheer and chin up but, you see, the boys left their training camp and shipped out to the Front a few days ago and a silly part of me worries terribly for them. I know I shouldn't, and that the newspapers are full of encouraging news of all our wonderful victories and our brave soldiers, but Charlie Gilbert wrote recently and his words troubled me (he didn't propose, in case you were wondering). He says war is very different to what he thought it would be and there is very little chivalry or heroism about it at all, regardless of what the newspapers report. He says the men are as cheery as can be expected but they all pray for conscription to come into force as they are in desperate need of reinforcements. I can't help worrying that things are not going as well over there as the newspapers would have us believe. The casualty lists take up more column inches every day. Am I silly to worry? Please tell me I am. And if I am silly to worry, then you mustn't either. I know how you were hoping for a dance with Will at Mama's Christmas Ball so we must trust that it will still happen.

The problem is I have too much time to dwell on things. I can't picture what war looks like, or where the boys are. When they were at Oxford it was different. I knew the dreaming spires and the Bodleian Library. I spent lazy summer afternoons punting on the Cherwell. Now, it feels as though they have gone to the ends of the earth—to some undiscovered land I know nothing about. And I can't help feeling terribly afraid.

I can't even go out for a decent hack to take my mind off things because the horses have been shipped out, too. I've asked Mama to give me permission to volunteer in some capacity—I hear women are getting involved in all sorts of ways: working on the omnibuses, serving as War Office clerks, delivering the post—but she won't hear of it. She says the best thing I can do to help is join her knitting circle. I can think of nothing worse. You know how useless I am with knitting needles. Perhaps if I have someone's eye out, she'll be happy to let me work on the omnibuses instead.

Anyway, I'm sure—as they say—it will all be over soon and we can get back to thinking about happier things. Christmas, for one. I still love the idea of Paris and hope you were serious

when you said you would come. Everything is always much
more fun when you're there, Alice.

Write soon. Cheer me up. Send me something wonderful or
shocking to read. Tell me about the latest unfortunate young
fellow to have fallen head over heels in love with you.

Much love,

Evie

X

P.S. I am now a lady cyclist. Terrific fun. You must try it.

From Evie to Charlie Gilbert

10th November, 1914

Richmond, England

Dear Charlie,

A few lines to thank you for your latest letter. You sound a
little blue. It must be terribly difficult for you there, but everyone back home is full of hope that we will see an end to it very
soon.

Don't worry about writing so often. I know it must be hard
to find the time, or the words. You must concentrate on staying
fit and healthy and leading your men to victory.

We are all very proud, and send good cheer to the troops.

Sincerely yours,

Evelyn

From Thomas to Evie

20th November, 1914

Somewhere in France

Dear Evie,

I'm in France now, and I think we're settled for a while so I can write again with our latest address. Things turned rather hectic after my last letter. They needed our regiment overseas immediately and cut our training short, though it continues here. They've got me set to be a machine gunner and Will is being trained as a grenadier. I must say, for the first time I feel like a man. No more boyish Oxford days. I have responsibilities to my troops, and I enjoy being in charge.

I still haven't worked up the courage to tell Will about the horses. I'm guessing he already knows, deep down. As for Charlie Gilbert, I assume he's still sweet on you? I think you're a little hard on him. He's a decent fellow and you could do a lot worse. If this war sees an end to us all, you might not have much choice in the matter anyway. I know he's your mother's first choice for a "suitable" fiancé, though I am the last to listen to my father so I suppose I can't very well comment on following parental advice, can I?

Things are tense here at ▆▆▆▆▆▆, but that's to be expected. We're no longer playing at war, it's the real thing. My toes are thoroughly drenched and aching, but my spirits are high. All is going swiftly now. There's still hope this will end by Christmas, and we can indulge in our Parisian plans for *vin chaud* and *boeuf bourguignon*.

Sincerely yours,
Lieutenant Thomas Harding

From Evie to Thomas

25th November, 1914

Richmond, England

Dear Thomas,

Bonjour, mon ami! What a relief to hear from you—and Will, whose note arrived on the same day (perhaps just use one envelope?). I hope the crossing wasn't too choppy. Will feels seasick on the Thames, let alone the English Channel.

Get the job done and come back soon, would you. All the reports in the newspapers are very positive and full of allied victories and good news. The censors struck out a few lines from your last letter, but I got the sense of most of it and I'm glad to hear you are all in good cheer.

I've enclosed a knitted scarf. It's my first attempt, so please forgive the rather unusual shape. If it can't keep you warm it might at least make you laugh. I'm attempting socks next, so prepare yourself!

Stay safe.

Bonne chance!

Your friend,
Evelyn

From Evie to Will

Richmond, England

Dear Will,

Bonjour!

A few words to let you know that your sister, Evelyn, has taken up permanent residence in your room. She sits for hours beside the fire, writing letters here, there, and everywhere. She says it prevents the tedium of knitting duty and is certain you'll find her letters far more comforting than badly constructed socks.

She spends a lot of time staring out of the window, too. She watched the swallows migrate one calm October evening and looks forward to their return. She watches the robins and blue tits now. Sometimes she sketches their likeness in the margins of her writing paper. She'd forgotten how much she likes to draw. She isn't too bad really.

She also asks me to tell you that the horses were taken to war and begs you not to be too heartbroken. They are the most wonderful animals and will give someone the best ride into battle. We all must do our bit, and she knows you will be as proud of the horses as she is of you. She insists you take good care of yourself because she finds herself feeling terribly fond of her only brother now that he, and his endless teasing, is far away.

She has also enclosed a few sheets of Basildon Bond which

she hopes you will be able to fill with cheery news of victories and your imminent homecoming.

With greatest fondness,

The Writing Desk

P.S. Evie has also become rather fond of your old bicycle (which she has christened Rusty). You would laugh to see her flying along the laneways. She still takes the occasional spill when she encounters a pothole, but is otherwise quite accomplished.

From Alice Cuthbert to Evie

1st December, 1914

Brighton, England

Dear Evie,

Greetings, love. I had just returned from a day of shooting grouse (only a few days left of the season and you know how I like to handle a gun) when I saw your envelope peeking out of my letter box. Unfortunately it was quite soggy. My room-mate never brings in the post, or hangs her coat, or shakes out her eternally soaked brolly before she comes inside and drops everything on the sofa. I should have known better than to ask Margie Samson to move in with me. I was desperate, though, as you know. There aren't many "respectable girls" from proper families who allow their daughters to live on their own. (Not that I've ever waited for a lick of permission for anything.)

Try not to worry too much about our boys at war. They'll be trained tip-top, do their thing, and be home in a jiff. We'll celebrate madly when they return. I bet your brother is handsome as ever in his uniform. My heart flutters to think of it.

I'll be in Richmond next Wednesday, so I'll call. Shall we sneak off for a little Christmas shopping? I don't have a fellow these days. It's time we both enjoyed a little mischief.

Alice

XX

From Evie to Will

7th December, 1914

Richmond, England

Dearest brother,

How are you? Please send word, even if you can only send one of those awful Field Service Postcards. Just to know that you are safe and in good spirits will be comfort enough. Or send a few lines in the letters Tom writes. He and I have become quite good pen pals these past months.

I often wander into your room, fully expecting to see you stretched out on your bed like a lazy cat. There's a strange sense of emptiness here, as if the walls ache for your return. I know you are a very private man and will no doubt hate to think of your little sister having unrestricted access to your room, but it somehow feels right to be in here when I am thinking of what to say to you. How silly, to have to *think* of some news to share. I miss the spontaneity of conversation. I miss seeing you; hearing your voice. Letters are so tricky to write when there is so much to say, and yet nothing to say at all. And the silence between replies is agony.

Mama is being unusually stalwart, organising endless fund-raisers and finding jobs where there are none. "We will not be idle while the men are away" has become her personal motto since we waved you off. I have a feeling this war may yet prove to be more dangerous for those of us left under the command of fretful mothers than for you soldiers under the command of your Generals.

It doesn't look as though it will be over by Christmas after all, does it? You'll be much missed around the dinner table, although I shan't miss your dreadful jokes.

Well, I must close before I start filling the pages with too much gushing fondness. Alice Cuthbert sends her regards. She came to Richmond last week and dragged me into London for some shopping. She really is a tonic. She insisted we take our minds off things with tea at Fortnum & Mason, although neither of us could quite summon up the enthusiasm for it. Everything tastes rather bland when taken with a dose of guilt and worry. You will drop her a line or two, won't you? She is rather depending on it.

Wishing you a *Joyeux Noël* from afar.

Your loving sister,

Evie

XX

P.S. I have enclosed tobacco, and a Christmas pudding from Cook. She put extra brandy in it especially for you. I hope the silver sixpence brings you all the luck in the world. More than anything, I hope luck and fortune bring you home very soon.

From Evie to Thomas

8th December, 1914

Richmond, England

Dear Thomas,

Hello again! How are you? We read plenty of good news in the papers, which cheers us, although we would far rather there was no news at all and we had you all home again.

I thought you might be amused to hear that with only three weeks until Christmas we have a crisis on our hands. A fox found his way into the Allenbury's huts and helped himself to our Christmas dinner. Poor Mama is beside herself. I honestly believe she has diminished in height by a good inch since hearing the news. And we are not the only household to find ourselves goose-less; practically half of Richmond is in the same predicament.

I wonder, will you celebrate Christmas at all? Celebrate seems like the wrong word. I suppose jolly occasions such as Christmas and birthdays have no place at the Front, although part of me hopes that an instruction will find its way down the wires to stop fighting, for Christmas Day at least. Our little plan to spend Christmas in Paris seems rather like a silly dream now, doesn't it. Next Christmas then?

How are your toes? You complained of them giving you trouble in your last letter, although I can never be sure if you are being serious or teasing me. Such is the burden of having a brother who was popular in school: having to tolerate the endless teasing of his wicked friends. In any event, I have sent you some socks (poorly knitted by my obstinate fingers, which would much rather have been sketching or writing than twirling wool around infuriating needles). Everyone is knitting comforts for the troops these days. Socks, hats, gloves. The entire nation seems to move to the *click clack* of knitting needles. It is all we women can do to help, and for those of us not blessed with nimble fingers and a steady hand, this is rather unfortunate. I hope the enclosed OXO cubes and tobacco make up for the "socks."

Cook has sent a pudding. She insisted, although I told her you were never especially fond of plum pudding. She's been steeping the fruit for weeks so I couldn't bear to decline. Also, I read in the papers that Princess Mary is raising funds to send a Christmas parcel to British troops. You must write to tell me if you receive one. Is there anything else you need? I hear lice powder is helpful, although I shudder to think of it. Is this true?

Alice Cuthbert visited recently. It was wonderful to see her again, but it was far too brief and only made me wish she lived closer. I could use a daily dose of her good cheer. We lamented the postponement of our plans for a Parisian Christmas, and settled on a stroll down Regent Street instead to look at the shop windows. They are very pretty, decorated with Union Jacks and patriotism and festive wishes to our brave soldiers. It brings a lump to one's throat.

Well, I must close. We have a goose to find or Christmas must be cancelled. Please send my regards to that dreadful brother of mine. We've still only had a few letters from him, and all of them too brief. Perhaps you could give him some instruction in letter writing. You have a particular talent for it.

With all good wishes for the festive season, and remember we are incredibly proud, and think of you often. More often than you might believe.

Your friend,
Evie Elliott

P.S. The lanes are too icy for cycling. My trusty steed, Rusty, has been stabled for the winter. My mad dash to Brighton will have to wait until the spring.

From Thomas to Evie

10th December, 1914

Somewhere in France

Dear Evie,

I'm sorry I haven't written the last couple of weeks. Lots happening here with new troops arriving, and my responsibilities have shifted.

The socks you knitted are jolly things! Perfect in their Oxford blue and white, even if the stripes are a bit jagged. I imagine Miss Needham would have rapped your knuckles each time you missed a stitch. She'd rap anyone's knuckles given half an excuse. What a mean old windbag for a governess you had. Will and I used to fill her wellies with sand, do you remember? We would do the dirty deed, and launch off the back porch, laughing so loud the whole house could hear us. She would tear after us then at full tilt, chasing us with a broom as we raced to the river's edge like rabbits. She never did catch us. Maybe secretly she wanted us to get away. She always had a twinkle in her eye when she yelled at us.

As for your poor fingers, I can understand a stabbing needle pain with the best of them. We spent three days in the trenches this week without sleep, and only a few stale loaves of bread to keep us company. The cold was mind-numbing, Evie. I could barely load my gun. That's not a good thing when the enemy is so close you can hear him pant in fear, or rummage through his stash of bullets. War is nothing like I expected it to be. An adventure, certainly, but I didn't count on the way it would destroy my easy view of things, make me ache for home and the simplicity I had taken for granted, like the solitude of my bedroom, or a cup of scalding tea first thing in the morning. I dream about taking my skiff out on the inlet behind the house, and watching the dandelion seeds float by until they descend and skate across the pond's surface. It all seems like a lifetime ago.

Tell Cook her pudding was the best I ever ate. There are few pleasures these days, but I appreciate her care. And the tobacco! I'll ration it into the New Year, if I can manage. You're a peach for sending. Speaking of tobacco, we all received the Christmas gift from Princess Mary: a tin with a sachet of tobacco and letter-writing tools. She tucked a signed letter under the lid as well. It was generous of her to go to such trouble for the soldiers. We're all very grateful for these small tokens from home.

Your brother is making a nuisance of himself among the nurses at the field hospital here. He seems to have set his sights on a French nurse. The poor girl will be heartbroken by the New Year, without doubt. But don't let on I told you. You know how secretive he likes to be about his girls. I may visit the nurse myself this week, show her my dreadful toes (which are slightly better because of the socks you sent).

I keep thinking about our plans for Christmas and try not to become discouraged. Still, I'll go on hoping that the war will end in the next couple of weeks, and that I'll be home to enjoy some festive cheer. I'd like to see that pretty smile on your face, reminding me there's still plenty of happiness out there waiting for us.

Sincerely yours,

Lieutenant Thomas Harding

P.S. I've enclosed a note from Will. I think he may have strained his hand writing it.

From Will to Evie

Dear Evie,

I'm not much for writing, as you know, but I'll try to make use of the stationery you sent. We spend long hours doing nothing at times, so your letters are a welcome distraction. Don't tell Papa, but I've been enjoying his stash of Cuban cigars. I took every last one I could find before I left. I figured a man at war needed something to look forward to.

You shouldn't spend so much time in the house, especially not in *my* room. It isn't good for you. You never were the idle sort. Less letter writing and more bicycling. I insist.

Your loving brother,
Will

P.S. Please pass on my regards to Alice. Tell her I will take her dancing when I return.

From Evie to Alice

13th December, 1914

Richmond, England

Dearest Alice,

Dreadful news. Charlie Gilbert is dead. Killed in action. Papa saw his name in the casualty lists yesterday. I'm afraid I'm taking it rather badly and Mama is distraught.

Poor Charlie. He may not have set my heart alight or my mind spinning with intellectual thought, but he was a good man. I didn't wish to marry him, Alice, but never did I wish him dead. And now I can hardly sleep for worrying about Will, and Tom Harding and the other boys. Any death is a sobering reminder of the dangers they face. The death of someone who might very well have become one's husband—it is all so terribly upsetting.

Goodness, Alice. However did this happen to us? To us?

Please come and visit again soon. I am in desperate need of your endless good cheer.

Evie

X

From Evie to Thomas

15th December, 1914

Richmond, England

Dear Thomas,

I'm sorry I haven't written in a while. You might have heard about poor Charlie Gilbert. He was killed in action. Shelling, I believe. I'm afraid I have taken the news rather badly.

It's difficult to think of you and Will in the trenches, hunkered down in your dugouts while I sleep in comfort. You'll think me silly but I slept on the floor last night, with only a thin blanket for warmth. A troubled mind and a cold hard floor do not make for the best bedfellows but I plan to do it again tonight. Every night, until you come home. It won't be long now, will it?

I expect you'll also have heard about the bombing of Scarborough. Seventeen innocent lives lost. Women and children among them. Ninety minutes of shelling from the German ships, the papers are reporting. What unimaginable horror. The War Office already has posters up saying: Remember Scarborough and Enlist Today. People are angry, Tom. And rightfully so.

Sometimes, when I wake in the morning, I pretend it is all a dream and that Will is taking breakfast downstairs and you'll arrive shortly with some outlandish scheme or other for an outing to Somerset to drink scrumpy cider. I don't even care for scrumpy cider, but I would drink it all the same.

At least you still have time to think of love and romance—or at least my brother does. I'm encouraged to hear he is making a nuisance of himself among the nurses. The poor girls won't stand a chance against his amorous advances. Is this French girl very pretty? There's nothing like a foreign accent to turn a man's heart—she must be quite impossible to resist. How quickly Will forgets his flirtations with Alice. You might remind him of the saying "absence makes the heart grow fonder." Alice still hopes to hear a few lines from him but I won't breathe a word to her of this nurse (does she have a name?). Promise to keep me fully informed of any romantic developments?

In less romantic news, we finally have a goose. Not as big as Mama would like, but a goose nonetheless. She forgets (or denies) that we have several fewer mouths to feed this year. I hardly dare mention it. She becomes wretched at the slightest mention of war. None of us can really believe you'll be away for Christmas, especially since they promised us it would be over. So much for our Parisian plans.

Join me in a little daydreaming, Tom, will you? Look, there we are strolling along the Champs-Élysées, marvelling at the Arc de Triomphe as fat snowflakes tumble from a soft sky. There we stand, watching the artists at Montmartre, the soaring majesty of the Sacré-Coeur behind us. *C'est si beau.* And look at us now, tipping our necks right back so that we can gaze up at the soaring heights of la tour Eiffel. There are three hundred steps up to the top, you know. I'll race you!

My foolish heart clings to these happier thoughts. But it isn't just the charm of the capital city that pulls me towards France. You'll think me silly to say it but part of me longs to be closer to the war. I need to *DO* something, Tom. Anything, except sit here wondering and worrying.

Do take care, and if I don't hear from you before, have the happiest Christmas it is possible to have there. We will be thinking of you at every waking moment, and in our dreams.

Joyeux Noël.

Yours,

Evie

From Thomas to Evie

20th December, 1914

Somewhere in France

Dear Evie,

As I sit here in my bunker, completing the never-ending paperwork for my superiors, I'm dreaming of oysters and champagne, roasted chestnuts dusted with sugar, a roaring fire. I never was one for dancing, but I'd give my right hand to be at your mother's Christmas party right now. Last year I only danced twice—once with you and once with your mother, if you recall—and then I scooted off to the fringes for another scotch. You wore a peacock-blue dress and sparkled like the tinsel on the tree. After a while, the heat in the ballroom had me running for the garden. You found me there and we shared a cigarette beside the rose bushes. Do you remember? I gave you my jacket to keep you warm. That's when we found your brother huddled behind the holly hedges with Hattie Greenfield. Will and his women!

Will's French nurse is called Amandine Morel. A pretty French girl named after an almond flower—a perfect opportunity for bad poetry if ever there was one. I have to admit, I envy him the distraction. I'm rather glum. Battles rage on, regardless of season or sacrifice.

My father wrote at last. He seems disappointed I'm not coming home for Christmas, which cheers me a little. The last time I saw him we had a dreadful argument and haven't spoken since, so his few lines show progress, I suppose. The thing is, Evie, I have little interest in running the *London Daily Times*. It's not the sort of work I see myself doing—I'm not interested in chasing the next story to make a few quid or become a star reporter. Nor do I care about status. Frankly, I don't see why we can't hire someone else to do it, or pass it along to the next of kin, but Father won't hear of it. He's never understood my passion for literature and yet, isn't that what he does, at least in the most basic sense—share stories with the public? Perhaps I'm a fool to think we can bridge this gap between us.

Forgive me for becoming sentimental. I'm certain this isn't the sort of thing you were hoping to read in my letters.

Paris will have to wait until next year, if it is still standing. I'm sure all will be well and done by then. This war can't go on much longer.

Think of me when you slice into that goose. I'll be imagining it and a fat helping of gravy.

Happy Christmas, dear girl.

Sincerely yours,

Thomas

Paris

15th December, 1968

Paris greets me like an old friend, open-armed and joyous. As our taxi navigates the winding streets, I sit in silence and watch the snow fall from a rose-tinted sky. The city never looked more beautiful.

After the long journey, I am relieved to see the familiar outline of the apartment building on the rue Saint-Germaine, our Parisian home-away-from-home, our own little corner of France, as she called it.

When Margaret finally concedes that I am comfortable and warm and not in any immediate danger of taking a tumble from the balcony, she heads out to discover the city for herself. I envy her the delight of seeing it all for the first time—taking a stroll along the Place de la Concorde, discovering the local delicacies, absorbing it all with the exuberance of youth—and yet I am grateful for the solitude her absence gives me; a moment alone with my memories. And what riches they offer.

I doze for a while, dreaming of walks in the rain in the Jardin du Luxembourg, smiling as she laughs and shakes the damp from her hair. They are pleasant dreams in which I am still a vibrant young man, utterly enchanted by her, and she is still here and not so recently taken from me. It makes waking so unbearable, but wake, I must.

Too soon, Margaret returns with a thud of the heavy front

door, bringing the sharp scent of cold and the aroma of roasted chestnuts inside with her. She chatters on with tremendous excitement about the market stalls and the patisseries, the lights along the Seine, the beauty of it all.

"Oh, Mr. Harding, how romantic it all is," she enthuses as she shakes out her polka-dotted headscarf. "No wonder they call it the city of lights. *J'adore, Paris!*"

I manage a smile. I know something of the romance of this City of Lights; how it can steal your heart as easily as a glance from the person you adore more than any other in the world.

Snowflakes pepper the mahogany strands of Margaret's hair, and dust the shoulders of her coat. Her cheeks glow with that rare kind of excitement one only gets in Paris at this time of year. Her arms are laden with Christmas treats and packages which she lays out on the kitchen table, recounting each of her prizes: wedges of cheese, sugared beignets and almond biscuits, rosewater soaps crafted in the luxuriant French style, and a bundle of holly berries tied with ribbon. But it's the spiced aroma of *vin chaud* that sends my senses soaring, and in the flames of the fire I see the woman whose smile could buoy me on the worst of days. There she is, cradling a goblet of warm wine in her hands, her gaze fixed upon mine, her cheeks aglow with life.

My heart thuds a painful beat. The irregular rhythm of grief.

"Oh! I almost forgot." Margaret pulls a letter from her handbag. "This was in the mailbox downstairs. I presume it is from Delphine. You were clever to have her send her response here. You would have missed it in London."

Nodding, I take the letter from her, noting Delphine's familiar handwriting on the envelope. Dear Delphine. I will be so glad to see her again. I open the envelope carefully and unfold the perfumed square of paper inside.

14th December, 1968

Dear Tom,

I am, of course, delighted to hear you are coming to Paris for Christmas, although I must admit, I am a little worried about you making the long journey. I would counsel against it, but I know you won't change your mind once it is already made up, so I will simply say that I am looking forward to seeing you again.

I know it will be especially difficult for you to be here this year, but it wouldn't be the same without you. We will make the best of things and find some of that *vin chaud* you're so fond of.

I will call the apartment in a few days' time to check you have arrived safely.

With warmest affection,

Delphine

My hands tremble as I fold the page and return it to the envelope. So many distant faces and memories flicker to life, stubborn flames that will not die.

"Is everything all right, Mr. Harding?"

I nod, and turn to my nurse. "Yes, Margaret. Except my cup appears to be empty. A little more *vin chaud*, perhaps?" She hesitates. I know the thoughts that cross her mind: What about his medication? Is a little more wine a good idea? "It seems a shame to waste it," I press.

She smiles and fills my cup, and her own, before raising hers to mine. *"Salut, Monsieur Harding. Joyeux Noël."*

"Merry Christmas, Margaret."

I cradle the warm mug in my hand and leave Margaret to admire her packages as I take the next bundle of letters from the writing table beside me. *1915.* She was so meticulous in her organisation. The next year of the war. The next year of our story.

Before I continue reading, I glance towards the window. Silently, I make a promise to the snow clouds that lace the sky, and wish a Merry Christmas to those I hold most dear in my heart . . .

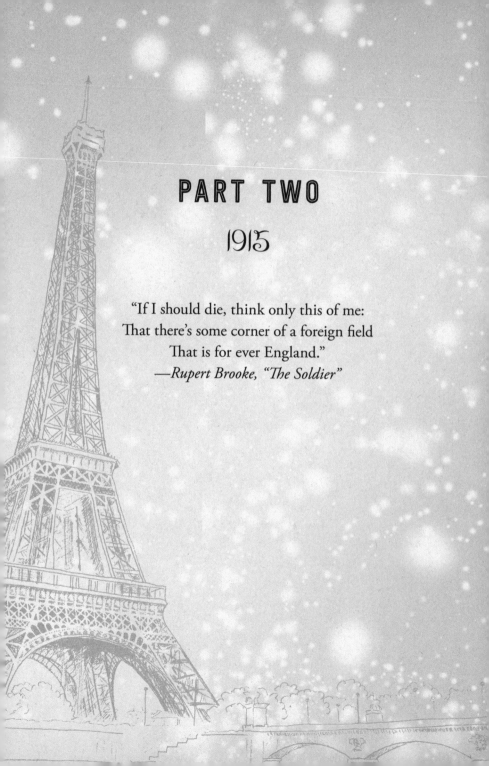

PART TWO

1915

"If I should die, think only this of me:
That there's some corner of a foreign field
That is for ever England."
—*Rupert Brooke, "The Soldier"*

From Evie to Thomas

1st January, ~~1914~~ 1915

Richmond, England

Dear Lieutenant Harding,

Bonne année! I still can't get used to your official title. Most unlike the young fool Tom Harding whom I remember shooting at sparrows on the lawn. So much is changing, Tom. I can hardly remember you and Will as rowdy young boys in short trousers, running among the flowerbeds with your peashooters. How could we have possibly known how real those boyhood games would become?

So, here we are in 1915 and I must wish you a Happy New Year, although I cannot find much to be happy about as war creeps on, and ever closer to home. There was more bombing here—on Christmas Eve, would you believe. We read about it in the papers. Thankfully nobody was injured or killed this time. A rectory gardener was thrown from the tree he was pruning. Poor chap. War felt so distant at first, but not anymore. What if they start to drop bombs on London? Hurry up and finish them off, would you?

Alice would tell me to be more positive—and she is right. I do hope my letters cheer you and make you smile and remind you of home, and what better time to look ahead than on the first day of a new year. A whole unblemished twelve months stretching out before us like a blank ream of writing paper waiting to be filled. I keep telling Mama to stop looking back on what was or what might have been (she still weeps at the mention of Charlie Gilbert and the marriage proposal he took with him to his soldier's grave). I remind her constantly that all we can do—what we *must* do—is look forward to better times, and dancing at The Ritz.

You are sweet to recall the dress I wore at last year's Christmas party. I had forgotten it entirely. I wore it again this year, in your honour, although nobody offered me a puff of their cigarette, or their jacket, or told me I looked bewitching beneath the winter moonlight. Do I make you blush, Tom? Had you forgotten how your compliments flowed as easily as the wine?

I only tease you because I have little else to do.

In other news, we have an infestation of mice. I hear them scampering behind the skirting boards and the chimney breast. It makes me shudder to hear the *scritch scratch* of their dreadful little claws. Mills has put traps down and I can tell you there is nothing more unpleasant than the *snap* and *crack* they make when they are sprung. It turns my stomach. So much so that I am on the hunt for a good mouser. I'm not especially fond of cats, but anything must be preferable to that dreadful sound. I've put a notice in the post office window and eagerly await a reply.

While I was at the post office, I had a rather interesting conversation with the postmistress. She told me that with all the men gone, they are looking for women to assist in the sorting and delivery of the post. Of course Mama won't hear of my applying for such a position, but I believe I could do the job, and rather well. I have my bicycle after all, and what I wouldn't give to get out of the house and away from Mama's continual scrutiny. She says I will never find a husband if I don't start taking more care in my appearance. With Charlie out of the picture she is on the lookout for a suitable replacement for my future husband. Be careful, Thomas. She may yet set her sights on you as a last resort!

I hope Christmas was bearable over there. How long we anticipate it and how quickly it passes. We did our best to keep things jolly here, but of course we felt the absence of friends and family around the table and found it hard to fully embrace the festivities. It's a curious thing, but we try not to talk about the war too much. We have developed a strange sort of code—"I wonder how they are getting on. You know. Over there." "Any news. You know. From . . . you know." We don't say "war." We don't say "France" or "Belgium" or "the Germans." Our words trail off, midsentence, so that I imagine a great hole in the ground where our unspoken thoughts and fears drift around, lost forever. Good riddance to them, I say.

Honestly Tom, I feel like an unworn dress, hanging limply in the closet, without purpose or shape or form. All I am good for is writing notices for the post office window and worrying about mice. Perhaps I'll read up on the care and treatment of toes so that I can volunteer as a nurse and join you and Will out there. Anything would be better than pacing the boards here at Poplars. The house is like a morgue. Truly. It is unbearable.

Did I mention I have the most wonderful surprise for Will when he gets home? I commissioned a portrait of Hamlet and Shylock, and matching miniatures set into a pair of cuff links.

They are so beautiful. I was hoping they would be ready for Christmas, but the artist caught a fever and has only just finished them. I'll keep them here to surprise Will as a welcome home gift.

Do take care, Lieutenant Harding, and don't worry. Before you can sing ten rounds of "It's a Long Way to Tipperary," you'll be back to plain old Tom Archibald Harding, sculling that little boat of yours lazily along the Thames towards Teddington Lock or Hampton Court. The herons will stand to attention on the riverbank and salute you for everything you have done for King and country. Such dreams we must cling to with all our might.

To quote William Blake: "The Land of Dreams is better far, Above the light of the morning star."

All best wishes,

Evelyn Maria Constance Elliott

P.S. More socks enclosed. I think I might be improving.

From Mr. Charles Abshire to Thomas

2nd January, 1915

London, England

Dear Thomas,

Greetings, my boy. I'm writing on behalf of your father. I don't wish to alarm you, but he has been rather unwell the last few weeks and is having difficulty in his recovery. I will continue to write for him when he requests, as well as see to things at the *London Daily Times* when possible. As you know, my duties are numerous already with the keeping of the books, but I will do my best for now. Should your father's health not improve in another couple of weeks, I may call in your cousin, John Hopper, to assist in running the office. I trust that will be acceptable?

Please take care in France. We look forward to welcoming you home.

Sincerely yours,
Charles Abshire

From Thomas to Evie

4th January, 1915

Somewhere in France

Dear Evelyn Maria Constance Elliott,

Happy New Year, though it sounds as if the newness has already worn off. I heard about the raids. We were outraged here at the Front, though a Frenchman put us in our places quickly enough. He pitched his cigarette butt to the ground and said, "You have a few air raids and you are angry. We lose our homes and families, the beauty of our country, our pride. We lose everything! When this war is over, you will return to a few broken buildings, and we return to desolation. *Rien de tout!*"

He's right. What the French have lost and continue to lose will leave a great chasm. Rebuilding for them may continue the rest of our lifetime. The Frenchman's tirade happened just before your latest package arrived. I patted the chap on the shoulder and gave him one of the precious pairs of socks you sent (I hope you don't mind). He smiled ruefully and nodded his thanks. He wears them as gloves. We're all in this together, as much as one can be.

Speaking of socks, thank you! Pair after pair of them. I can't tell you how glad I was to see them. I miss dry feet most of all. I'm lucky, though, being a lieutenant and all. They rotate my position more often than the privates. Poor bastards. I have to admit, I'm plagued with guilt and melancholy when I lose a man. With only around fifty in my command, I feel his absence keenly, and envision the King's letter arriving on his family's doorstep, announcing that he's gone. A wretched business.

Your brother's affections for Amandine do not abate. In fact, he seems pretty serious about her. I thought he would move on quickly enough, but hasn't. You know how he is. One flash of his smile and every girl within ten feet of him swoons at those baby blues. Me, on the other hand? A ginger-haired, barrel-chested giant isn't what most girls fall for, is it? It's just my luck to be a replica of my uncle—the most detested man in the family. I got his brains, too, though. That's something, I suppose.

You hoped we would cease our fighting for Christmas Day. Well, much to my shock and that of all the other men, my commanding officer called a truce for the day. We crawled out of our holes, the Germans too, and shared a biscuit or two sent from home, or a smoke. Evie, to lay down our arms and shake hands with the Germans like comrades—I can't describe how incredible it was. Here I was, sharing a few hours with the very men who caused so much damage in the first place. Imagine the trust we had to show, to step into no man's land unarmed and befriend the enemy, even if only for a little while. Feeling like men again made us all a little giddy.

The whole evening was pleasant, if one could call Christmas at war such a word. A hard frost killed some of the water, making my post in the mud more bearable. When night fell, I even saw stars and the moon, instead of more soaking rains. And you'll never believe this when I tell you, but we sang Christmas carols. Imagine it. A pack of filthy soldiers, German and English alike, serenading each other with hymns. All this after General Smith-Dorrien warned us off from fraternising with the enemy. I ask you this: How am I to hate a man when I smell his breakfast cooking each morning, or hear him crying out in anguish only feet away? It was a relief and much-needed reprieve to behave as I would in real life, away from this war.

Oddly, now I find myself asking, is "real life" what happens back in London? Cars jamming the streets, people rushing about, ladies tending their gardens and buying new hats, men knocking back a fine scotch after a round of billiards at the club. Or is the reality here, harsh and unspeakable? Blood and flesh and all that senseless death. It was especially brutal at

I'm sorry, Evie. I shouldn't speak of it to a lady, but for some reason, you make me want to spill all of my thoughts.

You say you're restless and anxious to play some part, but I'd hate to see you here at the Front. It's dangerous, soul-altering, and anyone who can be shielded from it should be. I want my best friend's sister as far from it as possible. Why don't you do some writing? I remember how much you enjoyed poetry. The volume of William Blake was in tatters last time I saw it, well loved. No one quite understood my love of literature as much you, Evie. I'm missing my library tremendously. Will you read enough for the two of us? Perhaps you might send me some reading material as well? There are long hours when we are idle, waiting for orders.

I'm missing my father, too, if you can believe it. He's quite ill and doesn't seem to be recovering in his usual way. I hope it isn't anything too serious.

I look forward to your next letter.

Sincerely yours,

Lieutenant Thomas Archibald Harding

P.S. Will is going to like the portraits very much. He mentions his horses often enough when we see them go down in battle. Such beautiful animals lost. Poor chap.

P.P.S. Have a look at the envelope. You'll see I've placed the stamp in a specific place. A lot of the fellows here are using the Language of Stamps when they send letters home. An extra message to decode for fun. Do you know what I'm saying to you?

From Thomas to his father

16th January, 1915

Somewhere in France

Dear Father (in care of Mr. Charles Abshire),

I was very sorry to learn of your illness, but you're a stubborn gentleman and I have no doubt you will soon rally and be in as good of health as ever.

I was grateful to hear from Abshire, and glad to know he is looking after the estate and the paper while you're under the weather. Perhaps we should go with his suggestion and bring cousin John on board if you do not rally? I don't care for the fellow, but he would do a fine job, at least temporarily. We must be running pages around the clock with the world at war. There's so much to report, although much is censored, I hear. There's a fellow here by the name of ███ who sends his reports to Fleet Street. He has to smuggle them out, he says. He has been writing from ██████. Do you know of him?

Rest and recover soon, Father.

I remain your loving son,

Thomas

From Evie to Thomas

14th February, 1915

Richmond, England

Dear Tom (I hope it is acceptable to be so informal),

Firstly, my apologies for not having written in a while. I've been suffering with a dreadful head cold and found myself incapable of anything other than bed rest and drinking a dubious restorative broth which Cook assured me would cure the very Devil. To give credit where credit is due, it did the trick.

I was very sorry to hear that your father is unwell but he's a vigorous man. I'm sure he'll recover in no time, so please try not to worry.

By my own admission, I have been a terrible patient. Fidgety and irksome, longing to bring Rusty out of hibernation and cycle off down the lanes. Mama tells me everyone is delighted to see me well again and back on my feet. Surprising, really, to know that I can cause her as much trouble when I am bedridden as I can when I am up and about.

To punish me, she's invited your aunt Josephine to dinner next week. Josephine's eldest—your cousin, John Hopper—is to accompany her. I fear meddling may be afoot. I will have to make sure to be on my very worst behaviour and portray myself as being entirely unmarriageable. You're not especially keen on Hopper if I remember, although I thought him agreeable enough when I met him briefly once before.

Awful news about more bombing raids. This time in Great Yarmouth and King's Lynn. Four people killed and over a dozen injured. Zeppelins did the damage. I hate the thought of them creeping silently over us while we sleep, like monsters in the dark. I read a newspaper report that suggested they are being launched from a secret base in England. I'm not ashamed to tell you that I'm frightened, although Papa assures me they won't come to London—just the coastal towns. Still, I can't sleep. Every sound wakes me and I rush to the window to check for zeps overhead. I suspect this was the cause of my illness. More worry than any disease.

I did, however, use the time in my sickbed to reacquaint myself with that volume of Blake's that you mentioned. How funny of you to remember it. He wrote such wonderful words. "Tyger! Tyger! burning bright, In the forests of the night, What immortal hand or eye, Could frame thy fearful symmetry?" And I found these lines from "Love's Secret," underlined. "Never seek to tell thy love, Love that never told can be; For the gentle wind does move, Silently, invisibly." I wonder whose unrequited love I was lamenting at the time. Silly notions of a lovesick schoolgirl, and yet reading such sentimental lines gives me hope that love and kindness will conquer in the end. I see so many hasty marriages taking place—men hoping to evade duty at the Front and young girls clinging to their marriage vows as if they were a shield to protect their loved ones. I find myself wondering if real, honest love can flourish in times of war, or if we are all just grasping desperately to the slightest suggestion of it, like drowning men clinging to life. What do you think, Tom? There's something to ponder while you lie awake at night, unable to sleep.

I was greatly cheered by the news that you had a short truce on Christmas Day. Can you really smell the enemy's breakfast cooking? Are you that close? I imagine you all miles apart, not practically neighbours. How awful. I can't imagine the terror you must live in, but I know how very brave you are and that those under your command are lucky to have you. I suspect you have them all shipshape and well presented—and improving their knowledge of Chekhov and chess, no doubt. You will lead them well, Tom. I know you will, even with poorly knitted socks and unhappy toes.

Are the rats a dreadful nuisance? We hear rumors of infestations bothering the men in the trenches. Do you remember the one we found in the woodpile that summer at Granny Kent's? I squealed so loud that you and Will came rushing to my rescue with the peashooters! Such dashing heroes.

Our own infestation of vermin is under control thanks to Tennyson (the new cat). He came with the highest accolades and I must tell you that he certainly lives up to them. He looks like a brute with half of one ear missing but I find myself becoming quite fond of him. Perhaps we all must find something to attach ourselves to in such unsettling times. Sometimes, I feel I could be blown away on the breeze like a dandelion seed if I don't grasp hold of something solid and permanent and unchanging. No wonder we all flock to church every Sunday. There is a comfort in such permanence as that offered by the centuries-old walls and a vicar who is nearly as old.

The Language of Stamps, you clever boy! Of course I know about it, but hardly thought you would bother with such a thing! Your message was "forget me not." Impossible, Tom. I've known you too long for that! I've sent a message back. Be sure to check your envelope.

Well, I will sign off for now because I have a cramp from writing so much and I have a charity luncheon to dress for (another fund-raiser) and then I'm going up to London to hear an address by Emmeline Pankhurst. You will remember her from the suffrage movement she and her sister started before the war. They have called an end to their militant activities and are focusing their efforts on galvanising the women of Britain to help in the war effort. I'm intrigued to hear what she has to say. I'm hoping to convince Mama to come with me on the pretence of buying a new hat. I'm hopeful that if she hears others speak with passion about the necessity for women to do their bit, she will acquiesce in her refusal to let me even discuss the matter.

Do write soon. I hate the days and weeks that pass without word from either you or Will. I never had to wait for anything in my life. I'm not very good at it.

Your friend,
Evie Elliott

P.S. I hope you like the gloves (despite the lack of fingers). A new knitting venture of mine. I recall that you have rather large hands, although looking at these I find it impossible to think of anyone having hands quite *that* large. I hope they will be of some use to you, if only for the unravelled wool, which I'm sure you'll be able to find some clever use for.

From Evie to Will

15th February, 1915

Richmond, England

My dearest Will,

Mama insists I write to you again. She can hardly bear to put pen to paper herself. It upsets her so much and sets off one of her headaches. We hear regularly from Tom, so at least we are assured that you are alive and well but you really must send word to Mama. She worries so, and you know how fragile her nerves are at the best of times. Please write a few lines to her, even if you can't find time to write to your favourite little sister who misses you dreadfully and still finds herself wandering aimlessly into your room for no other reason than to somehow feel closer to you.

We think of you every day and you are always in our prayers. Stay safe, brother, and remember we are all very proud of you.

Your ever-loving sister,

Evie

P.S. I have the most marvellous gift for you when you come home!

25th February, 1915

Somewhere in France

Dear Evie,

I apologise for the delay in replying, but things have been busy here. There are few moments I can truly relax, most of them when I fall into an exhausted sleep, unable to hold it together another moment.

I'm relieved to hear you're safe. I abhor the thought of those damned Germans raiding London. You can understand now, what it feels like here, if only a little. Be safe my friend, and well. You must be brave for others when the zeppelins come. Your family and friends need your strong spirit to see them through.

As for talk of love, I never took you for a cynic. Paul Humphreys really broke your heart, didn't he? There are plenty of romances built on sturdy foundations. Look at Queen Victoria and Prince Albert. She mourned his death for decades. Romeo and Juliet? I know you've read that one at least a dozen times. How about your parents? I've never seen an old couple so in love. Remember the day we were playing pontoon? They came into the study, and we hid under a blanket behind the sofa. When they started kissing, I blushed so hard I think every last freckle on my face burned up. Come to think of it, where was Will during all of that? Sometimes he disappeared to God knows where.

What they say about rats in the trenches is true. They're bigger than any I ever saw in London. Those were charming country mice in comparison. These rodents are well fed, practically the size of a small dog. The men take turns using them for target practice. I know how you like the hunt yourself, or I wouldn't mention shooting the filthy things, but then, you never were easily frightened, were you? I can see you in my mind's eye now, dark hair flying out from under your hat, gun in your hands. You were certainly made from a different mould to other girls, except maybe your friend, Alice. Your poor mother wanted nothing but a well-bred society lady. You've given her far more than she bargained for—good for you.

Are you writing again? I hope so. What's the latest from town? Tell me about Mrs. Pankhurst and the luncheon. I imagine tea cakes, marmalade and scones, ham slices, and all the buttered carrots you can eat. My stomach is groaning just writing these words. When I come home, all I'm going to do is eat. I'll eat until I'm fat as a sow, and enjoy every minute of it.

I suppose I should ask how dinner went with John Hopper. Did your mother take to him as you suspected? He's a handsome devil, but be careful around him. He's not known for treating a lady well. Do take care, Evelyn.

I badgered your brother to write. (See letter inside.)

Your friend,

Tom

P.S. My knowledge of the stamps is limited to say the least, but your brother assures me the positioning of your last means you think of me. I should think so, too!

From Will to Evie

Dearest Favourite (only!) Little Sister,

Please give Mama my love. Tell her I'm as safe as can be expected out here at the Front. As luck would have it, for the next three days I'll be away from the main action and staying at billets in a local town. Looking forward to bathing and shining up nicely for a change, enjoying a small piece of the normal life. Small accomplishments are rather important these days. I'm not sure how much longer I can put on a happy face. I'm missing home, and you.

Your brother,
Will

From Alice to Evie

26th February, 1915

Brighton, England

Dear Evie,

I had a smashing time with you last weekend—it always cheers me to see your face, and I was happy to see you back on your feet, cold banished. We really should make the effort to see each other more often. Brighton isn't the moon, after all, and neither is Richmond. Either of us can take the train whenever we like and be together in no time at all. Shame on us for making excuses. No longer!

To continue our discussion, I think it's important we get involved in the war effort somehow. I don't especially want to be a nurse. I'm not cut out for it. Far too clumsy for a start. I'd no doubt kill more men than I would save. But there must be something we can do to help, even if it's here at home working in the munitions factories. Let's put our heads together, shall we? Perhaps I'll register with the Labour Exchange. See what comes of it.

Thank you for your invitation to go cycling next month, but you know me, I would rather be run over by one than be caught dead exerting myself. I'm sure you're adorable on Rusty, just the same. Instead, I'm learning to drive and I'm quite good! If my mother knew, she'd have an absolute fit. Billy Peters, a friend of my father's, has been kind enough to teach me in exchange for a few dinners out. I think it cheers the old bugger up a little! A win-win, wouldn't you say?

All my love,
Alice
X

From Evie to Will

28th February, 1915

Richmond, England

Dearest Will,

How lovely to get a few lines from you. I know it must be awfully hard, but please try to remain strong in spirit, even if your body is battered and bruised. You, Will Elliott, already have the heart of a lion. Now you must find the temperament of an ox to accompany it. You *can* bear this. I know you can.

Mama was so relieved to hear from you. She says to remind you that we could not be more proud. You serve your King and country—what greater glory could there be? I know you will have dark days, but I know you, when this is over you'll be grateful for all of the goodness and long life before you instead of looking back on those difficult days. Also, I can feel spring is on its way, bringing brighter and warmer days to cheer us all. Everything seems worse in the winter. You must keep watch for the first spring flowers. Tulips, perhaps? Do they grow in France? Think about the tulips, Will, and keep faith in yourself. You command your own destiny. Not the enemy. Only you.

Stay safe. I will write again soon. Send word with Tom if there is anything I can send to help you feel more comfortable.

Your ever-loving sister,
Evie

From Evie to Thomas

1st March, 1915

Richmond, England

Dear Tom,

Pinch, punch, first of the month! Goodness, I think this must be the first time I've managed to get those words out before you. Perhaps there are small victories to be won in wartime after all.

March already. You and Will have been gone six months. Half a year. It feels more like half a lifetime. How much longer must we endure this, Tom? How much longer until the enemy is defeated and you can return to England, victorious? Perhaps you'll be able to apply for leave soon? It would be wonderful to see you. I think of you every time I see the soldiers on the trains, their uniforms still caked in mud. Some are home on leave, some are recovering from wounds, and all are ever-anxious to return to their brothers at the Front. They look so strange to me. Like ghosts, almost. So different to the hale and hearty men who left last summer.

At least there is some joy to be found in the improvement in the weather. Rusty the bicycle has emerged from hibernation! I took advantage of a pleasant day yesterday and set out for a long cycle in Richmond Park. I forget how beautiful it is when I haven't been for a while. I pedalled to the top of the hill and took in the view across Petersham Meadows and along the Thames all the way to the city. It looked so peaceful and I felt so safe sitting on my lofty perch. I imagined I could see all the way to France and I waved to you all and sent you good wishes on the breeze. I hope you know how often we think of you all; how often we take pause in our day to reflect and to pray for your safe return.

Mrs. Pankhurst was marvellous. She's a formidable woman and I was stirred by her words. She spoke of the need to support the government and has agreed to step down her campaign to secure the vote for women in order to focus on encouraging us to get involved in the war effort. She and her daughter, Christabel, are lobbying to bring about involuntary conscription. It is hard not to support her when you hear her speak in person. With every new report of heavy losses at the Front, and with the NCF (No-Conscription Fellowship) pacifists having recently opened an office on Fleet Street, one really doesn't know what to think anymore. Papa says the NCF's operation is a disgrace and will be shut down.

You also asked about my writing, and yes, I have started again. All I seem to do these days is write in one form or another. I take comfort from it, but find it infuriating at the same time. I pour my emotions into my journal, write lines of poetry, and yet nothing changes. I can express all the anger and fear and hope I have within me, use the most beautiful words in the English language, or write a stream of muddled rambling thoughts—it makes not one bit of difference. They are, after all, just words on a page. No matter what I truly think of this war, I cannot stop it.

I took my journal to Richmond Hill this morning and read my words out loud, shouting them into the wind, imagining them being heard across London and printed in the newspapers so that everyone might know how I feel about this war. It makes madmen of us all, Tom. Of that I am certain.

As for the examples of true love you shared in your last letter, I will admit defeat. Who could ever denounce Shakespeare's star-crossed lovers? You are perfectly right. I must not become cynical. I must believe in the inherent good within people. Not in the evil that drives them to war.

What news of your father? I hope he is feeling much better.
Stay safe, dear boy.
Write soonest.
Evie

P.S. I forgot to tell you about the dinner party with your cousin. I don't know why you are so down on Hopper. He was perfectly charming (I'm sure Mama would have me marry him tomorrow), and I found myself enjoying his company immensely. Then again, I am so starved of male companionship I suspect I would have enjoyed an evening with the gardener. You are too hard on Hopper. I can find nothing bad to say about him, I'm afraid.

From Will to Evie

10th March, 1915

Somewhere in France

Dear Favourite Little Sister,

You didn't even have to harass me and I've written. Surely there should be another surprise awarded for that?

I've been bursting with news and couldn't wait any longer to tell you—something you never thought you'd hear, I bet. I'm in love with a beautiful French girl named Amandine Morel. She's a nurse stationed at the field hospital close to the reserve trenches, so I see quite a lot of her. I can hardly think of anything else. I know—I've gone mad!

Don't tell Mama. Things have a proper order and war has thrown us all off-balance. I'm not ready to make any big decisions yet, but I thought you might like to know that all is not doom and gloom here. Pass on my love to the family.

Yours,
Will

From Evie to Alice

14th March, 1915

Richmond, England

Dearest Alice,

Lovely, as ever, to hear a few lines from you and yes, you are absolutely right, we *must* find a way to get involved in the war effort. The longer it goes on the more helpless I feel. So much so that I did something about it today and made enquiries at the post office, and guess who is to become a postwoman?! Rusty and I will soon be flying around Richmond delivering the post. I'm terribly excited. With all the letters I'm writing and receiving I know how important those few lines can be. To be entrusted with their safe delivery to loved ones and fretful mothers and lovers—it makes me feel prickly with pride. I start next week. Imagine it, Alice. Me, a postie!

Of course it has all caused a terrific row with Mama. She strongly believes that a family like ours should be above such menial tasks. I could slap her, Alice, honestly, I could. Papa is thankfully far more understanding and has given me his blessing. He's proud of me for wanting to help the war effort, and promises to talk Mama round. I hope he can. She is almost as bad as me when she's in one of her sulks and I hate it when we argue.

In other developments, I'm sorry to tell you that my brother is quite smitten with a French girl—a nurse. He wrote to tell me all about her and says he loves her. I know you'll be a little glum to hear this, but I also know you've given up all hope of him ever looking upon you as more than a friend—and rightly so. Much as I love my brother, I'm sure there's a far more suitable husband out there for you somewhere, and you know how Will is when he sets his mind to something—he could very well have the girl married by the end of the month.

Talking of marriage, John Hopper (Tom Harding's cousin) was the perfect gentleman at dinner recently. Mama can't stop talking about him and I find myself thinking about him more often than is healthy. I'm afraid I was a terrible flirt—a lack of male company has rather turned my brain, it seems. I hadn't appreciated he was working incognito for the government. He said he would prefer to be out there on the front line, but went to great lengths to explain how the war must be fought from the home front too. The poor chap has been approached by the White Feather Brigade on more than one occasion, despite the fact that he wears his On War Service badge. He finds it awfully frustrating.

Let me know if you register at the Labour Exchange. I would far rather you didn't become a munitionette. It's awfully dangerous work. Would you not consider nursing? I can't think of anyone better suited to it. You're always so wonderfully cheerful. Your pretty smile alone would have the soldiers well on the road to recovery. Bedside manner can be as important as any other medicine. Promise me you'll think about it? And please take care with Billy Peters and his truck (though I must admit the thought of you at the wheel, flying around his farm, makes me smile).

Much love,
Evie
XX

From Evie to Will

14th March, 1915

Richmond, England

Dear Will,

Well, well. I certainly wasn't expecting to read *those* words when I opened your letter, but I must say I am extremely happy to know that you have found a little time for romance amid such horror. This Amandine must be a very special girl indeed to have stolen Will Elliott's heart from all the other girls! Send me a photo would you? I should very much like to know more about this French enchantress.

Joking aside, I'm happy for you, Will. I know the midst of war is far from the ideal place to fall in love, but true love does not care for time nor place. It will strike whenever and wherever it is supposed to, however improbable it might seem. So, set your heart on a rampage, dear boy. I am full of joy for you.

A little news from home. I am to become a postwoman! I shall be cycling around Richmond, delivering the soldiers' letters. I start next week. As you can imagine, Mama is beside herself with shame that it has come to this. Her own daughter, working! She is convinced that becoming a postwoman is one step away from becoming a soldier on the front line. Please send a few lines to encourage her to support me. It would mean a lot.

Take care, Will, and mind your heart. I hope this Amandine Morel isn't going to break it. And don't forget about your little sister. I never tell you, but I do love you, you know.

Yours,

Evie

From Thomas to Evie

15th March, 1915

Somewhere in France

Dear Evie,

The Ides of March bring ill fortune. I never liked this day with its reputation of infamous foreboding, and today it was precisely that—one filled with doom. Evie, it was wretched, though the word barely scratches the surface of the truth.

More than half of my platoon was decimated. A shell exploded at the perimeter of our base camp. A dreadful fire raged, wiping out many of the supplies. When a group of German snipers rushed us, Will darted out like a Spartan warrior and said his piece in bullets. I raced after him to assist with half a dozen other men. We dispatched them swiftly but as we headed back to camp, another shell exploded. I threw my body over Will, bullets zipping overhead. This was far worse than the whizz bangs they fire from the smaller field guns, Evie. I'll leave that there.

Your brother was foolish, but heroic. In all, he pulled a dozen men to safety. The stretcher-bearers raced to their aid (Will insisted they treat his men first), while I cleaned up a nasty flesh wound in Will's leg. He's fine, recovering well now, so no need to worry.

Time stops in those moments. You move through them like a dream. When you look back, you can't believe it was you out there. I wonder when my time will be up? Will it be all white-hot pain, or the slow drain of life ebbing away? I keep a last letter in my jacket pocket—a lot of us do, just in case. I think about it often, who will read it first. Will the words have any meaning when I'm only a memory and in the ground?

In these moments I wish I had drawn up a will. It was foolish to leave my fate to chance. My father was so angry with me before I left, he said he'd cut me out of his will completely. I wonder if my ambition to become a scholar will mean anything to me in my father's last days. Is it a mistake to follow a young boy's dream, and one devised, perhaps, to rebel against a father's wishes? Or is it what I really want, and worth the cost of my relationship with him—and my inheritance? Things I ponder after months facing my enemy.

Father still isn't well and doesn't seem to be improving. Abshire said cousin John has been asking about the *London Daily Times*. We haven't approached him yet about helping out. Father fears Hopper will attempt to buy us out, and then it's all over for the family business. He believes Hopper will sell the paper to collect a fat cheque, and leave us to pick up the pieces. I'm not sure what to do. As much as I don't want to run the paper, I can't allow my father's hard work and joy to be sold off, and by a blood relation, no less.

I need to be there, at home. I need to protect what belongs to the Hardings, and decide how to proceed from there. I can't tell you how frustrating it is to be too far away to be of use. I find myself desperate to spend time with my father. I'm beginning to worry a great deal, our differences be damned.

On a lighter note, I'm glad to hear you're cycling again now the weather is improving. I can picture you flying along in your scarf and hat, cheeks pink, as the wheels whizz beneath you. And you're writing again! Good! You always seem happiest when you can put your thoughts on paper. It's rather funny how you and I fell in love with literature and writing separately, yet alongside each other. We're kindred spirits, my friend.

Speaking of literature, I will leave you with the words of my oldest friend, Shakespeare, from one of the few books I brought with me. It's from *Henry IV*. (Perhaps I should have brought something more upbeat.)

O war! thou son of hell,
Whom angry heavens do make their minister,
Throw in the frozen bosoms of our part
Hot coals of vengeance! Let no soldier fly.
He that is truly dedicate to war
Hath no self-love, nor he that loves himself,
Hath not essentially but by circumstance
The name of valour.

I'm sorry for the dark subject of this letter. It's been a dark day and Richmond—and you—feels so very, very far away.

Yours,

Tom

P.S. As for Mrs. Pankhurst, though I admire her, I can't say I agree with her insistence in dishonouring men who choose not to join the war. If given the chance to do this all over, I'm not sure I would enlist as readily.

From Evie to Thomas

25th March, 1915

Richmond, England

Dearest Tom,

Thank you for your letter, although I must tell you it has me awfully worried. To learn of you and Will being in the

thick of the action fills me with the deepest dread imaginable. Was it terrible? Did you fear for your life? Gosh, Tom,
I cannot imagine it. You are the best friend Will could ever
wish for. Thank goodness he had you beside him. Was he
hurt badly? I try not to think of it, but I imagine the worst.
He never could handle pain. The slightest nettle sting would
send him howling to Nanny. You poor things. How helpless
I feel.

Today is Lady Day—the start of spring—and the daffo-
dils look so lovely in the sunlight. It certainly helps to feel
the warmth in the breeze and to see the brighter evenings. I
hope you feel the sun on your face, too. Hopefully the better
weather will lift your father's spirits and see him on the road
to recovery. Try not to worry about the newspaper. I'm sure
things will settle down when you're back home and can talk
things through with your father face-to-face. You are a pair of
stubborn mules.

I mentioned your predicament to Papa (subtly, so he wouldn't
read too much into it). He knows Hopper quite well and believes he has a good head for business. Papa said he would get
him on board as soon as possible if it were his business at stake.
Certainly, from the conversations I've had with Hopper over
recent dinners, I can only believe that he would be a sensible
choice as a temporary stand-in to oversee things. What other
choice do you have? If relations are terribly frosty, your father
needn't know the full extent of Hopper's involvement, need he?
I could always ask Papa to drop by the offices to take a measure of things if it would help? He visits his club in London on

Wednesdays. I could ask him to make up some excuse or other to look in?

If only I could meet you for afternoon tea or for a stroll through Richmond Park, this would all be so much easier to discuss. Any news on a period of leave?

The *London Daily Times* has become my preferred source of news in recent months. The larger newspapers paint a very different picture of war to the one you describe in your letters. The editors would have us believe everything is perfectly jolly over there and war is nothing but continual victories and divisional concert parties. Your editor at least seems a little more willing to tell some of the truth of what is happening out there.

As for enlisting, I know you would do the very same if this were to happen again, because that is what brave young men like you do. Trust me, you would not wish to be on the receiving end of the White Feather Brigade. They are harsh in their condemnation and as the weeks and months pass, and we learn of more and more losses, I find it hard to have any sympathy for those fit young men I see walking down the street in their civvies. Some claim to have failed the medical examination, but most refuse to fight on moral grounds. Conscription is coming, Tom, I am sure of it. There is a palpable sense that we are in this for the long haul. I only hope and pray that you and Will and all our other friends and cousins will be away from the worst of the danger while it lasts.

Try not to think dark thoughts, Tom. We shall make a bonfire of your last letters when you come home, and we'll watch the sparks float up into the sky like fireflies and drink good wine. Think of that, and of how thankful we will be when victory comes. Think about Dover's white cliffs welcoming you home. Think of your boat on the Thames. Think of being in Paris at Christmas. Think of all the things you have never done, all the living you still have left to do. So much, Tom. So very much. You must not let death in. Shut it out where it cannot find you. Put down your Shakespearean tragedies.

> *Come, on wings of joy we'll fly*
> *To where my bower hangs on high;*
> *Come, and make thy calm retreat*
> *Among green leaves and blossoms sweet.*

(A few lines from Blake.)

Please keep writing. I find myself depending on your words more and more.

Stay safe, dear boy.

Evie

P.S. I believe the War Office has put in place an amnesty program for the little VPK cameras to prevent any images falling into enemy hands. Do you still have your camera? Take a picture of you and Will if you can before it is confiscated. I would so like to see your faces again.

From Evie to Will

25th March, 1915

Richmond, England

Dear Will,

Tom wrote with news of your involvement in some skirmish or other, and of your act of heroism and resulting leg wound. It causes me such anguish to learn of these things. It is just like you to think of others before yourself. To run headlong towards the danger when others would be running away. The British Army is lucky to have you on their side, Will, and we are lucky to have you in our hearts.

Please send word of your recovery as soon as you can. I hope your sweet Amandine is by your side to give you courage and proper treatment.

Please do take the greatest care.

Your loving sister,

Evie

From Will to Evie

FIELD SERVICE POSTCARD

NOTHING to be written on this side except the date and signature of the sender. Sentences not required may be erased. If anything else is added the postcard will be destroyed.

I am quite well.

~~*I have been admitted into hospital.*~~

~~*{sick   } and am going on quite well*~~

~~*{wounded   } and hope to be discharged soon*~~

~~*I am being sent down to the base.*~~

I have received your

    *{ letter dated   25th March '15 *

    { ~~telegram~~ _____

    { ~~parcel~~ _____

Letter follows at first opportunity.

~~*I have received no letter from you*~~

    { lately

    { ~~for a long time~~

Signature only.   Will Harding _____

Date _____ 31st March '15 _____

[Postage must be prepaid on any letter or postcard addressed to the sender of this card.]

From Thomas to Evie

1st April, 1915

Somewhere in France

Dear Evie,

Pinch, punch, first of the month. (I got you!)

It's Fools' Day here at camp, yet I can't find a thing to be jovial about. One of the privates thought it would be funny to fill my tea—if you can call it that—with dirt. I lost it, shouted at him and the lot of them. You've never seen a pack of men run so fast. It's a trivial thing to be angry about, but war does that to a man.

Now that I've complained I see I do have something to be happy about—your letters. I shouldn't admit this, but since I have no idea what lies ahead, I may as well be honest. I watch the letter carrier drive up from the road, over whatever humped terrain we're on, and walk swiftly to the mail tent. The minute he jumps back into his truck I amble to the tent, nonchalantly of course, and duck inside, secretly praying there's a violet-scented envelope with your elegant script. When I see one, I feel like I've won a prize. I look for letters from Father as well, but they never come, only the occasional update from Abshire. He is a silent sort of fellow, his letters are more like telegrams written in abbreviated, blocky sentences. It says a few things about him, doesn't it? Anyway, he doesn't write prettily, as you do.

As for the newspapers, when I return I'll see to it that ours prints the truth. I can see this troubles you and I value your opinion. At least the LDT is better off than most in this concern—being a smaller publication we're not watched as closely as the big boys like the *Mail* and the *Times,* although Abshire mentioned the *Globe* is suspended for two weeks after printing false reports about Kitchener's resignation. Relations between Kitchener and the Cabinet may be strained, and Asquith might well reduce the man's responsibilities, but he will never cast him aside completely. So much is censored now, it's a wonder I get any news to you at all. What good is it to a newspaper if the truth is glossed over? I suspect trouble will continue to brew on this front. We need to keep a close eye on how this sort of censorship develops.

Ho, dinners (plural) with John Hopper! Lucky fellow. He always was, even if he didn't deserve it. I'll leave it there for now.

I'll hold on, Evie. Don't worry. I have nothing to do but that.

Sincerely yours,

Thomas

P.S. Will enclosed a letter.

P.P.S. I hope you like the photograph. I had to bribe my commanding officer with my ration of rum to get it.

From Will to Evie

Dear Evie,

Don't worry your pretty head over my wound. It healed within days. Amandine took excellent care of me, cleaning and dressing the wound, and setting my spirits to rights again. She smuggled in sweets and tobacco for me as well and what is a fellow to do when he is helpless in his sick bed other than to let himself fall ever more madly in love. See? Nothing to worry about. Good as new.

I hear we're moving to ▆▆▆ or just east of there in two weeks. Could you send another pair of gloves before then? Mine are wearing thin.

Your loving brother,
Will

From Evie to Will

16th April, 1915

Richmond, England

Dearest Will,

What a relief to hear from you and to hear that you are well enough to march on. I have enclosed new gloves and socks for the journey. Will your lovely Amandine be able to go with you, or must she stay behind?

The censors got to your letter, so I don't know exactly where you are headed. I only hope it isn't closer to the Front. We've heard of awful casualties close to the Belgian towns of Ypres and Armentières. The Germans still hold Menin and are reported as getting the best of the Allies at the moment. I hope you are to march in the opposite direction. Dear God, Will. How did it ever come to this? I pray, with all my heart, that you are somewhere safe, at camp or in billets, and far away from the firing line.

England is all talk of the loss of 2nd Lieut. Gladstone, MP whose name appeared in the casualty lists. He had been in the trenches less than a week. Shot by a sniper's bullet when he reached up over the parapet to try and locate that very sniper. Papa says it was a senseless death and the result of inexperience as much as bad fortune. I take some comfort in knowing how experienced you are now and that you would never do anything so rash and foolish.

Tom sent a photograph of you both. So handsome, even if you do look a little thin.

Stay safe. We remain terribly proud of you all.

Evie

From Evie to Thomas

18th April, 1915

Richmond, England

Dear Tom Harding (Lieutenant),

I must apologise for the overscenting of my letters. It has become a habit to dab my bottle of violet water onto my fingertips and dot it about the paper before sealing it. I imagine such terrible smells in the trenches and hope that this little fragrance of an English summer garden will be a welcome boost. And you know how I adore the scent of violet—and rose and gardenia.

I long for the bushes to bloom in the garden so that I can cut a few sprigs for my bedroom.

Will writes of an impending march. I know you cannot tell me where to—or you can, but the censors will strike it out—and that you and your fellow officers censor the privates' letters, but who censors yours? In any event, I find myself poring over maps of Europe and newspaper reports in an attempt to follow the battle lines. Papa and I have a miniature War Office in the library here, trying to work out where on earth you might be. It would amuse you, I am sure, to see us puzzling over maps and no doubt reaching the wrong conclusions, but such is the way we occupy ourselves these days. It feels like a game and I only wish I could tip the board over in a temper and bring you all home.

As for propaganda, it is rife here. I can only guess at how little we are really being told. I, too, hope your father hasn't fallen foul to the pressures yet. Please don't shy away from telling me the truth and the detail of what is happening out there. I am made of strong stuff and can take whatever you have to tell me. I would rather know the truth of it than live in ignorance. We women are not as sheltered from the world as we once were. War is opening the world up for us. What sad irony is that?

Take care and write whenever you get a moment. Was there any news on your getting a period of leave?

Your friend,

Evelyn Elliott

P.S. The photograph is wonderful to have. You both look so relaxed and happy, arms draped around each other. I would so love to see you both again.

P.P.S. Regarding John Hopper—do I detect a hint of envy? Don't worry. I shan't abandon you. I will always write, no matter how many dinners I might have with him.

From Thomas to his father

23rd April, 1915

Somewhere in France

Dear Father (in care of Mr. Charles Abshire),

I haven't received a letter in some time. You have me worried, Father. I trust you've sent for the best doctors? Please continue to keep me informed through Abshire. I think it's time John Hopper take over for a while in your stead, since I cannot. He isn't the first choice or even the fifth, I'm afraid, but there's nothing to be done about it. Abshire needs the assistance and will keep me informed of what's happening there. I will certainly keep an eye on that cousin of mine as best I can, given the circumstances. I imagine this surprises you, that I should show concern for the LDT. In all honesty, I surprise myself.

Here at the Front, my commanding officer called a briefing this morning. There's a rumor we'll be wearing gas masks soon. We may even be fitted with them by next week. "Chemical warfare" they call it—a new and even more wicked version of "battle"—this is what the Germans have brought upon us. The cowards won't even fight man to man. They'd rather wipe out the enemy with noxious fumes at a distance, run away with their tails between their legs. Father, they decimated two French divisions and one of Algerian troops. I continue to ask myself how hell could be brought lower, how it could be made hotter, yet I continue to be surprised by what the Germans do next. The worst of the news is, we're headed to the scene of this horror next week, north of ▮▮▮▮ as backup.

I've lost too many friends these last months. "Every good man fights for a cause," you've always said, and I suppose that's true. Perhaps we'll be victorious swiftly now, and I'll come back a decorated hero as you did. A man can hope, and should, I've been told.

Wishing you well. Please rest so you may recover.

I remain your son,

Thomas

From Evie to Thomas

8th May, 1915

Richmond, England

Dear Lieutenant Harding,

Where on earth are you? I haven't heard from you—or Will—for weeks now (your last letter was 1st April) and I can't help but worry terribly. We read awful things in the papers about the gas masks and the Germans' so-called chemical warfare. Is it true? Dear God—what animals.

I'm delivering the post now and with every bag full, I pray

to find an envelope addressed to me in your own hand. It seems especially cruel to deliver so many letters, and still find nothing from you or my brother. The job is not quite the joy I imagined it would be. Most of the letters bring news of worsening conditions and dreadful battles. Some are simply returned "To Mother," stamped "Missing." It breaks my heart to see them.

These are anxious times. The casualty lists grow longer every day. I can hardly bear to read them for fear of seeing familiar names. We have suffered heavy losses among friends and neighbours—most during the battles at Gallipoli and Ypres (I'm not entirely sure how to pronounce it, but a soldier home on leave who I was talking to on the station platform said the Tommies call it "Wipers." He said they make up names for all the foreign places they can't properly pronounce.) Anyway, whatever the place-names, please be somewhere else, away from the worst of it, Tom. Please be somewhere safe, with my brother by your side.

You will, no doubt, have heard about the sinking of the *Lusitania*. Such atrocities. Such dreadful suffering among civilians. Over a thousand men, women, and children dead. They say it took only a matter of minutes for the liner to sink. It is too dreadful to think about.

Please send word soonest. I will even promise to stop having dinner with Hopper until I hear from you.

Keeping you ever in my thoughts and prayers.

Your friend,

Evie

Telegram from Thomas to Evie

```
                                        9TH MAY 1915


TO: EVELYN ELLIOTT, POPLARS, RICHMOND, LONDON SW
SENT: 10:00 / RECEIVED: 10:20


WILL WOUNDED. VERY BAD. PRAY FOR HIS RECOVERY.
PREPARE FOR THE WORST. MORE SOONEST.
LT. T. HARDING
```

From Evie to Thomas

9th May, 1915

Richmond, England

Dearest Tom,

I can barely write.

We all pray for Will's recovery. He is an Elliott. We are made of iron. Please stay with him, Tom. Don't leave my brother alone—not for a second. Keep him safe. He is all I have in the world.

Yours,
Evelyn

Telegram to Evie's mother, Mrs. Carol Elliott

10TH MAY 1915

TO: C. R. ELLIOTT, POPLARS, RICHMOND, LONDON SW
SENT: 10:40 / RECEIVED: 11:16

DEEPLY REGRET TO INFORM YOU LT. W. J. ELLIOTT
WAS LOST ON THIS DAY. PLEASE ACCEPT OUR DEEPEST
SYMPATHY. SGT. MAJOR UNWIN. 2ND OXFORD RIFLES.

From Thomas to Evie

10th May, 1915

Somewhere in France

Dear Evie,

I have started this letter twice and tossed it into the bin. How do I write these words? I am so sorry my dear friend, but he's gone. Will is gone. He fought like the devil, and was brave to the very end. These last few weeks have changed us all, even your shining, exuberant brother, but now he has nothing to fear, no pain. He is at peace.

He wanted me to tell you that he loved you very much, and to not be cross with him for eating all the orange jelly every Christmas. You know how he was, always a jokester, even until the last. God almighty, I'll miss him. He was my best friend, my family. I don't know how to do this without him.

Please write soon. Share a pretty poem from one of your books? Right now the world is dark, so dark. I need a reason to see this through, Evie. Anything. I don't believe in this war anymore.

My deepest condolences for your loss, to you, and your parents. Ever your friend,

Tom

Letter to Evie's mother, Mrs. Carol Elliott

12th May, 1915

France

Dear Mrs. Elliott,

On behalf of the Officers and men of my Company, I wish to offer my sincere sympathy in the bereavement you have sustained in the loss of your son, Lieut. William James Elliott. I feel that you would like to know how very highly regarded Lieutenant Elliott was amongst all his comrades, and that his loss was felt with great sorrow among the Company.

Lieutenant Elliott was wounded by a mortar attack on 9th May. At the time of his injury, Lieutenant Elliott was in command of a small patrol advancing against the enemy. His men survived the bombardment, having taken cover at his command. Although we were able to remove him to a field hospital, his injuries were too serious. His friend, Lieut. Thomas Harding, was by his side at the time of his death, which was peaceful and without suffering.

He is buried in a military cemetery with full honours. His personal effects have been sent.

Again, assuring you of all our sympathy.

I remain, yours sincerely,

Robert Harrison, Capt. R.E.

From Evie to Thomas

13th May, 1915

Richmond, England

Dearest Tom,

I can think of nothing to say, to write, to do. My heart breaks for us all.

Mama is inconsolable. Will's personal effects really brought it home to her. I left her alone with them and haven't pressed her to see them. She tells me they are the usual things—his battalion number, a packet of smokes, a photograph of his horses. Of course there was no last letter. Not from Will. He never was one for many words. His life was lived all in a look, and a touch, and that knowing smile.

Papa is ashen-faced and walks about as if in a dream. His only son and heir—gone. I heard him weeping in his study yesterday evening. It broke my heart all over again. My dear Papa. Weeping like a child. No sound could possibly be worse.

It is hard to find anything to be hopeful about, but I took

some small comfort in knowing that you were with him to the last. Oh, Tom. I am so desperately lost without him. My only brother. Our lives will all be darker without him.

I can write no more. Even poetry cannot cheer me. I hear only sorrow and loss within every line and verse.

Please keep safe, and do not feel alone. You have always been family to me—and I hope you will consider yourself my brother, now more than ever. Send word whenever you can. Your letters have become something of a life raft for me to cling to.

Never stop writing. We will fight this war together, you and I.
Evie

From Evie to Alice

13th May, 1915

Richmond, England

Darling Alice,

How on earth can I write these words? Will is gone, Alice. He is gone. He was unable to recover from his wounds and passed away with Tom by his side.

My heart is truly broken, as I know yours will be too. I only wish I could sit with you and hold your hands and tell you this in person. But war has no mind for such things and such is the way this saddest of news must now be heard: in a few meagre words scribbled on a flimsy piece of writing paper.

I can find comfort in nothing, Alice. I cannot eat. Cannot sleep. I don't know how to endure this. I don't know if I can.

What unimaginable sorrows we must face.

May God help us all.

Evie

X

Telegram from Alice to Evie

14TH MAY 1915

TO: EVELYN ELLIOTT, POPLARS, RICHMOND, LONDON SW
SENT: 11:55 / RECEIVED: 12:35

NO! MY DARLING GIRL. MY HEART ACHES, BUT I *CAN'T BEAR IT* FOR YOU. LEAVING ON NEXT TRAIN. WILL BE WITH YOU SOONEST. ALICE.

From Charles Abshire to Thomas

3rd June, 1915

London, England

Dear Thomas,

I am writing to update you on happenings here. Your father continues in his struggle for improved health, but manages to retain his stubborn nature. He sends you his good wishes, as always.

I don't know if you are aware, but our Secretary of War has, at last, allowed correspondents to report from the Western Front. This may change the nature of our reporting at the LDT, though we will remain vigilant with an eye to any new restrictions from Kitchener and all others.

My sincere condolences for your loss of your good friend, William Elliott. I am certain he will be greatly missed. May God bless his soul.

Sincerely,
Charles Abshire

From Thomas to Evie

5th July, 1915

Somewhere in France

Dear Evie,

I am sorry for the delay in letters. We're on the move again, and my boots are wearing thin, but at least it's warm. I'm desperate to walk barefoot in the warm summer grass behind my house, desperate to stretch out on the lawn and stamp out the image of the enemy lurking in the bushes. Day in and day out I find myself bargaining with God. If he would just see me home safely, I plead, I'd give up tobacco, volunteer for charities—adopt orphans! Whatever it takes. But one can't bargain with God, it seems.

Two images of Will keep flitting through my mind as I lay on my bed in the dugout: one, the day we went off to university together, arms full of books and our stomachs full of bees—all excitement and a bit of fear at the change of things—and the other, the day I returned from my mother's funeral. I was only thirteen and so forlorn, a complete mess, in truth. I confided in Will how hard it was to go on without her, how alone Father seemed, and how I suffered even being with him. I had never told anyone about my feelings. Will hugged me as boys do—awkwardly and without looking one another in the eye—and said, "You're never alone, Tom. You've got me and Evie, and my parents. You're part of our family, too." And so I was, and always have been.

I can't believe he's been gone for almost two months already.

Now I'm alone again, among all these soldiers, medical workers, and volunteers. Alone because each of us walks our own path towards death; no one can do it for us. Lately, as I face each day, that path is all I can think about.

I'll keep writing, Evie, if that is acceptable to you. It's the only thing I have to hold on to.

Your friend,

Tom

11th July, 1915

Richmond, England

Dearest Tom,

How happy I was to find your letter in the morning post. I tore it open the moment I saw it in my postbag. (Yes—I kept up my position as postwoman after having threatened to abandon it.) You were right. Alice was right. Will would have wanted me to continue, and—silly though it may sound—I feel a sense of duty to make sure the letters are safely delivered. It gives me purpose, and purpose gives me hope.

I'm sorry to hear you are finding things so difficult. It must be unimaginably lonely so far away from home and from everyone and everything you know. Of course Will was right. You *are* part of our family, and I am glad you remembered his words just as I am glad of your letters, which I would happily receive from you every day.

I know you do your best and write as often as things allow. I, on the other hand, have no excuse, other than to tell you that sitting at the desk in Will's room became unbearable for a while. I felt I had nothing to say to you. The truth is, these past weeks I have felt like a rag, wrung out. But time passes and the pain eases a little each week, and although there isn't a day when I don't think about Will, we must somehow find a way to go on, mustn't we? Your memories of him made me smile, so thank you for sharing them with me.

Increasingly, there are brighter days when I wake with more courage and fortitude than the day before. I call these my "Letter to Tom" days—days when I feel able to put pen to paper and write about things past and share with you my hopes of things that are yet to come. Today is one of those days. We are blessed with sunshine after days of endless rain, and I have taken myself out to the garden for some much-needed fresh air and birdsong. (Did I mention I have taken to sketching birds to pass the time? I stumbled across a very pretty book of British Garden Birds in Papa's library and set myself a challenge to draw a likeness of each bird from the colour plate illustrations. There are forty-five plates in total. I've started on a wren, it being the smallest. Perhaps I will send it on to you when it is done.)

You asked, a while ago, whether my knitting has improved—a little, but not as much as Mama would like. Her knitting circle expands faster than Papa's stomach at Christmas. We can hardly keep up with demand from the local War Chest and Comforts for the Troops Appeal. A dozen of Mama's lady friends call to the house every day, knitting all manner of things: socks, hats, mufflers, mittens, balaclavas, and such. I'm still all fingers and thumbs and hopelessly slow so I am now in charge of organising the individual packages to be sent to each soldier—all POWs. I must say that I enjoy the stroll into town on little errands to collect donations for the parcels. I wonder why we always relied on the maids to do such simple things for us.

We hear the POWs are being fed only on cabbage soup and

black bread and many are in danger of starving or freezing to death. Poor chaps. I've started up an Adopters scheme (lots of people are doing it), where each of us knitters "adopts" an individual soldier to knit for. We include a personal note each time we send a parcel. It's such a small thing and can hardly make much of a difference, but I do hope it gives them some hope to know that someone back home is thinking of them. I have adopted Private James Kent from East Sheen who was captured at the start of the war, last October. The poor boy has been a prisoner for as long as you have been a soldier, Tom.

One final thought before I close. I wonder whether Will's lovely Amandine heard of his death. I imagine not, with everyone moving around so often. Would there be any way to get word to her do you think? He really was terribly fond of her, and I would very much like her to hear the news from someone who knew Will, rather than from a list (although it may already be too late). Still, I would like to try. Do you think it might be possible to send her a few lines through those you know in command? I know it would mean the world to Will if you could.

Stay safe, dear boy, and do write often to let me know you are well.

Yours, Evie.

X

P.S. New socks enclosed. Don't be too hasty to put them on. There is a packet of Virginia tobacco inside each!

From Thomas to John Hopper

12th July, 1915

Somewhere in France

Dear John,

Greetings, cousin. I trust you are well and that Hopper En-
terprises flourishes under your astute supervision. I write to you
from the trenches out of concern for my father. His illness isn't
retreating (the doctors tell us it is a cancer), yet he has stubbornly
refused both mine and his bookkeeper's suggestions to apply for
your assistance. I'm afraid I must overrule him at this juncture.
In short, I am worried about both him and the future of the
newspaper, but there isn't a bloody thing I can do from here.

Charles Abshire is a competent fellow with the books, but
he's a gentle soul. I worry he may need someone to look in on
him, ensure all is running like an oiled machine at the LDT.
Our Editor-in-Chief, Jack Davies, is a tough old bird and runs
our reporters hard. He needs some guidance from time to time,
or some boundaries laid, shall we say. Could I ask you to pop by
Fleet Street, see to things and report back? As you well know,
the Press Bureau is coming down hard on anyone who pushes
the boundaries of war reporting too far, and Davies has never
been one to listen to authority. All in the family, I say.

I would owe you a great debt that I will repay the moment
I am able.

Regards,
Lieutenant Thomas Harding

From Thomas to his father

13th July, 1915

Somewhere in France

Dear Father (in care of Mr. Charles Abshire),

Forgive me, but I've taken the liberty of contacting cousin John. I know you don't see eye to eye with the Hoppers, but I thought it time to put the family feud aside. This appears to be an emergency—me, on the battlefield in harm's way on a daily basis, and you, laid up indefinitely. I've asked Hopper to look in on things. (Charles, I thought you might like some assistance since your workload has increased tremendously.) I've warned him about Jack Davies as well, and have also written to Davies to tell him to treat the man with a modicum of decency.

Please send word of your condition. I find myself more and more worried for your welfare, Father. Take care of yourself.

Your son,
Tom

From Evie to Tom

14th July, 1915

Richmond, England

Dearest Tom,

I find myself waking to another "Letter to Tom" day, so consider yourself a lucky fellow to have two letters on their way to you. You see, I am anxious to share some rather exciting news with you. It concerns your cousin, John Hopper, so grit your teeth and bear with me.

John made a very interesting proposition over dinner last night. I was telling him how frustrating it is to always read the news from a male perspective, and that I would be far more interested to read about the war from a woman's point of view. I'm afraid I found myself talking rather too passionately about Nellie Bly, whom I greatly admire (she is reporting for the *New York Evening Journal* from the Eastern Front, Nellie Bly being a pseudonym). Anyway, my comments to John about the newspapers offering a female perspective on the war were really just casual observations made over too many glasses of wine, but he rather took to the idea and suggested that I might be the one to write such a thing. I laughed at first, but by the time we were having dessert I realised he was entirely serious. He doesn't know why anyone hasn't done it sooner, and that since women are reading the newspapers more than ever with the men being away, it makes perfect sense to have a woman write about the war.

I said I would sleep on it before agreeing. What do you

think? Is it absolute folly, or fate? Please tell me what to do, Tom. I have always trusted your good sense and calm judgement of a situation while I flap about like a headless chicken.

If I do take John up on his idea, I quite like the column title: "A Woman's War." Of course I'm thrilled at the prospect of writing my own column (quite the step up from the parish newsletter), but I worry I shan't be able to think of anything interesting to say, other than to make a few remarks about the temporary demise of the suffragists and the dangerous work conditions faced by the "canary girls" in the munitions factories.

I've been trying to think what Will would advise, and in his absence, I find myself asking, what would Tom advise? It is, after all, something I've always wanted to do—write—and if I can find anything good to come from Will's death, it is a renewed determination to grasp every opportunity life throws at me. At the very least a column would take my mind off things and stop me eternally stewing on what might have been if this wretched war had never started. Please tell me—honestly—what you think I should do. I value your opinion and good sense, especially at a time when my heart is already running away with me towards Fleet Street and the clatter of the printing presses.

I hope you are able to find some small moments of comfort and happiness. We hear reports of divisional concert parties and troop entertainment. Do you have time to enjoy any of that? And what about the French towns. Is there anything pretty left to look at? I've always imagined the French countryside to be full of rustic churches and terra-cotta-tiled barns and farmhouses. Please tell me it is still, that somewhere you can find a little beauty to cheer you and brighten your day.

Do write often to let me know you are well.

Yours,

Evie

X

P.S. I finished Miss Jennifer Wren, my first sketch, and have enclosed for purposes of decorating your dugout. I do hope you like her. I've become rather fond of her these past weeks. I hope you might care for her as much.

From Thomas to his father

20th July, 1915

Somewhere in France

Dear Father (in care of Mr. Charles Abshire),

I will not apologise for having John look in on you and the press, regardless of your admonitions. We both need the assistance at this point, and he accepted my proposal willingly. I know his history of bullying the competition, but I can't imagine he would do such a thing to the LDT when it isn't formally his business, and especially when doing so would mean I could lose my inheritance. Have a little faith, Father. Neither you nor I have given Hopper permission to take over completely. If he tried, Jack Davies wouldn't keep quiet about it. We both know our editor would be on your doorstep first thing. Hell, he might even write to me over here.

If you are truly worried that John will try to take over, consider reinstating me as coexecutive alongside you. As you know, I have other plans for the future, but I won't make any serious decisions until I'm home and settled and better able to find the best solution for us both. I won't let your pride and joy falter into ruin.

Please be well.

Your son,

Thomas

P.S. If there's more to this family feud that I should know about, now is a good time to tell me so we can approach the issue in the most resolute way possible. No more secrets.

From Alice to Evie

21st July, 1915

Brighton, England

Dear Evie,

Please forgive me. I know that weeks have passed since Will's tragic death but I haven't written to give you a little space, dear. Every time I put pen to paper I felt all I had to say was so silly and pointless. I hope you have recovered from the shock. You know—life and all it throws at us.

Did you receive the journal and book of poetry I sent? After my last visit and darling Will's passing, I've been unbearably restless. And you know how I can be when restless—spending all Father's money and drinking one too many gins. I had a particularly dark evening three nights ago where I suddenly felt like such a useless, silly thing sitting here in Brighton, worrying about zeppelin raids. It doesn't suit me to be so melancholy. So I've done it. I've signed up as a VAD nurse. I lied when they asked if I had spent at least three months in a hospital, but really, why can't I learn in France? I hope they'll let me try a few of the "easier" less gruesome tasks, but at this point, I'll do anything. So tomorrow, I'll wave goodbye to my roommate Margie with a final salute and head into my future.

I'm thinking of you, my favourite girl. I hope you're holding your head up.

With love,

Alice

X

From Thomas to Evie

25th July, 1915

Somewhere in France

Dear Evie,

As always, thank you for your letters. They are like a hot loaf of bread for a starving man. (Good God, does hot bread sound divine!) You can't know what your words mean to me these days; far more than ever before.

You were right in your letter—I've been terribly down. It isn't just Will's death. It's the fear that is my constant companion, the stench of bodies left for the crows and the rats. Also, it's the continual sense of trouble brewing at home. Father shows no signs of recovery and he yelled at me via post if that is possible, and let me assure you it is. The paper may be in trouble, both from falling profits and an old family feud. Father isn't thrilled John Hopper will be looking in and neither am I, but he is the only choice. And then he laid the guilt on rather thick that I shouldn't abandon his business and him. At some point I need to get home, sort this out.

There's a rather nasty battle raging in ██████, from what I hear. The French are leading. You can mark that on your map if my superiors don't strike out the name. I know better than to state where we're headed, but since this battle is already going on and surely in the news, I assume it's fine. To be frank, I'm praying they don't call us in for reinforcements.

My friend, I would be thrilled to have you join the staff of the LDT—you have my complete consent. *"A Woman's War"* is a tremendous idea, and you'll be brilliant. You should use a pen name to protect your identity (like your Nellie Bly). What do you say to Josie Hawk, or perhaps Genevieve Wren? There we have our brave journalist, snapping up the latest news for her faithful audience. Tough, yet feminine enough for our heroine. You'll see my crude sketch of a war hawk on the back of the letter. I've even given it a helmet with a ribbon. An impetus for a laugh, I'm sure, but I'm not the artist you are. At any rate, congratulations are in order! Little Evie is going to be a star journalist. I'd ask you for your autograph, but I've already had the pleasure of seeing it on every letter. (Really, I'm very pleased for you.) Just beware of Hopper, would you?

I see you're putting your drawing into practice. I sliced the envelope open along the top with a knife to preserve the trio of wrens you drew on the flap. It's tucked neatly inside my notebook now, for safekeeping. Did you know wrens symbolise strength? I wonder which bird will be next. Perhaps one that symbolises dinner. I'm starved.

Did you read the *Report of the Committee on Alleged German Outrages*? I heard it's a real dinger; lists all the wretched things the Germans are doing at war and in the towns they've captured. Not that I need to read the account, since I see it first-hand, but I wonder at the word "alleged" in the title. Maybe the newspapers have become too loose in their fact gathering. It's hard to say since the journalists don't seem to be allowed near us out here. I hope your column brings the truth to light.

I sent a telegram to Amandine Morel at the field hospital back in ██████, to tell her of Will's death, but the reply I received said that she had taken ill and returned to her home in Paris. I hope the telegram was forwarded on to her, poor girl.

Do keep me informed of your writing successes. I am so very proud of you. You're like a sister to me, and I want nothing more than to see you happy.

Your friend,

Tom

P.S. Have you heard any news of the Americans joining the war? We talk about it constantly here.

From Thomas to John Hopper

30th July, 1915

Somewhere in France

Dear John,

Greetings from the Front. I wanted to commend you on your suggestion to add the column *"A Woman's War"* to the LDT. Miss Elliott has a natural talent and quite the passion for writing. I can think of nothing better to encourage a family friend, as well as expand our anemic circulation figures. I trust that you and Jack Davies will monitor Miss Elliott's articles for proper tone and content. However, in the future, would you do me the honour of informing me of any other changes you have in mind first? I'd like to be involved in the decision-making process while my father is ill, before new directions are implemented.

Also, take care to see all articles meet the standards of the Press Bureau. Abshire tells me more and more papers are being issued with "D" letters for violating the bureau's standards of reporting about happenings at the Front. I am not certain I agree with this sort of monitoring, but who am I to say when I'm so far afield. We must do what they ask to protect the interests of the paper for now.

Sincerely,

Lieutenant Thomas Harding

From John Hopper to Tom

5th August, 1915

London, England

Dear Thomas,

Thank you for your letter. Rest assured I have the paper's—
and Miss Elliott's—best interests at heart. I must say you kept
her rather well-hidden. She is quite the tonic, not to mention
very easy on the eye. If it pleases her to write a few little lines
every now and then, I am happy to give her a go. If her views
on war don't quite hold up to the quality of our male journalists, I'll have her write up some wartime recipes, or items on
household thrift. Something a little less challenging.

Don't worry about the paper. You get on with defeating the
Germans and I'll keep the presses running here.

Sincerely,
John Hopper

From Evie to Tom

5th August, 1915

Richmond, England

My dear Tom,

Thank you for replying so quickly. I can't tell you how happy
I was to hear of your approval for the column (not least be-

cause I have started working on ideas for the first piece!). Your encouragement means everything to me, since you're the only one who really understands my desire to write in order to make sense of the world. Alice is all enthusiasm for the idea, too, but Alice would be all enthusiasm if I told her I was going to put on a uniform and rush into battle. I can't tell Mama (she will entirely disapprove), and although Papa will be more supportive, I think it best to remain anonymous for the time being. I do like your suggestions of a pen name. Josie Hawk has quite the ring of derring-do about it. More like the heroine of a *Girl's Own* adventure story than a respected journalist though, don't you think? I think Genevieve Wren is the one. A wren for strength. Isn't that what you said?

As for the report you referred to, yes, I did read it, although I rather wish I hadn't. Alleged Outrages or not, it makes me furious to hear of the Germans' disgraceful activities.

To the rest of your letter. Hot bread? Really? Never did I think I would see the day when you were fantasizing about a loaf of bread. Do you get nothing decent to eat at all? It makes me cross to think of you all starving. Men need a full stomach to march on. Even I know that. I have sent chocolate and cough candy. I remember how fond you are of both.

How strange that we have known each other for so many years and know so many little things about each other, and yet only in these past months, since writing to you, do I feel that I've really begun to know you at all. Letters make one uncommonly honest, don't you think? I've told you things in words that I would have been far too shy or distracted to tell you in person. I wonder if I will have anything to say to you at all when we see each other in the flesh again. Will it be soon? Any news on home leave? Or will it be Christmas at the earliest? At this rate, we will have to settle on Christmas in London and make do with a decent French restaurant. There are already concerns here about food shortages. Mama is sure rationing will become compulsory before much longer.

I'll be visiting London next week for lunch with John Hopper. He wishes to discuss my first piece for the new column before I send it to the editor. Davies, isn't it? If I remember correctly you have great respect for him. I hope my piece will impress.

I also plan to look in on your father while I'm there. I should like to see him. It has been too long. I'm sorry to hear you are still so worried about things back home. It seems dreadfully unfair for you to have matters of business to worry about when you have so many greater worries facing you every day. It would seem to me that Abshire (although well intentioned) isn't really up to the job of running things until your father recovers. I'm sure John will do a much better job, family difficulties permitting.

Yes. The wrens. I found myself doodling on the envelope as it was the closest thing to hand. The time passes quickly beneath the nib of my pencil, and there's a lot to be said for that. I had no idea the wren is a symbol of strength. It was purely through my own laziness that I selected the smallest bird to draw first. Now I know that each bird has a weightier meaning I will have to choose my next subject very carefully or you'll be drawing (excuse the pun) all manner of erroneous conclusions. All this talk of birds and symbolism has driven me to my poetry books. I'd never appreciated how often the bird is written about. Dozens of works jumped from the page. I like this one by Thomas Hardy. Lines from "The Darkling Thrush." Are you familiar with it? It fits my mood perfectly today.

> *At once a voice arose among*
> *The bleak twigs overhead*
> *In a full-hearted evensong*
> *Of joy illimited;*
> *An aged thrush, frail, gaunt, and small,*
> *In blast-beruffled plume,*
> *Had chosen thus to fling his soul*
> *Upon the growing gloom.*

Whenever I hear the song thrush, I think of Will and imagine that both he and the thrush are singing songs of hope—and you must do the same. Listen for the birds, and when you hear them, know that I am thinking of you.

Well, I must go. Keep hearty and hopeful. And do try to eat. I imagine a starving man is almost as dangerous as those Howitzers and whizz bangs you write of.

With much love,

Evie.

X

P.S. I missed yesterday's post, which gives me the opportunity to add, by way of a postscript, the joyful revelation that the lark is a symbol of luck and harmony. I think you could do with the former and the world could do with the latter, so here is my best attempt (done—in my defence—in a hurry, before I miss the post again).

From Evie to Alice

12th August, 1915

Richmond, England

My darling Alice,

How on earth are you? I am so very sorry for not having written to you for so long. For many weeks after Will's death I found myself quite unable to write anything that wasn't desperately sad or smudged by my tears. But I feel a little brighter of late, and I am spurred on by the thought of a few lines from you in return.

I also have a little news to share with you. I am to write a column for the LDT! It is all John Hopper's doing (he really is terribly persuasive when he sets his mind to something—and is still Mama's current favourite for a suitable husband for me, by the way). Tom thinks the column is a splendid idea and encourages me wholeheartedly. I'm not sure when the first piece will be printed but when it is, I will send on a clipping for you to read. I'm to write under the pseudonym Genevieve Wren (partly to prevent Mama knowing I am behind the words—she would never agree to it). What do you think? I rather like it.

Tom and I are still exchanging letters faster than he is exchanging gunfire with the enemy. I must tell you that I find myself thinking about him often and longing to hear a few lines from him. What is this, Alice? This is *Tom Harding*, for goodness' sake! Since he went to war and we started writing all these letters to each other, I find myself wishing, ever more, that I could see him. It makes no sense at all. Perhaps I have a fever on the way. I must go for a lie down after posting this off.

Anyway, I ramble.

It seems futile to talk of other news, but life, as they say, must somehow go on. Tell me, how is the nursing going? We hear such marvellous things about the VADs. Diana Manners was all over the newspapers in her uniform, encouraging ladies to enroll. I am so terribly proud of you. When will you ship out?

Do write soon, and let me know when you might be able to get to Richmond again. Perhaps we could take a walk along the river like we used to as young girls. Such simple pleasures. Who would ever have thought they would become such impossibilities.

Yours,

Evie.

X

From Thomas to Evie

15th August, 1915

Somewhere in France

Dear Evie,

Your letter made me laugh! I haven't laughed in ages so I thank you. I should have known the one person on this Godforsaken earth to cheer me in the darkest of times would be you. Little Evie who tied my bootlaces together before I boarded the train to Brighton one summer. The very same girl who told her governess she was sick so she could miss her lessons, only to help her brother let toads loose in the drawing room to bother the mean old spinster. What a mischievous character you were.

Also, thank you for the chocolate and cough candy. My commanding officer cracked his tooth on one of those blasted Huntley & Palmers biscuits they're feeding us, and the Maconochie I'm forced to eat is about the foulest version of tinned stew you've ever smelled, much less tasted. Sometimes I think I don't deserve your kindness. The thick horror of my day-to-day existence has a way of making me see things through a queer light.

Bird analogies are quite useful, you see? The wren puffs its little chest for fortitude and strength, the lark for luck, but what of the peacock with its proud turquoise chest and fancy tail feathers? You're like a bird yourself. An eagle, meant to soar above, yet never losing keen sight. You are not a woman to be caged, are you? One day, you won't be able to control that fire inside you and you will be off, on the road and unstoppable. Your column is the perfect start.

I know the Thomas Hardy poem you sent—it's as darkly beautiful as the name suggests and particularly apt just as you said. You know my ardent fervour for Shakespeare, of course. Did you know he used bird imagery in his work more than any other? His most obscure poem and addendum to another writer's piece is called (at least now—it was published untitled initially) "The Phoenix and the Turtle." It stars a pair of birds, a phoenix and a turtledove, whose love creates a union so perfect it defies concrete sense and earthly logic, and overcomes any obstacle. When I return, I'll show it to you. I have a copy among my school things.

How is your first article progressing?

Tomorrow we move again.

Ever Yours,

Tom

From Thomas to his father

20th August, 1915

Somewhere in France

Dear Father (in care of Mr. Charles Abshire),

I received your letter and positively fumed at our relations, especially Uncle Arthur. I wish I had known all of this family history before. I'm sorry Hopper took advantage of your friends, and pulled our good name through the mud, but he would call it simple business practices, would he not? That seems to be his way, but I'm curious. If you and your brother-in-law had already gone your separate ways, how did John come to own stock in the business? I gather this means he owns rights in deciding the paper's future. If he's not to be trusted, as you suggest, we may find ourselves in a very precarious situation.

You may also be troubled to learn that Hopper is looking into why the paper is losing money. Apparently the other two presses Hopper owns are booming (he is well set up with his connections at Wellington House, after all) so he insists his points are valid. He suggests we begin a column entitled "*A Woman's War*." For now, I'm on board with the idea as Evelyn Elliott is to be the authoress, but under a nom de plume. Remember the poems she used to write, how we kept them in a drawer in the kitchen? She'll be brilliant at it. I must confess, however, that with Hopper steering things, I'd prefer you to be involved somehow. As soon as you're well enough to receive visitors, perhaps you and Evie may discuss a variety of topics. I'm certain she would enjoy that immensely. She respects you, nay, loves you like an uncle.

I wish you a speedy recovery, Father.

Your son,

Thomas

P.S. I've included a short note to Abshire.

Dear Charles,

If Hopper is poking around in our books and looking into financial matters, I should also keep up on them as much as possible. I need to be on my toes where he's concerned. I'd like a copy of the summary sheet from last year and the first six months of 1915 as well: business expenses, wages, stocks, and profits. There are hours I am not in battle and I would like to use my time wisely.

I hope you are well, friend.

Sincerely,

Thomas

From Evie to Thomas

28th August, 1915

Richmond, England

Dear Lieutenant Harding,

I am much heartened by the news that I can still make you laugh, even from so far away. I imagine laughter is in short supply over there, along with a decent meal and a comfortable bed. The "Maconochie" stew you write of sounds awful. Can you put a dash of rum in it to liven it up (or a dash of rum in yourself to numb your taste buds)? I always had an ability to bring a smile to your face, didn't I, although it wasn't always intentional. How you and Will used to tease me and get such great delight from your wicked tricks. If I have grown up to be full of mischief, I must place the blame firmly at your feet for setting such a dreadful example to an impressionable young lady.

You say that you are on the move and I find myself anxious. I have grown to hate those words "Somewhere in France" at the top of your letters. It might as well say, "Somewhere in the World," for all the reassurance it brings. Thinking of you marching closer to danger is unbearable. If only I knew where you are. If only Papa and I could consult our wretched maps and know with some certainty which direction you are moving *in*.

We place black buttons on the areas where we believe you have been and red buttons on the locations where we know the worst of the battles have already taken place, or are likely to take place soon. Those black and red buttons have come to represent my greatest fears, Tom. I keep a blue button firmly on London. It fell off the blue dress. The one I wore to Mama's Christmas party when we danced together. I must admit that I never especially cared for that dress, but now, whenever I see it hanging in the wardrobe, I think of you, and of laughter and dancing. I think of happier times. Which is why the blue button will remain on London until you are home and I will ask Sarah to sew it back on, and we shall dance again. Perhaps I will wear that dress to dinner in Paris. We will get there one day, won't we Tom? This Christmas. Next Christmas. One day. Promise me?

Oh dear. I am becoming hopelessly sentimental. War, it seems, can soften as well as harden people. And with all your words about Shakespeare's "The Phoenix and the Turtle," it would appear that you are still the same old Tom with a wordsmith's heart and a book always tucked under his arm, and not just a soldier at war with a gun and a bayonet. "It stars a pair of birds, a phoenix and a turtledove, whose love creates a union so perfect it defies concrete sense and earthly logic, and overcomes any obstacle." I wonder, is such perfect love possible? I do hope so Tom, or what on earth are you all fighting for?

In other news, I had the pleasure of visiting with your father at his home in Bartholomew Close. He was pleased to see me and was in reasonably good spirits, if a little frail and easily tired. We spoke of you (with great fondness, might I add) and briefly discussed your concerns for the newspaper. I know you and your father have had your difficulties over the years, but I must say, he is most concerned for your safe return. He is also incredibly frustrated by his poor health—frustrated that he cannot help in the war effort, frustrated that he cannot protect you. You are still his only son, whatever your differences of opinion.

I know he would dearly love for you to take the helm at the paper when the time comes. Couldn't you tell him you will? Make your peace with him before it is too late? I know your heart is in the scholarly, and back in the hallowed halls of Oxford, but it would give your father such comfort to know that you will do the honourable thing, so to speak. If only to ease his conscience, can't you say it will be so?

I have probably said too much, so I will close.

Stay safe, dear friend. You remain in all our prayers.

Evie.

X

P.S. My first column is to be printed towards the middle of September. I feel quite sick at the thought.

From Thomas to Evie

1st September, 1915

Somewhere in France

Dear Miss Evelyn Elliott,

We're back to formalities, are we? Yet you sign with your Christian name without a care. I do like contradictions. It is what fiction is made of, is it not? As for your writing, I'm certain your column will be a smash, just you wait and see. Courage, as the French would say!

You mentioned adding rum to my food, so I must tell you about this "rum" we are given (and which I, as a Lieut., distribute) in rations. It isn't a sweet, tawny liquid mixed well with fruit, or drunk cool. It's so strong it almost walks from the bottle, burns your eyes and nose, and slides down your throat like a violent tar, assaulting your stomach as it settles. But there's no doubt it does the trick, dulls the mind. In fact, it's a scourge. I've witnessed too many men stagger from the trenches in front of enemy fire to be struck dead instantly, without so much as their hand on their gun. Sure, the rum numbs the pain of loss for a time, but it's short lived and as it dissipates, it seems to intensify the aching. It leaves a man in a darker place from where he started. I know, sadly. After Will, I remained in a stupor for weeks. It's a miracle I survived it, Evie. But since, I've given it up completely. It's too dangerous.

We've had a slight reprieve the last two weeks, outside the usual daily sniper incidents. (Who knew I would consider a random shooting a relief?) I call it a reprieve, but the trench foot, typhoid, and pestilence make up for the lack of heavy bombing, and there are Blighty wounds, of course. I suppose I should explain the military lingo. Blighty wounds are serious injuries, in which a Tommy is in bad enough shape to be sent home, but the injury isn't fatal, or even crippling. In truth, many of the men hope for them. I know some injure themselves on purpose. It is a measure of how desperate we have become.

Thank you for visiting Father. I'm sure he enjoyed seeing you, as always. I must admit, it makes me a bit green. I should be home right now, caring for him, and looking after the LDT. Maybe I will tell him I'll run the paper as you suggested, though I'm not ready to commit to such a permanent change in direction yet. At least through your letters, I'm coming to understand the real value in news, the honour in seeking truths. I had never thought of journalism that way before. Father has always focused on it solely as a vehicle to make money.

Do you know what would make me happiest right now? Visiting a friend of mine who goes by the name of Genevieve Wren and talking about all of this over a roast and Yorkshire puddings.

I am making myself hungry again. I'll focus on that blue button instead.

Yours,

Lieutenant Thomas Harding

P.S. The badge enclosed was Will's. He slipped it into my hand before he died and I kept meaning to send it. I found it in my greatcoat pocket and wanted you to have it.

P.P.S. I do hope you'll send on a copy of your first column. I can hardly wait to read it.

From Alice to Evie

3rd September, 1915

Somewhere in France

Dear Evie,

How happy I was to receive your letter! Only a month away and I feel as if my life has taken on new meaning. I don't mind nursing half as much as I thought I would; I've grown accustomed to the sight of blood, and am actually quite good at changing dressings, though I do hate to see our boys suffer. I fear many will never recover their wits fully. And the empty look in their eyes, Evie. It keeps me awake at night. I hope you never see anything like it.

My mother is proud to see me doing my bit, but she scolds me in her letters as always, warning me to remember what I am there for and not to fall for the officers (it happens more often than you might believe). What good will it do, she says, if I go losing my heart to someone and then a German shoots out his eye or he loses an arm? Worse, what if he loses his soul to war? I suppose she's right, but I ask you this—what valiant young man hasn't stolen my heart, at least for a week or two? We both know the answer to that! And we are, after all, still human beings, even when we are in this hell.

I can't believe it has taken you so long to admit it, dear girl, but I knew you felt something for your ginger Tom! Perhaps you have always had feelings for him? He has been your friend since we wore pigtails and he's a lively fellow with that big grin and wicked sense of humour, yet gentle somehow, and so scholarly, too, which you've always admired in a person. And like you, Tom loves nothing more than a little adventure. What could be more perfect?

I can see you shaking your head all the way from here. Don't deny it. You as much as said it in your letter. Fall madly in love, Evie. Have a little fun! You need it now, more than ever.

Give my love to your parents (and Tom, wink wink).

Love,

Alice

From Evie to Tom

5th September, 1915

Richmond, England

Dearest Tom,

Thank you so much for Will's badge. I will treasure it. Such small tokens become incredibly precious when they are all you have to remember someone by. A badge. A button from a tunic. A letter. A lock of hair. A crumpled photograph. I am sure I have delivered them all to a grieving mother or wife along with the final words of their loved ones. I'm not sure what else was returned to us with Will's personal effects. Whenever I mention them, Mama bursts into tears.

Whatever my personal feelings about losing my only brother, I cannot imagine the grief Mama suffers having lost her only son, so I do not press her on the matter. I'm sure she will show me, when she feels able to.

I must say that your letters are being heavily censored by your superiors of late, so I cannot know where you are or what battles you refer to. (Can you not use an Honour envelope? A friend was telling me how her husband writes to her and uses the Honour envelope to prevent any intrusion by those in command. She says his letters are hopelessly romantic, so it is the contents of his heart, rather than any great military secrets, that he wishes to protect.)

I scour the papers daily for reports, but more often than not all I find are words of positivity and encouragement. "We are very close to victory." "In our finest hour of this war." "A day of promise." It is so different to the picture you paint in your letters and all your talk of disease and near-starvation and Blighty wounds. It is hard to know whether we are reading any truths at all, or simply the words the government wishes us to believe. For that alone I think you must press on with your interests in the newspaper. Financial gain is one thing. To tell the truth is a far nobler prospect.

I try to cheer myself with your letters. It might sound silly but I have come to think of your handwriting as you. Each loop, each flowing curve and flourish is like looking at a familiar face. The contours and undulations so definite and unique. There is quite a substantial pile of letters now. I keep them bound together with a red ribbon. They must form a stack four inches high already (and a good inch higher than the pile of dance cards I kept from my debut season). I tell myself that before your correspondence reaches five inches in height, you will be home. Time, you see, can be measured in means other than the ticking of a clock.

What news of the nurses there? Alice Cuthbert is now serving as a VAD. Can you believe it? Our flighty Alice?! I imagine she will be a real tonic to the injured soldiers with those eyes and lips, and that wicked sense of humour of hers. Do you have time to think of such things as pretty girls? I expect you are as deprived of affection as you are of fresh bread. Hot bread and love. You will be ready to consume both greedily and without restraint when you get home!

I am still sketching—a jackdaw this time. Slightly gloomy in all his funereal attire, but handsome nevertheless.

Be safe, my friend.

Yours, Evie.

X

Telegram from Charles Abshire to Thomas

9TH SEPTEMBER 1915

TO: LIEUTENANT THOMAS HARDING, 2ND OXFORDS
SENT: 7:25 / RECEIVED: 7:55

FATHER INJURED IN ZEPPELIN RAID. TRANSFERRED TO
HOSPITAL. WOUNDS DON'T APPEAR FATAL. LONDON HOUSE
ALL BUT DESTROYED. ONCE DISCHARGED WILL STAY WITH
RELATIVES IN RICHMOND. WILL KEEP YOU INFORMED.
ABSHIRE.

From Evie to Tom

9th September, 1915

Richmond, England

My dearest Tom,

I assume you have already been informed of the dreadful news that London suffered a zeppelin raid in which your father was injured. Bartholomew Close was one of the worst places hit, with many of the houses destroyed. He was lucky to have been spared the worst of the explosion (twenty-two are dead and over eighty wounded). I rushed to the hospital as soon as I heard. He is being remarkably matter of fact about it all, but he is in a pretty bad way I'm afraid.

Everyone in London is terribly nervous and calling for the government to bring in anti-aircraft defences. My hands tremble as I write these words.

Will you be able to come home on compassionate leave? It would give your father great strength to see you.

For now, I will pray for his speedy recovery, and for a swift conclusion to this damned war.

Yours in prayer,

Evie

X

From Evie to the Editor of the London Daily Times

10th September, 1915

Richmond, England

Dear Mr. Davies,

Please find enclosed my first column for "A Woman's War." We had not yet settled on a nom de plume and I hope you will be happy with Genevieve Wren. I have taken the liberty of using the name in the enclosed, although you will, of course, have the final say. I found myself so stirred by the recent zeppelin raid on London that I rewrote some of my piece as a result.

I can come to your offices in London any time to discuss the progression of the column in person, although I understand I will submit all future copy to John Hopper for editorial clearance in the first instance.

Sincerely,

Evelyn Elliott (Genevieve Wren)

A WOMAN'S WAR

by our special correspondent in London,
Genevieve Wren

"Waving the Boys Goodbye"

How long ago it seems since we waved our boys goodbye, off on their grand adventure to serve King and country and do their duty—heroes all. We were told it would be over by Christmas, but Christmas came and went and still our boys didn't come home. Nor did they return to us that Easter, nor Whitsuntide, nor for the summer solstice. And still it goes on.

We write words of love and support—incredibly brave, terribly proud, onwards to victory—pages and pages, never knowing if our words will be read, or any reply will be forthcoming. Those of us who are lucky enough to find a letter on the doormat devour the words inside with the appetite of a starving man. Those of us whose doormats remain empty must somehow find the courage to step over them and go out into a world we no longer recognise. We smile at a neighbour, share news with the postwoman, thank the bus conductor in her smart uniform, but in quiet moments, when we're alone, we ask the same questions: What is this war without end? How much longer will it be?

Questions without answer. Hope without fulfilment.

We have now passed the first anniversary of our nation's involvement in the "war to end all wars." Twelve months they've been gone—brothers, fathers, husbands, lovers, uncles, cousins, friends—and as we face the prospect of empty places around the dinner table again this yuletide, it is difficult to find the courage and resilience to go on. But that is what we must do. Courage and resilience are our weapons. They alone will help us fight this battle of never-ending dread. We must keep the home fires burning for when our men return to us.

In writing this column, I speak to all the women of Britain, whether in sculleries or parlours, farmhouses or country manors. I hope to share with you stories of courage and resilience, fortitude and heroism—small acts of bravery or kindness that may not lead to medals of honour, but are important nevertheless. With all the losses we must endure, let us never forget that the kindness of a stranger can help a person in more ways than we can ever know.

Do not feel that you are sitting idly by, knitting comforts or mixing another pudding for the Christmas parcel. Take a moment to comfort a friend. Check on elderly neighbours. Such small acts, when multiplied across all the streets and counties of our great nation, can become acts of immense importance. They can have as much impact as the bombs the enemy dares to drop on our cities.

A woman's war may not be fought on the battlefield, but it can be won in small victories every day.

Until next time—courage!

Genevieve

From Thomas to Evie

11th September, 1915

Somewhere in France

Dear Evie,

Thank you for alerting me at once about Father. Abshire informed me by telegram. I can hardly believe our misfortune. As if his poor health wasn't bad enough.

Evie, I would never admit this to another soul on this earth, but I'm afraid. Not just about what's happening out here in battle, but about losing my family, losing my livelihood. I can't think straight.

I have applied to my superiors for a period of leave as soon as possible. Thank you for being such a good friend. It means more than I can say.

Yours,
Tom

From Evie to Alice

15th September, 1915

Richmond, England

Dear Alice,

How are you? I am desperately worried. We were all rattled by the recent zeppelin raid on London. The warnings seem to go up nightly now. I say warning, but the sum total of that is simply a policeman pedalling furiously on his bicycle while blowing his whistle and shouting "TAKE COVER! TAKE COVER!" It is so frightening. I had to take shelter in the underground station just yesterday. The sight of those zeps looming in the distance is the stuff of nightmares.

Tom's father was badly injured in the raid last week. I really don't think he'll pull through, although I can't bear to tell Tom that, not after losing Will so recently. It will destroy him to lose his father, too.

So, I am sorry that I am not in the mood for jokes or silly remarks about my alleged affections for Tom. All I know is that I would love for him to come home on leave. He hopes for the same and has put in his request.

I find myself growing weary of letter writing with nothing but bad news to share. And I grow ever-restless and more determined to do something practical to help. If somebody doesn't dispatch me to the Front soon, I might dispatch myself. Mama was talking about arrangements for Christmas the other day and I'm afraid I spoke to her in a rather curt manner, telling her she was a fool to think of such things as place settings when men are dying in the thousands. She said people will die whether she plans Christmas or not, and that perhaps, by looking ahead she is offering some hope instead of dwelling in the past. If I wasn't as stubborn as an ox, I might very well have conceded that she made a fair point before I stormed from the room and slammed the door behind me. But I *am* as stubborn as an ox and we haven't spoken a civil word to each other since. I really don't wish to be a difficult daughter, but it seems that I cannot help myself.

In brighter news, my first piece for the LDT went to print. The editor was quite impressed with my efforts. To be honest, I rather think he had alternative plans for me to write about knitting patterns or some such nonsense, and I'm rather proud to have proven him wrong. I've enclosed a clipping for you. Having worried that I wouldn't have much to say, I found myself with far more words than I was permitted column inches for. I hope you enjoy it.

With much love,

Evie

X

From Alice to Evie

20th September, 1915

Somewhere in France

My dear Evie,

What dreadful news. I can't imagine our beloved London is under attack. It shocks me still.

No matter how bad it is there, Evie, you don't want to be here at the Front. The shine wore off quickly after several weeks of treating men for skin sores from the wretched mustard gas, and other wounds too gruesome to describe. I've also seen quite a few men suffering from nervous disorders. One poor fellow refused to follow orders and became hysterical, hallucinating and rampaging through the dressing station. He sprinted straight into the line of German sniper fire and was shot dead. Or so I hear. Thankfully I missed the shooting.

Bad news, indeed.

I understand if you feel you must be here to do your bit—I did, too—but be very certain, Evie, because I've already lost an innocence I didn't know I possessed. I fear the experience will change me forever, and not in a good way. The only positive news I've heard is that the Americans are finally furious with the Germans, following the sinking of the *Lusitania*. All those innocent people dying. It makes me so cross to see how low the Germans will go. Tragic though it was, I hope the incident will see the Americans take up arms soon and join the Allied forces. After a solid year of fighting, there appears to be no end in sight, and we could desperately use some reinforcements.

There is a small piece of brighter news to share with you. I've made a new friend named Jeremy Rollins, a private from Birmingham, and he's quite the ham. He makes me laugh every time I tend to him, and laughs are in rather short supply here. I met him at the dressing station. He has multiple bullet wounds, but appears to be recovering quickly, in spite of our limited Dakin's solution (used as antiseptic), or sodium salicylate (painkiller). We're hoping to get another shipment soon. Those poor buggers writhing in pain without any assistance. Sometimes I don't know if I can bear it, darling.

Your mother is quite right about diverting our minds from this misery. You are too hard on her. Let her have her festive fun. What harm? You should try to have some as well. It isn't good for you to be endlessly moping about that rambling old house. Could you do a little more at the post office? Do they need telephonists, or wire operators to take down the tele-grams? Just a thought.

I'll stop teasing you about Tom Harding—for now—though I think you should make jolly sure he visits you, as well as his father, if he does get home on leave. Nobody will expect you to have a chaperone with Tom being a long-standing family friend. Ask him to take you to Simpson's for oysters and champagne, and dancing at The Savoy. Then tell me everything!

With much love,
Alice

From Evie to Thomas

25th September, 1915

Richmond, England

Dearest Tom,

Any further news on your coming home on leave? We are all so eager to see you. Your father has rallied a little. He is a very resilient man (the doctors think he is a marvel), but I would dearly love for you to be able to see him.

I had a dream about you last night (I probably shouldn't tell you such things, but if war has given me anything, it has given me a keen sense of impulsiveness). The dream was so real I had to pinch myself when I woke up to be certain that I was at home in Richmond and not actually with you in Paris because that is where we spent the night, dancing beside the Seine (an accordion player provided the music). I wore my blue dress and you were dressed to the nines in black tie. We ate escargots and drank the finest champagne and the stars dazzled like a million jewels above us until the sky turned rose-pink beneath a new dawn. It was so beautiful, Tom. You recited poems of peacocks and turtledoves and I forgot that anything bad had ever happened in the world and in that moment it felt that if only every night could end, and every day could begin that way, nothing bad could ever happen again.

How annoyed I was to find myself waking to the murky drizzle of an English morning in autumn, with Paris—and you—so very far away.

With so much happening recently, I realise I never sent you a copy of my first column, so here it is (a little crumpled I'm afraid). Having tried for so long to have a piece published in the national press, I now feel rather shy and nervous about people reading my thoughts. I hope you like it. Your approval means a lot to me. Jack Davies was suitably impressed (I met him over a brief lunch with Hopper). He is quite a formidable character, isn't he? Not one to mince his words. I found myself quite nervous and rather lacking in appetite. I now understand why he commands such respect throughout Fleet Street.

The months march on and the leaves in Richmond Park have turned their stunning golds and reds. Nature puts on such a stunning show at this time of year. I think autumn is my very favourite season. The fires are lit again and the tang of smoke in the air sets my mind longing for cosy evenings in the library. It won't be the same though. Not without Will's company. Or yours.

I do wish you could get home on leave. I often see men in uniform—rather gaunt looking—strolling arm in arm with a loved one. It is a heartbreaking sight—at once so encouraging and romantic, and at the same time so unbearable, as we all know they will be on their way back to the Front within a matter of days, and the heartache of separation and the pain of worry will begin all over again. Still, I imagine it is worth it for those few snatched hours of normality, and affection.

Do write soon. I will pray for news of your coming home.

With much love,

Evie

From Thomas to Evie

3rd October, 1915

Somewhere in France

Dear Evie,

I have good news, at last! I've been granted seven days of home leave. First thing tomorrow I depart and will be in London, if all goes well, by early evening. Feels like a dream. I don't think I can endure the anticipation. Though I must admit, I'm anxious about seeing Father in his current state. I'll need to spend some time on his affairs, the books, and the newspaper as well, to which I do not look forward. You, on the other hand, I can hardly wait to see. If you're available that is, Famous Journalist Adventuress, Miss Genevieve Wren.

With warm affection,

Tom

P.S. That dream of yours will come true, if I have anything to say about it.

Telegram from Thomas to Evie

5TH OCTOBER 1915

TO: EVELYN ELLIOTT, POPLARS, RICHMOND, LONDON SW
SENT: 18:35 / RECEIVED: 18:55

IN LONDON. WILL VISIT MORNING AFTER NEXT. IF NOT
SUITABLE, SEND WORD C/O ABSHIRE. WILL BE WITH
HIM TOMORROW. I'M THE CHAP WEARING DRY SOCKS, AT
LAST! TOM.

Telegram from Evie to Thomas

6TH OCTOBER 1915

TO: LT. T. HARDING ℅ ABSHIRE, 34 LOVELACE
GARDENS, BERMONDSEY, LONDON SE
SENT: 09:13 / RECEIVED: 09:37

TERRIFIC EXCITEMENT HERE. DESPERATE TO SEE YOU
AND YOUR DRY SOCKS. UNTIL TOMORROW. E.

From Evie to Thomas

7th October, 1915

Richmond, England

Dearest Tom,

How ridiculous I am. The dust thrown up by your car tires has barely settled on the driveway, and here I am, writing to you. Old habits die hard.

I cannot think of anything to say that wasn't said over the past few hours, other than to say, again, how absolutely wonderful it is to see you. To *see* you! It hardly seems possible that you were here. To wrap my arms around you and feel your bones was such a delight. But my goodness, how many bones you have. You are too skinny by far. We must put some meat on them before you even think about going back. So, what do you say to Simpson's for lunch one day? Their roast beef is extraordinary. You can order two portions because one will clearly not be sufficient.

What a joy it is to have you back. I feel ten years old again, and were it not an unbecoming thing for a lady to do, I would turn cartwheels in the library.

E

X

P.S. I am inspired to write a column on the joy of a soldier's return. It will give others hope, do you think?

Telegram from Evie to Thomas

8TH OCTOBER 1915

TO: LT. T. HARDING % ABSHIRE, 34 LOVELACE
GARDENS, BERMONDSEY, LONDON SE
SENT: 09:45 / RECEIVED: 10:10

SENT LETTER YESTERDAY. TOO RESTLESS TO AWAIT
REPLY. LUNCH? 1PM. SIMPSONS? ROAST BEEF IS
DIVINE. E.

Telegram from Thomas to Evie

9TH OCTOBER 1915

TO: EVELYN ELLIOTT. POPLARS, RICHMOND, SW
SENT: 11:45 / RECEIVED: 12:12

SPENT MORNING AT OFFICE WITH HOPPER, AND HOURS
WITH FATHER LAST NIGHT. DESPERATE FOR A PRETTY
FACE. WALK THROUGH REGENT'S PARK AND PUB AFTER? T.

Telegram from Evie to Thomas

9TH OCTOBER 1915

TO: LT. T. HARDING ℅ ABSHIRE, 34 LOVELACE
GARDENS, BERMONDSEY, LONDON SE
SENT: 12:15 / RECEIVED: 12:40

MEET AT FOUNTAIN. 2PM. WILL BRING PRETTIEST FACE
I CAN FIND. E.

Telegram from Evie to John Hopper

9TH OCTOBER 1915

TO: JOHN HOPPER, 23 PATERNOSTER ROW, LONDON EC
SENT: 12:30 / RECEIVED: 13:40

CAN'T MAKE DINNER TONIGHT. RATHER UNWELL. RAIN
CHECK TO NEXT WEEK? EVELYN.

Telegram from Thomas to Evie

10TH OCTOBER 1915

TO: EVELYN ELLIOTT, POPLARS, RICHMOND, LONDON SW
SENT: 08:00 / RECEIVED: 08:25

MORNING WITH FATHER, BUT MEET AFTER? T.

Telegram from Evie to Tom

11TH OCTOBER 1915

TO: LT. T. HARDING % ABSHIRE, 34 LOVELACE
GARDENS, BERMONDSEY, LONDON SE
SENT: 08:15 / RECEIVED: 09:00

WHAT A WONDERFUL EVENING. SIDES ACHE FROM
LAUGHING. FEET SORE FROM DANCING. YOU ARE A
TONIC. E.

Telegram from Thomas to Evie

11TH OCTOBER, 1915

TO: EVELYN ELLIOTT, POPLARS, RICHMOND, LONDON SW
SENT: 18:25 / RECEIVED: 18:50

LAST AFTERNOON WITH YOU TOMORROW? BOATING OR A
DRIVE. BRING BIRDER MANUAL. PICK YOU UP IN SWIFT
AT TWO O'CLOCK. PROMISE TO WEAR NICE TROUSERS.
ONE DAY LEFT. HOW AM I TO RETURN TO IT? T.

Telegram from Evie to Thomas

11TH OCTOBER, 1915

TO: LT. T. HARDING ℅ ABSHIRE, 34 LOVELACE
GARDENS, BERMONDSEY, LONDON SE
SENT: 18:52 / RECEIVED: 19:23

LOOK FORWARD TO IT—ESPECIALLY THE TROUSERS. WILL
WEAR BLUE DRESS, AND A GARDENIA IN MY HAIR. E. X

From Evie to Alice

11th October, 1915
Richmond, England

Dearest Alice,

My apologies, in advance, for the nonsense I am about to write but I am dreadfully confused and I need to tell someone.

Tom finally came home on leave last week. It was all very sudden. He was anxious to see his father, and to meet with his business associates to make sure the LDT is in safe hands during his absence. But between his meetings and hospital visits we saw each other every day. Lunch at Simpson's, cocktails at Archer's, walks along the Thames. It was bliss.

The thing is, Alice, for those few hours I spent with Tom each day, I felt like the old Evie. The Evie who laughs and jokes and always sees the joy in things. When we were together it felt—for just a little while—that we are not a country at war, and that Tom was just a regular Oxford scholar, not a Lieut. in the British Army. It was all so easy and wonderfully normal. A little too wonderful, perhaps. Nothing at all was said between us on matters of affection, but I cannot help feeling that so much was left *unsaid*.

I know you are already convinced that my heart was stolen by Tom Harding years ago while I wasn't paying any attention, and I'm beginning to think you may be right, darling. Still, it makes no sense at all, not least because John Hopper sent a telegram this morning inviting me to have dinner with him to-night, and I'm being dreadfully indecisive about what to wear (a sure sign that I am not just going along for the food).

What if I am falling in love with him, Alice?

Please send some words of advice. You were always much better at dealing with affairs of the heart.

With much love,

Evie

X

P.S. Do not show this to a soul. In fact, burn it.

P.P.S. I am so wrapped up in myself that I forgot to ask how the nursing is going. I hope it isn't dreadfully gruesome. x

From Alice to Evie

22nd October, 1915

Somewhere in France

Dear Evie,

I knew it! You always get cross before you admit you like a boy. But *love*! My friend, I never thought I'd hear you utter the word. You *liked* Tim Smith and Peter what's-his-name. You *liked* Jonathan Sawyer. But my goodness, you might be falling in *love*?

And with whom would that be—Thomas Harding or John

Hopper? I noticed you left that rather ambiguous in your last letter, you tease! But really, how could it ever be anyone but Tom. Of all the fellows, he's the one. He's charming without knowing it, intelligent without being boastful, and kind without expectation. He's known you most of your life and the spark between you two is immediately apparent to everyone in the room.

I wonder how he kisses. You'll have to tell all when you get to that!

I'm not so certain about this Hopper fellow. Didn't you say Tom has some reservations about him? Also, he isn't at war, is he? I must say, this gives me a seed of doubt as to his character, though if my Evie likes him so well, I'm sure I will grow to like him too.

As for me, I've been transferred out of the dressing station. I'm to drive an ambulance! I've seen a few other nurses doing the same, though not a large number. But imagine *me* behind the wheel, barrelling down the road at top speed—the girl who crashed a bicycle each time she rode it. Sometimes I wonder if they're mad to give me such responsibility, but they are in dire need. How glad I am for Billy Peters's tuition earlier this year! I'll help load the injured and race to the hospital trains with my precious cargo. Just think of it! I'll be a heroine. If this wasn't such a dreadful set of circumstances, I would don a pilot scarf, maybe a little rouge to look the part. Alas, this is no time for my silly antics. It's a serious business, saving lives.

How are things at home? I miss you horribly.

Gros bisous (as the French would say),

Alice

From Thomas to Evie

28th October, 1915

Somewhere in France

My dear Evie,

I couldn't bring myself to write to you the last fortnight. I've been sullen and angry with nothing nice to say. Despair. That's what I've felt. Despair that this blight on humanity continues and that I am in the middle of it; despair that Father is failing rapidly and I can't be there for his final days. It eats away at me.

Though a short reprieve, my trip home spoiled me quickly and I can think of nothing now but fine meals, sleeping in my warm bed, and your bright laughter. It's quite infectious, you know. The waiter at Simpson's was taken with it—and you—though perhaps it was your scandalous dress which drew his attention. Really, when you wear blue, you don't give menfolk a chance.

I've taken to card tourneys with the Tommies after dark. We use pebbles as tokens, and trade goods from home. To the winner goes the spoils. It's about the only time I don't feel like screaming until my lungs pop or someone shoots me. Whatever comes first.

Thank you for being there when I came home. Really being there. Beyond my poor father, it was a week of perfect days. I hope there will be more of them someday soon.

Yours,
Tom

From Evie to Tom

5th November, 1915

Richmond, England

My dearest Tom,

I have never known the weeks to drag so awfully. One minute you are here and it is as if we don't have a care in the world, and the next you are gone and there is nothing but a dreadful silence and endless worry. Every day since your return, I searched for my name in my postbag. Every day I had to endure the disappointment of finding nothing. You cannot imagine the relief when I received your letter, and yet now I face an entirely new anguish as you sound so awfully glum. Unusually so.

Is it unbearable to be back? Did your time here not lift your spirits and remind you of everything you are fighting for? Try to recall that roast beef and think of a time when we'll go to Simpson's again. If only Will were still there to jolly you along. He would tell you to stop stewing and to buck up and no doubt make you laugh with one of his ridiculous yarns. I miss him dreadfully, Tom. I miss so many things.

You will no doubt have heard the awful news about Edith Cavell being executed in Brussels for helping POWs escape to the Netherlands. It was all over the papers. The country is up in arms. Anti-German sentiment is at an all-time high. Men are rushing to the recruiting offices. I was very shaken by the news. I foolishly imagined women like Cavell would be immune to the German bullet. It seems that nobody is safe. Nobody. I worry dreadfully for Alice. She writes with news that she is to become an ambulance driver. She never ceases to surprise me. For someone who struggled to master control of her bicycle, I really don't hold out much hope for the poor men she transports. Then again, Alice always did love a bit of drama, didn't she? Ever the girl to go rushing headlong into some madcap adventure. I only hope that war will not prove to be an adventure too far.

Did you notice the date at the top of the letter? Bonfire night. The bonfire on the green is much smaller this year— you'll remember how impressive it usually is. We have become quite efficient at conserving everything, wood included. What would Fawkes and his conspirators make of this war we find ourselves in, I wonder? It makes their few barrels of gunpowder seem rather paltry. Remember, remember. Gosh, Tom. All I want to do is forget.

I will make sure to visit your father whenever I can manage time away from my duties here. He is in the best place and there is nothing more you can do for him, other than to make him proud to know that you are doing wonderfully well over there.

I must close. Mama is calling for me to help with her latest fund-raiser. If I drink much more tea I'm sure I will drown in the stuff.

Yours,
Lady Evelyn Elliott

P.S. I must apologise for all the wretched snivelling on your shoulder when you left. I don't know what came over me. In my despair, I forgot to give you my latest sketch, so I have enclosed it here. This little fellow is a brambling. I think him rather adorable.

P.P.S. As for my dress being scandalous! Really, Tom, you are terribly old-fashioned at times. Your eyes would pop out of their sockets if you saw the munitionettes. They wear trousers, Tom. *Trousers!*

P.P.P.S. (Sorry, I should probably have started another letter.) Latest column enclosed.

A WOMAN'S WAR
by our special correspondent in London,
Genevieve Wren

"When the Boys Come Home"

There are brief moments when it seems as though we are not a country at war. Those occasional hours when we might share a cup of tea with a friend or take a walk in our favourite park, laugh at a joke or a shared memory and almost forget what is happening across the Channel. Almost forget, but not quite. However briefly we may feel the burden of worry or grief lift from our aching shoulders, it is always there, like a shadow following close behind.

Perhaps we feel this the most when a loved one comes home on leave. They walk back into our lives and our homes as if they'd merely popped out to collect the milk or the newspaper. Like a ghost they appear in our sculleries and hallways, and we cannot quite believe they are really there at all. We can't stop touching them, eager fingers desperate to make sure they are real.

What blissful agony it is to have them back. All our hopes and dreams come true. Those long months without them, fading into nothing. They are here—in our arms and our beds, at our tables and by our sides. And yet, something is different because part of them is not here with us at all. It is still over there, with their pals. With their brothers in arms. And for all that we love them with every bone in our bodies, part of us daren't get too close because it is always there, lurking in the shadows: the knowledge that they must go back, and that when they do, our own battle with hope will begin once again.

We might never understand the life they have lived while they've been away. We might never understand their longing to return to life in the trenches, or their desire to relieve the man whose turn on leave is next. We might never understand the horrors they see in their dreams and shout about in the dark as we try to comfort them and remind them they are safe. We might never understand any of this.

They return to us as husbands, lovers, brothers, friends—but they also return to us as soldiers. War is part of who they are now. Part of who they will

always be. And we will love them while they are here,
and we will love them when they go back.

We will love them until we see them again, because
no matter how far away from home they are, they will
never be far from our thoughts or our hearts.

Until next time—courage!

Genevieve

From Thomas to Evie

10th November, 1915

Somewhere in France

Dear Evie,

Please ignore the brown smudges. I have a cut above my eye
that won't stop bleeding. Got hit by shrapnel this afternoon.
I'm low on paper or else I'd toss this and start again. We followed orders from Lieutenant Colonel Duncan, my superior,
and stalked through a patch of forest not far from the ▬▬▬▬
river. Barbed wire ran along the hill right to the water's edge
so we knew the Boche (French slang for Germans, in case you
didn't know) were nearby or had set a trap. We scooted around
the edge of the wood, glad to find it vacated. But we didn't
know we were standing in a minefield—until it was too late.

Two mines went off and took out a dozen men. I ran around
the outskirts of the field like a madman, ordering my men to
follow me. We were either going up in flames in an instant or

getting the hell out of there. Walking gingerly on tiptoe, sweating after each measly footstep, would have been too excruciating. Thankfully, we lost only one more soldier as we pulled out.

Make a mad dash for it, Will used to say. "Like we should in life, Tom. Always make a dash for it." It was his voice I heard as I ran. I swear to God he saved my life.

I was pretty ragged after, wretched with disgust at the senselessness of it all, and these weapons we've devised to annihilate more, and more, and more. A good friend was shipped off to the hospital. He lost at least one limb. His face looked pretty bad as well, but I think he'll pull through. I can't imagine what he'll do with himself when he discovers he's bound to a wheelchair the rest of his life. He was a champion rugby player at university. He'll be crushed, poor chap. At least he's alive, though I'm not sure that's much of a consolation to some.

I heard about Edith Cavell. What kind of man shoots a woman, in particular one who has devoted her life to helping others? Had I been on that firing squad, I would have walked away, faced punishment for disobedience. It isn't honourable, and in the midst of all this suffering, a man's honour is what distinguishes him from the beasts.

On a lighter note, I have a little scrapbook of your bird sketches now. You notice this time I didn't attempt to replicate one. With a buggered hand and a bleeding brow, my attempt at a brambling or a robin would likely make you laugh. It's difficult to write today as is.

Evie, about your tears. It was nice to feel appreciated and missed, feared-for even. I will reserve my shoulder for the curve of your cheek anytime. I hope I am lucky enough to feel it again.

Yours,

Tom

P.S. I'd be lying if I said I didn't feel like weeping the day I set foot on French soil again. Also, I miss Will, too. Every single day.

From Evie to Alice

20th November, 1915

Richmond, England

Dear Alice,

Apologies. I seem to have no time to put pen to paper. I am very busy at the post office with the approach of Christmas, which brings a flurry of new letters every day, and with the pathways too icy to take Rusty out, my round must be done on foot. Also, my column takes more time than I'd imagined. I fall into bed at night exhausted and barely have a moment to think, although when I do, it is the same thoughts I keep returning to and I remain as confused as ever when it comes to matters of the heart.

You do not know John Hopper, so I cannot expect you to be as sympathetic towards him, but I can assure you he is the perfect gentleman: handsome, witty, intelligent (and not without considerable wealth in his various businesses). He makes it very difficult not to be charmed in his company (I can only imagine those eyelashes of yours fluttering under his gaze). What is a girl to do when otherwise wholly deprived of male company? John encourages my writing and talks of opportunities that might present themselves when the war is over. He firmly believes women will find themselves better placed to continue in the roles they have adopted during the men's absence. He talks about the future a lot, Alice. He has hinted, on more than one occasion, that he would very much like me to be part of his.

As for Hopper not being at war, he assures me he would like to be, but is on official war duty with the War Office at Wellington House (don't ask me to explain what he does there. It is all rather secretive). We must remember that the war is being fought from many angles, and not always with a rifle in hand. After all, they do say the pen is mightier than the sword.

And then there is Tom. I'm certain he still sees me as nothing more than Will's sister and a good friend, and yet there were moments when we were together recently, moments when I thought he might take my hand, or look at me a certain way. His latest letter referred to "a week of perfect days" that we spent together during his leave. He also says that he hopes his shoulder can be used for the curve of my cheek again sometime soon. Much as I adored the time we spent together, when I think about it with a level head, much of it was occupied with the usual lighthearted banter that has always existed between us, and not of anything one might misconstrue as romance. You know how we like to poke fun at each other—always have.

With Hopper it is different. I feel more like a woman in his company, but then I feel more like myself in Tom's.

Oh, Alice. It is ridiculous. Why must love be so complicated? I suppose I have only myself to blame for bringing matters of the heart into it at all. Why I can't simply do business with Hopper and send words of encouragement to Tom, I don't know. But apparently we cannot choose with whom, or indeed when, we fall in love. My feelings for Tom come as much as a surprise to me as they would no doubt be to him, were he ever to find out. And he mustn't. This is to be our secret, Alice.

Do take care in that ambulance. You never were the best at direction and control when it comes to things on wheels.

Much love to you.

Evie

X

From Alice to Evie

22nd November, 1915

Somewhere in France

Dear Evie,

Just a quick note to say, what a lucky girl you are to have choices in love. I am happy no matter whom you choose—I adore *you* and that's what matters (even if you know my preference. Wink wink). I won't be the one lying next to the fellow every day, devoting myself to him for all eternity, etc., and you would. Imagine such a thing! I've never thought myself the marrying type, in spite of my boy-crazed mind, but who knows? My private has made a full recovery and has become a bit friendlier than usual of late. I quite like it. More soon.

Alice
X

From Evie to Tom

25th November, 1915

Richmond, England

My dear Tom,

What an absolute fool I am. I just found a letter I had written to you a fortnight ago in reply to your latest—but I never sent it. I was wondering why there was no reply. Now I know. Things move and change so quickly in this damned war that when I reread my letter, my words hardly make sense anymore, so I have thrown it into the fire and started again.

What I wish to say is that I think you terribly brave to be in the midst of such awfulness. You say you ran—made a mad dash for it. That we always must. I agree with Will on this. We must make a mad dash for everything in life, mustn't we? Why sit back and let it all pass us by? More than ever, I simply do not know what the world will look like when I wake up each morning. It all feels so fragile. Like silk beginning to fray, and once that thread begins to unravel, it is so difficult to stop it.

War makes me question everything. It makes me feel brave and then foolish and then reckless with my emotions so that I don't quite know who I am anymore.

I'm afraid I must tell you, that in the two weeks between my intended letter and this new attempt, your poor father has gone downhill rather rapidly. I'm sure Abshire has been in touch to tell you the same. I think he is giving up the fight, Tom. I hate to be the bearer of bad news, but I believe you must prepare yourself.

Wishing you some moments of peace among all that is so difficult.

Yours,

Evie

X

Telegram from Charles Abshire to Thomas

1ST DECEMBER 1915

TO: LT. THOMAS HARDING, RANSART, NORD-PAS-DE-CALAIS, FRANCE
SENT: 18:10 / RECEIVED: 18:45

DEEPLY REGRET TO INFORM YOU OF YOUR FATHER'S PASSING. DIED PEACEFULLY. DID NOT SUFFER. WILL SEND ON A LAST LETTER FROM HIM. WILL STAY ON AT LDT UNDER DIRECTION OF JOHN HOPPER UNTIL YOU RETURN. GODSPEED. YOUR FATHER WAS ETERNALLY PROUD OF YOU. ABSHIRE.

From Charles Abshire to Thomas

2nd December, 1915

London, England

My dear Thomas,

My sincere condolences for the loss of your father. He was a great man and a wonderful friend to me. He will be greatly missed by many. As promised, I've enclosed the letter from him, which he dictated to me just hours before he died.

Best wishes,
Charles

Letter from Thomas's father to Thomas

My dear son,

If I could muster the strength to laugh at the irony which has put me on death's door, I would. My confounded illness crippled me, but God sent in the Germans to finish me off. I'd had too much luck in battle those years in the South African War, I suppose. Now my time has run its course, but I am at peace. Cherish the good as it comes, Thomas. It slips away when you least expect it.

I know our disputes in the past led you to believe I lost faith in you, but I never doubted your character for a minute, or your intelligence. You make the world a better place by being in it. Have courage, dear boy. You will survive this ghastly war because you are strong—all heart as your mother was—and you will live a rich life. War has a way of making everything on the other side of it all the sweeter. Do not think of our quarrels or your inheritance when you make your decisions about the future. No matter what, you must walk your own path, just as I have. Nothing could make me prouder. Please know I will be with you always, looking after you.

With all my heart besides,
Father

From Evie to Thomas

5th December, 1915

Richmond, England

My dearest Tom,

I am so dreadfully sorry. I heard the news of your father's death from Hopper. He told me that Abshire sent word to you immediately. I believe he slipped away quietly in the end which, I suppose, is all that we can hope for when it comes. I hope you can draw some comfort from that, Tom, although I know you will be desperately sad to be over there and not here.

I will admit that I have been avoiding writing to you since I heard. There simply didn't seem to be any words to express my feelings adequately. We have been here before, haven't we? I seem to have used up any ability to write eloquently about death and grief. But each day since I learned of your father's passing I felt ever more awful for leaving you with no word. So this is my best attempt.

The funeral was a very dignified affair. You would have been very proud. I know you and your father had your difficulties (what child and their parents don't?), but when all's said and done, you would have been—and should be—a very proud son. If nothing else, war must make us value life, with all its frustrations and disagreements. I find myself more forgiving of Mama's "ways." Sometimes I even feel quite fond of her.

And for all that I dearly love to receive your letters, I hate to learn of your skirmishes and the dreadful injuries that fall on your troops. I would ask you to be a little less descriptive, but that would be cowardly. I must know the truth of it from you because we hear very little of it in the newspapers. Everything is still bolstered by talk of bravery and victorious battles against the enemy. The government would have us believe you are all enjoying a jolly holiday over there. The headlines are nothing more sinister than "Making Steady Progress" and "A Day of Promise." Cavell's execution was, of course, used to stir up patriotic sentiment among those who haven't signed up yet. Leaflets and posters are everywhere. "REMEMBER CAVELL." "GO NOW!" Women are shamed into encouraging their sons and husbands to go. There is talk of conscription coming in the very near future. Hopper believes the act will be passed early in the New Year and then everyone will have to go. We will be a nation of women, alone.

I'm afraid I have no bird for you this time, but I am working on one and will send it soonest. When I study my field book or watch the birds in the garden, I find myself wishing *I* were a bird. And you, Tom. And all the poor souls out there. What freedoms we would have. What joy to spread our wings and fly away, to choose our own direction, to catch the thermals and soar. What are we compared to the birds of the air? We are but worms, tunnelling blindly through the earth. We, who think we are so superior, are the greatest of fools.

I may be silly to do so, but I still imagine our Christmas in Paris and pray, with all my heart, that this Christmas will not be our last. I imagine all the many peacetime Christmases stretching out before us, waiting to be filled with mirth and merriment and carolling and good brandy. I imagine a winter's afternoon stroll along the Seine, just for the thrill of it. They say the light in Paris is extraordinary. I imagine a little sliver of it, resting in my heart, to brighten these darkest of days.

Yours in deepest sympathy for your loss.

Evelyn

X

P.S. A few lines from Blake. Goodnight, my friend.

The sun descending in the west,
The evening star does shine;
The birds are silent in their nest,
And I must seek for mine.

From Evie to her editor

6th December, 1915

Richmond, England

Dear Mr. Davies,

Please find my latest column enclosed (John Hopper has seen it, but I would greatly value your opinion as to whether it needs a bit more work). I know you asked me to steer clear of matters of death or anything too morbid, but this is war, sir, and I'm afraid the two are rather unavoidable.

I have already lost my only brother in this war, and recently a very dear friend of mine lost his father as a result of the recent zeppelin raid on London. It isn't enough, sir, for the mothers and wives and sisters of the dead to be expected to carry their grief silently. Therefore, I find myself encouraging us to talk about those we have lost.

I am heartened by the news that you have received several letters in support of my first two columns. Dare I consider them fan mail? I would very much like to read them and wonder if you might be so kind as to forward them to me.

I find myself more certain than ever that I would like to make a career as a journalist when the war is over and things are settled once again. I hear there are female reporters at the Front—Nellie Bly for one, reporting for the *New York Evening Journal* from the Eastern Front. Wouldn't it be something to have a Nellie Bly all of your own, reporting for the LDT? I never was one for knitting, and the sight of blood makes me feel faint, so I am not really cut out for nursing either. Perhaps reporting on the war is to be my most effective contribution.

I had the misfortune of reading a book recently by the writer Arnold Bennett who is of the opinion that "journalists and women-journalists . . . [are] about as far removed organically from the other as a dog from a cat." He believes "the female journalist" to be unreliable and to have a disregard for deadlines. He goes on to accuse "the female journalist" (as if we were all one person) of inattention to detail; a slipshod approach to spelling, grammar, and punctuation; and a lack of restraint in her prose. If you ever find yourself in this Mr. Bennett's company, I might ask you to correct him on his "opinions" before giving him a firm slap on the cheek on my behalf.

I shall send more next week (female inadequacies permitting).

Yours sincerely,
Evelyn Elliott

A WOMAN'S WAR

by our special correspondent in London,
Genevieve Wren

"Notes on Loss"

Life goes on, we are told. But I am not so sure.

Yes, we wake up each morning, we wash, we dress, we talk, we go about our day, we pray, we sleep. The endless repetition of the things we must do in order to survive. But I ask you, women of Britain, is this *life*, or is it simply survival? It appears to me that we do not fare much better than our men over there in the trenches when it comes to living life to the full. We endure. We fight. We survive. Soldiers all.

Life does not go on when our loved ones leave us. Life departs in all ways. The life we have known, the life we have anticipated, the life we hoped for—all of it disappears in an instant when the dreaded telegram arrives. "I regret to inform you . . ." Were any words ever more painful?

We read the condolences and the brief description of our loved one's death. We sink to our knees and our heart aches with a pain—a physical pain—the likes of which we have never known. And yet we somehow stand up again, and we remember how to breathe.

We carry on.

Life, in another form, carries on.

We are encouraged not to talk about our losses, to lock them away behind closed doors and suffer in silence. We see it everywhere—in the pale faces of our friends and neighbours, in the reluctance to look each other in the eye—but we do not talk about it, or dwell on it.

We carry on.

We must stop this silence and talk and shout and scream and cry. I encourage you to talk about your loved ones, to share happy memories, to remember those fond little moments: a joke, a nickname, a favourite toy or book. We should not consign our brave men to a silent unspoken past where, in years to come, they will be forgotten, never spoken of. They deserve far more than that. They deserve our strength and our bravery. They deserve to be remembered. We must keep their memory alive through our words and our reminiscences, both in private and in public.

Our losses in this war will be the hardest we will ever have to bear, but we can bear it together, over a cup of weak tea or sitting beside the fire, where happy memories burn bright if we can find the strength to share them.

Until next time—courage!

Genevieve Wren

From Thomas to Evie

10th December, 1915

Somewhere in France

Dear Evie,

Thank you for your kind words about my father. I still didn't know, until now, whether or not he had decided to leave the paper to me, but I'm relieved to discover all is in order. I'm not certain the direction I'd like to take, but I wanted the choice at least. I made him so angry that I thought he may well have left the business in its entirety to John Hopper instead. I'm hesitant to explain why he has taken issue with Hopper in the past since you are good friends and colleagues, so I will just leave it at that.

Sometimes I think about the young man I was before this all started. How could I have been so blind, so optimistic and clueless about the way of things? I didn't have a care in the world outside cricket and my studies. At least I treated everyone with respect, women included. Speaking of treating women with respect, what happens out here on a daily basis is shameful. Prostitutes hang around the barracks and are bussed out to the field hospitals. I've seen quite a few French soldiers offer their sisters to the other men. It's crass, I know, but a reality of war, I suppose. I can't say I'm interested. I don't know how some chaps do it. If they respected their mothers and sisters, they wouldn't treat women the way they do. I'm not interested in much these days, I'm reluctant to admit. The view from here is rather grey, what with my father's passing, and several more friends laid to rest this week. The only relief comes in sleep. When it comes, I'm so exhausted I don't dream and I'm grateful for it. It's an escape for a few hours.

I hope you enjoy the journal I sent. I bought it at a little shop in a nearby town. The monsieur makes the paper himself and his wife does all of the artistry you see on the cover and on the inside pages. The birds made me think of you. The handkerchief I enclose is for future tears. I hope none are caused by me. And I wish against all else that you are happy, safe, and hopeful, my strong, dearest friend. I'm not sure I can be.

Affectionately,

Tom

From Jack Davies to Thomas

15th December, 1915

Fleet Street, London, England

To Lieutenant Thomas Harding,

I write to you with dire news. Since your father fell ill, Charles and I have run the paper, which is to say, I have run the paper—until of late. John Hopper has inserted himself firmly into the LDT's affairs.

Let me be plain. Your cousin is mucking about the office, creating small fires by insulting the staff. Only yesterday he dismissed several of my columnists without checking with me. The paper shortages mean we need to consolidate our columns, it's true, but to do so out of hand without consulting the rest of us—and in such a manner! Also, he has threatened Charlie Abshire, and has plans to hire his own writers when we can expand again. The staff is outraged, and, frankly, so am I.

In short, Tom, we're at war here on Fleet Street and all is bullocks.

You've always been an intelligent, industrious fellow. I have full faith in your ability to right things again. It's time you were the man at the helm as your father always wanted you to be.

Please instruct me how to proceed, or I may have a few choice words with your cousin, and you'll have an Editor-in-Chief tossed out on his behind.

I await your reply.

Sincerely,

Jack Davies

From Thomas to Jack Davies

16th December, 1915

Somewhere in France

Dear Sir,

Thank you for your candour, as always. I didn't want Hopper in the office at all, but had no choice with this bloody war. I'll write to him immediately, remind him of his duties—and his boundaries. The last thing we need is him making a mess of things when the world is up to its breeches in horse shit, as is.

Do me a favour and keep an eye on Evelyn Elliott, would you? She's a good friend and the thought of Hopper leading her astray makes me incensed. I might start my own war on Fleet Street if it comes to it.

Keep up the good work, Jack.

Sincerely,

Lieutenant Thomas Harding

From Thomas to John Hopper

17th December, 1915

Somewhere in France

Dear John,

It has come to my attention that columnists have been dismissed without consent, and the paper's contents have been changed at the LDT. I have also been informed that animosity is at an all-time high among the staff. Hopper, I appreciate all you are doing to help in the office, but causing a mutiny with my Editor-in-Chief, insulting Charles Abshire, and making decisions about the paper's future without me involved are not what I had in mind. Nor is it acceptable. Once again I ask you to consult me before making such decisions, and should I decline them, to respect my word in following through as requested. Should these grievous reports continue, I will seek help elsewhere.

I hope I have made myself clear. I have no interest in going to such extremes, but I will do what is necessary to protect the interests of the LDT.

Sincerely,

Lieutenant Thomas Harding

From Evie to Thomas

18th December, 1915

Richmond, England

Dear Thomas,

What can I say that hasn't already been said? I wish I had some words that could cheer you up, warm your feet and hands, and bring solace to your broken heart. You must not trouble yourself with the actions of the other men. Stay true to your own principles. While I cannot understand the urges of men, nor the despair you must endure every day, I can remind you of those who miss you and think of you and long for you to be home.

And I can also tell you how very touched I was to know that you thought of me when you saw that beautiful journal. I will cherish it, and I promise to fill it only with happiness and hope, not with sorrow. Sorrow has no place inside something so beautiful. The lace handkerchief I will keep in a drawer until such time as I can wipe away my tears of joy when I learn that the war is over and we are victorious and you are returned to us safe and well.

I think of you every day, Thomas Archibald, and I know you will endure. Cast aside those dark thoughts. Cast aside your fears and hunger. You must stay strong. I absolutely insist.

Write soon and often. I become very irritable when I don't hear from you for a while.

Yours in hope.

Evie

XXX

From Evie to Alice

18th December, 1915

Richmond, England

Dear Alice,

A sad note to let you know that Tom's father died at the start of the month. Poor Tom is dreadfully upset and seems without purpose or hope. I feel helpless with him so far away with only his worries and the enemy for company. He writes of strange things: prostitutes and the inappropriate behaviour of the troops. And yet he sent me the most beautiful journal, decorated with birds, and a handkerchief—for my tears, he said. Did you ever hear such a beautiful sentiment?

I'm more confused than ever. One moment I dare to believe Tom has feelings for me. The next, I seem to be nothing but a friend to him again. I write little hints in my letters to him, giving him an opportunity to declare any feelings for me, but he either doesn't notice them (you know how very useless men can be in matters of subtlety), or chooses to ignore them. I keep his letters under my pillow now. Like the princess disturbed by the pea beneath her many mattresses, my sleep is disturbed by his words. While he struggles to sleep in restful peace, so will I. And among it all is John Hopper with his interesting conversation and Turkish cigarettes and expensive cologne and ambitions. He means to run half of Fleet Street, I'm sure of it. He makes it ever harder to resist his charms.

Where are you now? Can you say? I pray that you were no-where near the gas attacks on the French troops. It is hard to believe we will soon mark our second Christmas at war. Do you remember Lloyd George's rousing speech, "The war to end all wars"? They said it would be over by Christmas. They didn't say which one though, did they?

My bones ache with cold and anxiety. Papa and I scour the papers for the names of the Missing, Wounded, and Dead every day. How easily we pass over the unfamiliar names. List after list. Page after page. And yet every one, every single name, is a person, a much-loved son, brother, husband, lover. I was so angry yesterday I took the newspaper to the top of Richmond Hill and shouted out each name to the wind. I don't know how many there were in total, but I was there for a long time. The wind carried their names away over the meadows. I hope they soar on the breeze for all eternity. Gone, but never forgotten.

Wishing you a very happy Christmas, and wishing us all a brighter, happier, and victorious New Year.

Write soon—and remember that the brake pedal is in the middle.

Much love,

Evie

X

From Alice to Evie

24th December, 1915

Somewhere in France

My dearest Evie,

Thank you for sending news of Mr. Harding. Such a shame for Tom to miss his father's funeral. And I'm sorry you feel Tom's absence so keenly. He will survive! Say it every day in your heart and aloud on that hilltop. We have to believe passionately, with all our might, to will things to happen sometimes. You have never lacked will and optimism. Don't bow to the shadows now, my girl. We need our Evie to be strong, and inspire others with her new column.

You should see me drive this ambulance. I'm a natural now. I barrel over the roads at top speed, dodging gunfire and all else. We load the wounded carefully from the field hospitals and I race to the hospital train with one thing on my mind— cheat death! Sometimes I'm successful, sometimes I'm not, but I try like mad. As thrilling as it is, I find myself dreadfully homesick. I would give anything to be home for Christmas this year.

Chin up, love. We'll get through this. Happy Christmas.

With love,

Alice

From Evie to Thomas

24th December, 1915

Richmond, England

Dear Thomas,

No word from you for a while. I suspect it is far too cold to hold a pen.

Even though I know this won't reach you in time, I wanted— once again—to wish you a happy Christmas, and to let you know that I am thinking of you, and will think of you especially on the 25th. When I hear the carol singers in the town square I will join in, and sing for dear Will and for you, and for all the brave men fighting, and I will pray for happier times and victory ahead.

With fondest wishes, and three cheers for the Allies.

Evie

X

Paris

20th December, 1968

An early morning fog lingers on the Seine, painted rose-gold by the frail winter sun. These were her favourite times: just after sunrise and just before sunset. The bookends of the day, she called them. She had so many elegant ways to look at things. She taught me to see the world so differently.

But my thoughts this morning are with Will. My childhood friend, my counsel, and my conspirator. The man who stood shoulder to shoulder with me when we went over the top the first time. His presence was a blaze of light in a bleak world. Of us all, why did he have to be the one to go? I have never understood the choices Fate made on the battlefields.

Margaret fusses with the blanket wrapped around my legs. She mutters about my not catching a chill before she resumes her position at the helm and pushes me on. The indignity of a wheelchair is unbearable for a man with such pride, but if it is the only way I can get to the places I want to go, then so be it.

We make easy progress, it being early yet. Pigeons strut and coo as we go. The snap of their wings as they take flight brings me back to the trenches and the carrier pigeons we took to the Front in wicker baskets, to dispatch with messages back to base. I had always thought them nothing but vermin, but I suppose everyone finds their true calling in times of war. Even the brave pigeons were decorated and hailed as heroes.

Apart from the birds, all is silent along these Parisian boulevards. Cars don't yet clog the streets. Only a single bell rings in a nearby church tower. The quiet hours are a gift, I think.

I feel for the cuff links in my pocket. She wanted me to leave them at his grave, but it is too difficult a journey for me to travel out of the city to the military cemeteries, especially with the heavy snow. I hope my solution would please her.

Margaret buys Christmas roses from the flower market and it is among the velvet petals that I place the cuff links. I leave them at the Arc de Triomphe, at the Tomb of the Unknown Soldier. It is the best I can do. With misty eyes I look to the tomb and read the inscription.

Ici repose un soldat mort pour la patrie. 1914–1918

Margaret lays the roses at the foot of the stone slab, beside the eternal flame, and for the last time I wish dear Will a Happy Christmas, and the fondest of farewells.

"He was one of the bravest men I ever knew, Margaret."

She dabs at her cheeks. Tears glisten in the sunlight. "I know, Mr. Harding. I know."

But she doesn't. Nobody can, unless they were there. Only those of us who lived those days will ever truly know. It is a sorrow that has never left me, and I am glad of this place, this tomb, this eternal flame. A reminder of what was lost. A reminder, so we will never forget.

It is why I am grateful now for the letters. They, perhaps, are the starkest reminder of all.

Back at the apartment, with the fire crackling in the grate, I sit up in bed, my head propped against too many pillows, and I read on . . .

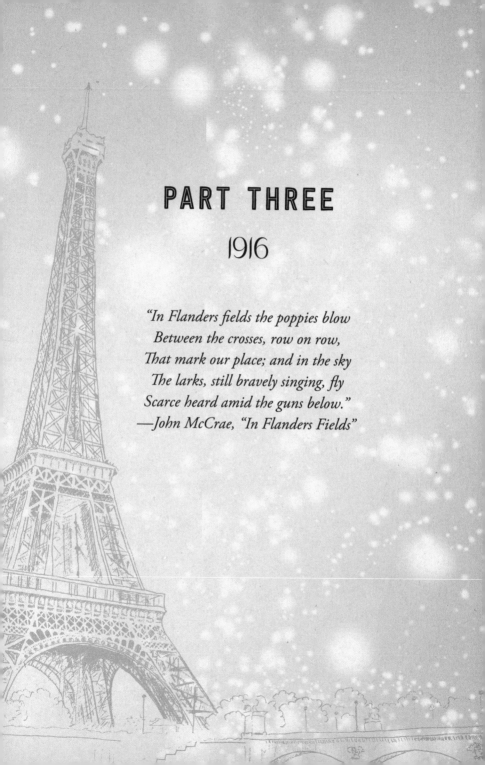

PART THREE

1916

*"In Flanders fields the poppies blow
Between the crosses, row on row,
That mark our place; and in the sky
The larks, still bravely singing, fly
Scarce heard amid the guns below."*
—John McCrae, "In Flanders Fields"

From Thomas to Evie

1st January, 1916

Somewhere in France

Dear Evie,

I hope you enjoyed Christmas, or rather, that you made the best of it, given how things are. I know your family will have struggled this first Christmas without Will. I thought of you often.

Thank you, as ever, for your encouraging and kind words last month. A heavy cloud has hovered over me these last weeks, and I've been unable to shake it with Father's passing. Another Christmas at war exacerbated things, but I'm breathing easier now that the festivities, and the incessant reminder of all I have lost, are behind me. A new year lies ahead. Though I am losing hope every day that I will ever return to England in one piece—or at all—at least time marches forward, paying no heed to the follies of men. There's something oddly comforting in that truth. The world goes on. Once more around the sun we will travel.

On a lighter note, you won't believe this but I ran into Alice Cuthbert! She was at the field hospital, ordering everyone about like a mother hen. I believe she may have found her calling in life. She was her usual charming self, though her immediate optimism has dimmed a bit. No one can escape the gruelling realities of war. Nonetheless, we shared a few stories and fond memories of happier times and raised a Christmas glass to absent friends.

Would you mind sending on a new pair of gloves? We've been told we'll be on a long march in the coming weeks and mine are shredded and too thin. Trying to ward off the infernal frostbite.

You're a star, Evie. About the only light I see in these endless nights.

Yours,

Tom

From Evie to Thomas

10th January, 1916

Richmond, England

Dearest Thomas,

Happy New Year!

As always, wonderful to hear from you. I thought of you often this past week and am much cheered to hear that you and Alice found each other and shared a glass of something. Fate works in strange ways, doesn't it. I can easily picture her bossing everyone around, charming them all with that smile of hers. I imagine her easy company made for a wonderful Christmas gift. I only wish I could have shared that moment with you both.

As you suspected, Christmas was a rather subdued affair here. Our eyes were all drawn to the empty chair where Will used to sit. It isn't right without him here, without his laughter and teasing. I don't think I will ever get used to his absence. I feel it like a shadow has settled on my heart. I was glad when Boxing Day arrived and the few remaining staff were given their gifts and we could move on.

No other news as such. Nothing much happens during the festivities, does it? I'm working on my next column. Hopper is terribly enthusiastic about it all. He says he has plenty of ideas for future topics should my well of inspiration run dry. By the way, did I mention I get "fan" mail now? Or rather, Genevieve does. It is hard not to feel a little important when you realise your words have reached out and really touched someone—helped them even. It makes me more determined than ever to keep writing.

I have enclosed a package of new gloves, socks, tobacco, tea, and brandy. What more could a fellow want?!

Write soon, dear.

Yours,

Evie

X

From Evie to Alice

11th January, 1916

Richmond, England

Happy New Year, dearest girl!

What news from France? I had a short note from Tom yesterday—he tells me you two happened upon each other and shared a Christmas drink. How was he, Alice? How did he look? Was he in reasonable spirits? I envy you to have spent that time with him. Please write and tell me what—if anything—was said, because if I know you at all I suspect you won't have been able to resist the chance to meddle and draw something from him with regard to his affections (or lack of them) for me.

I must tell you that the falling of the snow, the fire in the grate, memories of Will, and a large sherry got the better of me and prompted a great outpouring of emotion. I wrote a rather sentimental letter to Tom on Christmas Day. I meant every word, but now I cannot find the courage to send it. For the time being I have placed it for safekeeping inside a beautiful journal he sent me, along with a lace handkerchief. Perhaps it is best there, and not in his hands. Unless, of course, you have news for me?

Did you mark Christmas at all, apart from your drink with Tom? It was a wretched affair here. The jolly gatherings I remember so fondly seem to slip further and further away. I wonder if we'll ever know true happiness again. Of course, I wrote a thoroughly uplifting piece for the newspaper—life must go on, it is our duty to keep our spirits up, that sort of thing. I have never felt less connected to my words. It was almost as if someone else wrote them for me. It's so desperately hard to believe in these endless sentiments of hope.

How is your ambulance driving? Are things improving there at all for the Allies? We hear such conflicting reports in the newspapers and in letters from the Front. When the men come home on leave they have such terrible stories to tell. What of the brave animals, Alice? Do you see the horses and dogs? I hate to think of them suffering, but I hear the most dreadful accounts of horses drowning in the thick mud. Is it true? The fields are so empty here. One could almost forget how many beautiful creatures used to run free on the land. All of them gone, except for the ones that were too old and lame to be of any use in the first place. I wonder whatever became of Will's beloved Hamlet and Shylock. I hardly dare imagine.

In other news, the conscription act has been passed so it seems that all the men we have left must go to fight, apart from those who are married. John Hopper tells me he has been asked to remain on war duty at Wellington House. He is itching to see some action, and is damned frustrated by it all. I don't wish to sound unkind in encouraging him to go, but I hear so many stories of men finding all manner of clever ways to get around the system and sign up, regardless of height and age restrictions and health. The army are desperate for any man they can get at this stage. I'm sure Hopper will get his chance soon.

Well, I must close. I am due to report at the post office shortly and the postmistress does not tolerate tardiness.

I will write again soon.

Stay safe.

Evie.

X

From Thomas to Evie

20th January, 1916

Somewhere in France

Dear Evie,

Thank you for the gloves and socks. I bow to you in gratitude. And the tobacco and brandy! I'll make good use of them.

How are things at home? Your column is going well, I hope. I've heard some disparaging reports from Jack Davies about the state of affairs in the office at the LDT, and wondered what you make of it all. I wrote to him, urging him to take the reins when he can, Hopper's authority aside. He might be a blustery old bird, but he's one of the best damn editors in London and I trust his opinion. I hope the hullabaloo isn't affecting your writing, at any rate.

I would tell you more of what's happening here, but it's so black, I fear you'd stop writing to me. You'll have to settle for a few lines of poetry from Shakespeare's *Twelfth Night* instead:

> *Come away, come away, death,*
> *And in sad cypress let me be laid.*
> *Fly away, fly away, breath;*
> *I am slain by a fair cruel maid.*
> *My shroud of white, stuck all with yew,*
> *O, prepare it!*
> *My part of death, no one so true*
> *Did share it.*

Not a flower, not a flower sweet,
On my black coffin let there be strown.
Not a friend, not a friend greet
My poor corpse, where my bones shall be thrown.

Ever yours,
Tom

From Alice to Evie

28th January, 1916

Somewhere in France

Dearest Evie,

Happy New Year, darling! I have only a few quick minutes
to write. We've been working flat out the last week, and short
staffed. I keep hoping the Americans will join us. We're lacking supplies, ammunition, men . . . and we desperately need
more nurses. It's a mess here. Sanitary conditions in the huts
are truly awful, and even the duckboards we walk on are now
covered with mud. I've taken more than my fair share of spills.
You wouldn't believe the state of me. I am well, though, and
missing you!

Tom is thin as a twig, poor fellow. I got the feeling he doesn't
eat much, even when there's enough rations to be had. Melancholy seems to press on him, Evie, and in truth, I fear he may
be suffering from some sort of emotional or nervous distress. I

encouraged him to apply for leave. And his reply? "Why should I go home when my demons will follow me there? I would think only of my men that I leave behind to face their doom." Goodness, I encouraged him to drink a large glass of wine after such a speech. I mentioned that you would help restore his spirits. He looked at me then, from hollow eyes, and said, "I wish she could save me, Alice. I feel myself slipping away."

I told him you cared for him a great deal and would help him find his way, that he should lean on those who love him. I'm not certain he took my meaning, sadly. He is in a desperate way at the moment.

I must go, but sending lots of love. Oh, and the ambulance driving is still a great challenge, but I think I've finally mastered that devil of a machine. Just don't tell anyone I've put a few dents in the bumper. I keep hoping no one will notice.

Alice

X

From Evie to Thomas

30th January, 1916

Richmond, England

My dear Thomas,

We are to have Shakespeare again, are we? Please try to find something happier. A comedy, maybe. Wasn't *A Midsummer*

Night's Dream always a favourite of yours? Spend some time with Puck and Bottom and the fairies rather than stuffy old kings and raging storms. I don't like to hear you dwell on death so much.

Alice wrote. She said you are finding it all rather difficult at the moment. I wish there was something I could do to help, other than send brandy and letters. I've enclosed a little volume of sonnets to help keep your mind occupied in the bleaker moments. Look to it when you find the going tough, when you feel you can't bear it any longer. *You can,* Tom. I know you can—and you will. Even in the blackest hours remember that a new dawn is racing towards you. We must be victorious soon. Surely, we must.

As to the situation at the LDT, I try my best to keep out of the continual tussle for power. Honestly, you would think grown men would act with a little more dignity. Are you quite sure Hopper is the cause of the disruption? He speaks with nothing but passion and good intent whenever we discuss the LDT—or you. He only wants what is best for the paper, although I know he is ambitious and isn't afraid to challenge the staff to go further in their reporting. I do know he finds Jack Davies rather impossible to deal with. Are you sure Davies isn't spinning you a yarn? Playing on old rivalries between cousins? I shouldn't give it another thought if I were you, Tom. Leave the boys to play in the schoolyard while you and all the real men fight it out on the battlefield.

All remains relatively peaceful here. The occasional hasty

marriage and a baby born out of wedlock keep the gossips' tongues wagging. The world keeps turning. Life goes on. We must take courage from that.

Never be alone, Tom. Know that I am thinking of you.

Yours,

Evie.

XX

From Thomas to Evie

22nd February, 1916

Somewhere in France

Dear Evie,

Just a quick note as we're packing up and heading out towards the ▆▆ river. We've got quite a march ahead of us. You may not hear from me as often for a few weeks, but I do intend to write when I can. Send up some prayers, friend. We're headed into the belly of the beast and I'll need all of your courage and strength behind me as I lead the battalion. I'll be thinking of you.

With affection,

Tom

From Evie to Thomas

28th February, 1916

Richmond, England

Dear Thomas,

Godspeed, my friend. I so hate to hear of you heading out on a long march, but I know you will lead your men well, and bravely.

We hear the French are in a tense battle with the Germans at Verdun. Terrible losses. I pray you aren't there, friend. I had a dream last night that you'd happened upon a comfortable French *pension* somewhere in the countryside far away from the sound of shelling and sniper fire. A wonderful old lady (Madame de Carteret was her name) fussed over you and made you a local peasant stew to warm your bones. She was terribly kind and you grew stronger every day on the settle bed beside the fire. You took to whittling wooden animals for her from firewood and Madame de Carteret was delighted with the little treasures you made for her. Her husband and son had been killed in Belgium, so she was glad of your company.

I hope it might come true, Tom, and that you might find such comfort and kindness. Do you remember how you were always scraping at a piece of willow with your pocket knife, insisting you'd carved an elephant or some such when all Will and I could see was a lumpy piece of wood? We were cruel to tease you but all those memories are my richest treasures now.

Such carefree happy times. Perhaps you will whittle me a bird someday?

So many men are gone now. Only those who are married, or in reserved occupations remain—and the "conchies," of course. How they can bring themselves to walk the streets while everyone else faces conscription bravely is beyond my comprehension. How can they be so selfish? Why should they be spared when millions will not be? There are lads as young as fourteen and fifteen who have forged their date of birth and gone out like brave men. We read reports of tribunals in the papers every day, some poor chap or other stating his case for refusing to take up arms. Some are sent out to do noncombatant work like stretcher bearing. Others are imprisoned for their morals. It truly breaks my heart when I see the shadows their mothers and sisters have become. They hunch over like hags when they walk, always looking at the ground, ashamed to look anyone in the eye.

Stay safe, my friend. I comfort myself with reading the many letters you have sent to me since the war started. Do you remember how naive we were? How this was a grand adventure and you would be home in weeks, if you ever got to see any action. Who would ever have thought so many months and years lay ahead, or that we would ever have so much we needed to say to each other. And there is so much more to be said, Tom.

I live in hope that another letter from you will be on its way to me soon.

Evie

XX

Telegram from Thomas to Evie

15TH MARCH 1916

TO: EVELYN ELLIOTT, POPLARS, RICHMOND, LONDON SW
SENT: 17:22 / RECEIVED: 18:34

BATTALION DECIMATED. SURVIVING FEW JOINING
ANOTHER. NOT LOOKING GOOD. WILL SEND WORD
SOONEST. ACHING FOR HOME. TOM.

From Evie to Thomas

17th March, 1916

Richmond, England

Dearest Tom,

What anguish to read your telegram. I will pray for your safety, wherever you are. If this letter reaches you, please know that you are in all our thoughts. I cannot fight these battles for you, but I know you are a strong leader and that your men will look to you for direction and courage. Think only of that. Think of the men you have already saved, and those you will save yet.

You are so very brave and we are all so proud.

Victory will be ours soon and then a lifetime of peace awaits.

Yours,

E

X

From Evie to Jack Davies

2nd April, 1916

Richmond, England

Dear Sir,

Please find enclosed my latest column in which I address the issue of conscription. I hope you and the newspaper's readers will find it satisfactory. Given the mutinous reaction of groups like the NCF since the Military Service Act came into law, and with recent news concerning the imprisonment of Edith Smith for printing an NCF leaflet without submitting it for censorship, I am rather nervous about this latest piece, and its subject matter. But perhaps now, more than ever, a column written by a woman and dedicated to women is very appropriate.

You mentioned previously that you would send on some of the correspondence "Genevieve" has received. I would very much like to see the letters, if they are not too numerous, or too damning of my opinions.

Yours sincerely,

Evelyn Elliott

A WOMAN'S WAR

by our special correspondent in London,
Genevieve Wren

"We Who Are Left"

Conscription has seen the last of our men dispatched to war. Whatever our individual thoughts on the morality of compulsory conscription, fate (and politics) will always have the final say. Men of all ages and standing are gone.

The farmer no longer tends his crops. The bus driver no longer smiles a cheery Hello. The postman no longer cycles along the lane. We are a nation of women, and we that are left must now stand taller than ever before, dust off our pride, roll up our sleeves, and do our bit. We may think that we lack the skills, the strength, the physical ability to do some of the jobs required, but how do we know if we do not try. "Give a man a fish and you feed him for a day. Teach a man to fish and you feed him for a lifetime." We choose to learn how to fish, don't we, brave women of Britain?

Just as our courageous soldiers must learn to fight and to kill and to survive, so must we learn to keep this country on its feet. To bring food into the home and maintain law and order on the streets and keep everything running like clockwork, ready for when they return.

I urge you all to find a way to help, however small

it may seem. Together we can do extraordinary things and keep the home fires burning.

Until next time—courage!

Genevieve.

From Jack Davies to Evie

12th April, 1916

London, England

Dear Miss Elliott,

As requested, please find enclosed a selection of "fan letters" for your attention. Your Genevieve Wren is causing quite a stir. There is a sackful of letters, so this is just a small selection for your perusal.

Regarding the other matter we discussed recently, I am still making enquiries. If it were up to me, I would be happy to dispatch you and your notepad to France right away. You connect with people in a way most journalists cannot. You speak to them as if you were having a friendly natter over a cup of tea. I have no hesitation in knowing that you would write with passion and honesty and be an enormous success. However, as you know, women and journalism are an unconventional combination. Put a war zone into the frame and we have a very difficult—if not impossible—path to navigate. I'm also meeting with resistance by those involved in the running of the paper—and with Tom Harding away, I can't make a decision without the consent of someone in a position of authority.

I will keep trying—if you are still certain. I don't need to spell out the risks to you. If I can't get you there in any official reporting capacity, my only other suggestion is that you find a way to go over in some other—more acceptable—capacity (nurse, telephonist, etc.) and send your reports to me covertly?

I know you have dismissed the idea before, but if you are determined to go, it may be the only possible way. I'll wait for your word.

Yours sincerely,

J.D.

Fan letter to Evie

Dear Miss Wren,

I have never written to a newspaper before, and I am nervous to do so. I have been reading your column in the *London Daily Times* and had to write to tell you how much I look forward to it, and how much your words mean to me. I have lost two sons and a brother in the war. My husband and two other sons are still out there. I have an elderly mother to care for and am lucky to have very kind neighbours, but the house—once filled with noise and laughter, and life—is so empty. I do my best, but it isn't easy. Your words are a comfort to me. It is almost as if you know me, as if you are speaking to me personally.

I just wanted to let you know that you are helping many women with your honesty.

I don't know who you are, or what your circumstances might be, but it doesn't matter. Whoever and wherever you are, when

I read your words you are right here with me in my humble little kitchen, and for that I am very grateful.

May God keep you and your loved ones safe.

Marjorie Barrow

From Charles Abshire to Thomas

20th April, 1916

London, England

Dear Thomas,

I urge you to check in with Jack Davies at the LDT. Neither he nor I have heard from you in weeks and I'm concerned both for the paper and for your welfare. Please respond at once.

Sincerely,

Charles Abshire

From Evie to Thomas

26th April, 1916

Richmond, England

Dearest Tom,

A month has passed now without any word from you and I'm terribly worried. It is so unlike you not to write for so long.

You were so eager with your previous replies, and now the days drag with the quiet agony of not hearing from you, not knowing where, or how, you are.

Papa assures me you will be on the march and too exhausted to do anything other than slump into an exhausted heap. Mama says the best I can do is keep writing to you. And I will. Always.

I pray for your safety, dear.

Yours in hope,

Evie

X

From Evie to Alice

30th April, 1916

Richmond, England

Dearest Alice,

How are you? What news?

I am desperately worried. There has been no word from Tom for over a month now. Nothing since his telegram saying his battalion had been all but decimated, that he was joining another battalion and was on the march. I fear he may have been at Verdun from where we heard such awful news of casualties, and I cannot stop stewing on what you said about him being in a bad way when you saw him.

I feel very uneasy. I cannot eat, or sleep. I find myself imagining the very worst of things—that he is a POW at the mercy of the enemy, alone and afraid. Or worse. And yet I try to remind myself that if anyone can survive this war, Thomas Harding can. I must believe in him, mustn't I? Now, more than ever. His absence, and his silence, makes my heart grow ever fonder. Meanwhile, I see John Hopper with increasing regularity. The stark disparity between their worlds twists my stomach into knots and makes me more determined to play some vital part in the greater cause. You will think me mad, but Jack Davies and I are hatching a plan for me to get to France and report back to him. I feel like a spoiled child here in my ivory tower, shielded from the realities of life. I must know it, Alice. In all its guises. It does not frighten me as it does Mama.

Please write, if even a few lines.

Yours,

Evie

XX

From Evie to Thomas

16th May, 1916

Richmond, England

Dearest Tom,

Where in the world are you?

I keep writing and writing and still no word from you. I

scour the newspapers, but can find no news of you or your battalion. I hardly know which battalion you are with now. How can you simply disappear? How can I bear this dreadful silence?

I beg you to write. It is so dreadful not to hear from you and although I doubt you will receive this, I must write to you anyway just to let you know that I think of you every day and pray for your safety.

Yours, always,

Evie

X

From Charles Abshire to Thomas

1st June, 1916

London, England

Dear Thomas,

It has been weeks since your last letter, dear boy, and we are more than worried here in London. Please respond, even if via telegram or through someone else.

Godspeed,

Charles

From Evie to Thomas

4th June, 1916

Richmond, England

My dearest Tom,

How can anyone be so utterly lost? No word. Not even so much as a whisper from you. I find myself almost hoping to find your name in the newspaper lists now. Wounded at this stage would be preferable to missing. At least then I would know you were in the care of the nurses. I beg Alice to keep a careful watch, to be always looking for you, but she finds nobody with your name or number, nothing with which she can comfort my tormented heart. And still more recruits ship out. Married men are now under conscription. Only those on essential war work at home and the staunchest of objectors remain: stubborn in their defiance.

With the warmer weather I have taken to sketching my little birds again. Here, for you, is a kingfisher. Did you know they only have one partner for the whole of their lives? What wonders nature reveals when one chooses to observe it. I think him rather handsome and beautiful. What beauty there is all around us, waiting to be noticed. All we have to do is stop and look—and notice. How I would love to stroll with you along the river and see the flash of a kingfisher's wing.

I have added to my responsibilities as postwoman and am now a telegram messenger. You cannot know how heavy my postbag feels when weighed down with the dreaded telegram from the King. So often I must deliver a bundle of letters, the envelope simply marked "Return to Sender." Will my letters to you be returned, I wonder? Will you ever return to us?

I continue to pray for you, and I will keep writing.

Evie

XXX

From Evie to Alice

10th June, 1916

Richmond, England

My dear Alice,

I must apologise for not writing in an age. I can hardly bear to put pen to paper. It all seems so pointless.

My heart aches with worry for Tom. Still no word. Three months now, Alice. Three whole months. It is the most awful anguish. Not knowing. Never hearing.

I have tried to distract myself with my postal duties and my columns and luncheons with Hopper, but I only find myself growing ever more incensed by the fact that he is still here in London, living in comfort and safety, while Thomas is nowhere to be found. I challenged Hopper on the matter and I'm afraid he became rather cross. He said he hoped I wasn't turning into one of the bloody White Feather Brigade and that he will ship out as soon as his superiors will allow it, and why can't people mind their own bloody business. He apologised profusely after

(I think he'd had rather too much to drink). He says war makes madmen of us all and that he is frustrated to be deemed a coward when it is a matter out of his control. In the meantime, I hear rumblings via Papa that all is still not happy families at the LDT. Poor Tom would be horrified to know it. I wish there was something I could do.

Alice, you are right. When I think about Tom never coming home, I find an awful darkness where once a bright future beckoned. My anguish is not just for the friend I have known since I was a child. My anguish is for the man I have watched him become, and for the man I want him to be. I can think of nothing but him, of his smile, of his arms around my waist as we danced. What on earth will become of me if it is too late?

War makes me reckless with my heart so I posted the letter I wrote to him on Christmas Day. Should he ever receive it, it will leave him in no doubt as to my feelings for him. I hope I did the right thing in sending it. The fear of never seeing him again is suddenly far greater than the fear of rejection should he tell me he does not feel the same way.

Will you get home on leave at all? I feel desperately lonely and would so much love to see you.

And what absolutely dreadful news about Kitchener's death on the HMS *Hampshire*, and all those who perished with him. Papa says it is nothing short of a national disaster. Nobody is safe, Alice. Not even those in the highest ranks. What hope can there be for someone like Tom?

Evie

X

Telegram from Alice to Evie

5TH JULY 1916

TO: EVELYN ELLIOTT, POPLARS, RICHMOND, LONDON SW
SENT: 10:34 / RECEIVED: 11:36

TOM ALIVE AND WITH BATTALION! LETTER TO FOLLOW.
ALICE.

Telegram from Evie to Charles Abshire

5TH JULY 1916

TO: CHARLES ABSHIRE, 34 LOVELACE GARDENS, BERMONDSEY,
LONDON SE
SENT: 12:30 / RECEIVED: 13:14

TOM FOUND SAFE AND WELL. WILL SEND MORE SOONEST.
EVELYN ELLIOTT.

From Alice to Evie

6th July, 1916

Somewhere in France

Dear Evie,

Wonderful, stupendous, jolly news! I have found your dear Tom. He is alive and well! A doctor I've recently befriended sent word to a colleague at the location of some of the heaviest battles. Just as we feared, Tom was there, in the thick of it ████████████. By some miracle, he wasn't badly hurt, just a wound in his arm requiring a few stitches. You must be asking yourself why he hasn't written, but *he is alive*! Now for the more difficult news.

I've been told Tom is afflicted with a severe melancholy, the sort that makes one go numb, become listless. He's having difficulties facing the day, doing his duties, poor fellow. I've seen this a lot among the soldiers who have been here for long stints, and given how he was at Christmas, I'm not surprised. At the ████████ they say the dead and wounded were in the tens of thousands. But he is alive! I say this again, because it is a marvel in this war. And his spirit will recover, in time. I've forwarded a note to a nurse stationed near him to prompt him to write. I told him all at home are worried sick and so forth. I've also enclosed an address on the inside flap of the envelope (must conserve as much paper as possible).

In rather sad news, my friend Private Rollins was killed. He was struck blind by an explosion, then wandered aimlessly through a minefield. Isn't it the most pointless death you've ever heard? I've cried for weeks, but it's a waste. It won't bring him back. He was lovely, but I've moved on because I must.

More sad news. I'm no longer on ambulance duty. I rather preferred being behind the wheel to being based at a field hospital, but it seemed the many dents caught up with me.

Are you joining us here as a war correspondent? I would warn you of the dangers and urge you to stay at home, but I know it would be futile. Stubborn Evie Elliott will see it through. I know she will.

Keep me abreast of any news from Tom.

Alice

X

From Evie to Alice

19th July, 1916

Richmond, England

My dear Alice,

What incredible joy! What tremendous relief to know that Tom is safe! My hand trembles just writing these words. I have thought the worst for so long and to hear that he is alive answers all my prayers. Even when I hear that he is afflicted with a melancholy, I cannot be too sad. His melancholy will pass, I am sure of it. He is here, and that is all that matters.

I must write to him immediately, but I don't wish to be insensitive. I have heard people talk of the men who are affected by their nerves and how they seem incapable of thought or speech. Do you think Tom will be considered bad enough to be sent home to recover? Please excuse all my questions. How frustrating it is to not know if the answers will ever come.

I was dreadfully sorry to hear about your private. Must we lose everyone? I will admit, however, that I'm relieved to hear you're out of the ambulance. Far better to be in the field hospital. You must see the most ghastly sights. I just cannot imagine how you're managing. You didn't even like to see a grazed knee.

Although it seems of small significance now I know that Tom is safe, I must, of course, tell you that all is as well as can be expected here at home. I am still enjoying my job as a postwoman, although the weather has been horrid and Mama insists that I'll catch influenza being out in it all. I haven't, of course. Never have. Never will. She forgets that I have the constitution of an ox.

My column has become something of a sensation and—you won't believe this—I get fan mail! Honestly, Alice. I know you will be laughing as you read this, but dozens of women write to the newspaper every week to tell me how much they enjoy reading my words and how helpful they find them. It is really quite extraordinary and very touching. Some of the letters would break your heart. Of course, I can't reply. I don't have the time for one thing. But I suppose it is rather nice to know that I am helping in a small way.

My editor is still trying to find a way to get me out to France so I can write from there with firsthand accounts. He thinks the only way I can get over is by joining up as a nurse, or some such. I feel that I can't do anything until I hear word directly from Thomas. For now I must put thoughts of my own prospects out of my mind and get on with day-to-day things here.

Stay safe, and thank you, my dearest friend. You have bandaged a broken heart and I do believe it might, with the right care, make a full recovery.

Evie

XXX

From Evie to Thomas

19th July, 1916

Richmond, England

My dearest, dearest Thomas,

I had word from Alice that you are alive and safe and I am not ashamed to tell you how many tears of relief I have shed.

It has been torture not hearing from you, but I understand that you have been deeply affected by so many months at war and find it difficult to put words on paper. I would so very much love to hear from you but just to know you are not captured, or worse, gladdens my heart beyond expression. It is enough for me to know my letters are not disappearing into thin air. Have you been receiving them? I sent several these past months and I would love to know whether you received them.

Knowing you are alive gives me the courage to write on. Even though you might not find the strength to reply, please know that I think of you.

I will not burden you with too much news.

When you are ready, send me yours. I will be waiting.

Yours in hope,

Evie

XX

From Jack Davies to Thomas

22nd July, 1916

London, England

Dear Tom,

I believe you're not in the best of shape at present, but I felt compelled to write again. Things continue to dissolve here at the paper between Hopper and me. I shudder to think where the *London Daily Times* will be by year's end.

The bright side? The paper is generating serious revenue now. We have two columns about the war that are wildly popular. One hundred and fifty fan letters or more per week flood into the office. Many women are finding comfort and inspiration from our new columnists, including your friend Evelyn Elliott. I am glad for it, of course, but I am not thrilled Hopper now aims to push our columnists into dangerous territory in terms of the subjects they are writing about. The government wants the opposite, mind, and calls for more propaganda. We quarrelled about it heatedly and I nearly got myself sacked. I must admit, I fear Hopper's position here may be the end of my time at the paper. I mentioned this before, but the truth becomes more obvious daily.

I hope you're safe, my boy.

Sincerely,

Jack Davies

From Captain James Edwards to Evie

30th July, 1916

Somewhere in France

Dear Miss Elliott,

I write to you on behalf of Lieut. Thomas Harding, 10th Battalion. Harding is suffering from nervous exhaustion and is resting, at present, in a field hospital. He sends his regards and wishes to send assurances that he is being well cared for and hopes to be back in action very soon.

I wish to add that he is a highly valued and much respected member of our company, and we all wish him a speedy recovery so that he can rejoin our continued quest for victory.

Sincerely yours,

Captain James Edwards, 10th Rifles Battalion

From Evie to Thomas

5th August, 1916

Richmond, England

Dear Tom,

I received word from your captain. Dearest boy, I am so greatly relieved to know that you are resting in a field hospital. After the horrors we heard about the battles at the Somme, and Verdun, I hardly dared hope to hear from you again. So many men fallen. All of England, it seems, is in mourning.

I hope you will soon be feeling a little better, but do not rush back into the fray. Take your time.

I drew you a bird today. I hope you like him. He is a wagtail.

Send word as soon as you are able. I will be waiting.

Thinking of you always.

Evie

X

From Thomas to Evie

10th August, 1916

Somewhere in France

Dearest Evie,

It's me, Tom, your long lost friend. By the time you get this letter, I'll be on my way to Scotland, to Craiglockhart War

Hospital for Officers. It's in Edinburgh, and I'm to be treated for emotional weakness while there. I suppose it is ironic that I have so often longed to return to the country of my birth. Never did I think it would be under such circumstances as this.

Please forgive my prolonged absence and all the worry and trouble I've caused you. If I could think or see straight these past months, I would have written line after line.

I don't deserve your reply, but I saw these embroidered silk postcards (enclosed here), and I thought of you instantly. There were many varieties, but mostly of flags and patriotic sentiments. I thought the beautiful little butterfly suited my lovely friend.

Ever yours,
Tom

From Evie to Thomas c/o Craiglockhart Hospital

14th August, 1916

Richmond, England

My dearest bravest Thomas,

Your letter arrived and I cannot stop my tears. To see your name, your writing, your few words on a scrap of paper have made me the happiest girl in England.

There is so much I want to say to you but words seem so inadequate and my emotions so poorly expressed, and yet I had to write back to you immediately. I must catch the afternoon post. My hands tremble with relief at seeing your familiar script, and the beautiful silk postcard with the butterfly has captured my heart, and yet I feel such an ache there too, for you and your ailment.

For all these months of silence, time has dragged and now the minutes rush past too quickly and the post office will soon close. It feels as though I have thought of nothing and nobody these past months. Morning, noon, and night—even in my dreams. It was always you, Tom. I am sorry to gush (and please know that my cheeks flare as I do). It is so unlike the very private Evie of old to be such an open book, but to know that you are safe and on your way to the hospital in Scotland gives me the most intense sense of relief. They will have you back on your feet in no time, I am certain of it.

Now, I must run to catch the post—I am in danger of saying far too much if I write more.

I will pray for you. Dare I even hope we will see each other soon when I once thought you lost to me forever?

Stay safe, Tom. I will shout your name to the moon tonight. Look for me there.

Evie

XXX

From Evie to Thomas c/o Craiglockhart Hospital

16th August, 1916

Richmond, England

My dear Tom,

I hope this finds you safe and well in Edinburgh. I took the liberty of writing straightaway so there would be a few lines from a friend waiting for you when you arrive. Do you remember how eager I was to write to you and Will when you first set off for the training camp at Mytchett? I seem to recall my first letter arrived before you did.

I am sure you will soon rally under the care of the doctors there. You are in the best place, Tom, and while I know you will hate to be away from your men and are no doubt already wishing to be back among them, I pray that you can take this time to rest and recover fully. Others have stepped out for a while. Now it is your turn. Take all the time you need.

Send word when you are able? I will continue to write anyway. I hope that is acceptable. I don't wish to overwhelm you.

Much love,

Evie

X

Telegram from Thomas to Evie

17TH AUGUST 1916

TO: EVELYN ELLIOTT, POPLARS, RICHMOND, LONDON SW
SENT: 14:45 / RECEIVED: 15:27

ARRIVED SAFELY. PLEASE KEEP WRITING. YOUR WORDS
ARE A BEACON IN THE WOOD. T.

From Evie to Thomas

23rd August, 1916

Richmond, England

Dear Thomas,

How are you? Is Scotland as pretty and wild as I remember? Having visited that part of the country when I was a little girl, I can picture you breathing the fresh sea air that blows in off the Firth of Forth. Are you permitted outside? Does the hospital have gardens and grounds for you to stroll in? I do hope so. I know how fond you are of the great outdoors and hate to think of you cooped up like a messenger pigeon in an airless ward.

I have enclosed some of your favourite cigars, which I hope

you will be able to enjoy beneath the balm of a summer's evening while listening to a nightingale sing. You see—in my imagination you are not really a soldier at war, damaged by its horrors. You are just the same old Tom, enjoying the breath of Scottish air against his skin. Until I can see you for myself, I have to paint such pictures.

Would I be able to visit, do you think? Are visitors allowed? Are women permitted in the hospital at all?

I asked Papa to look into the location of the hospital and he tells me it is not too far from my cousins in Leith. Perhaps I could ask my uncle to look in on you if it isn't possible for me to come in person? Papa says the best way to help you recover is to leave you with the doctors who know best, but I am sure a friendly face would be the very best medicine of all.

Let me know? I would come tomorrow if I thought it would help.

I will pray for your good health. Do not trouble yourself with a long letter if you find it irksome and tiring. Just a line or two will suffice. "Dear Evie" is enough for me.

Yours,

Evie

X

P.S. I had a dream last night that we were in Paris for Christmas. You, me, Will, Alice. The snow fell in thick fat flakes as we strolled along the Champs-Élysées, the lights of the Eiffel Tower twinkling in the distance. It was the most perfect dream, Thomas. I know we will get there one day. I promise we will.

From Thomas to Charles Abshire

1st September, 1916

Edinburgh, Scotland

Dear Charles,

My letter is long overdue. I apologise for frightening you. The last few months I was in a very bad way. Recently, I was transferred to Craiglockhart War Hospital for Officers here in Edinburgh. It's a specialist hospital for officers with neurasthenia, or a sort of war neuroses. I will be here for an indefinite period.

I'm afraid I'm in no position to do much about the problems at home. Like Father, I place my trust in you. Please continue to keep me updated.

Sincerely yours,

Thomas

From Thomas to Evie

1st September, 1916

Edinburgh, Scotland

Dear Evie,

Thank you for understanding. I am a pitiful friend these days, but please know I hold you close to my heart. No one on this earth knows me as you do. Not anymore. They are gone, but I thank God you aren't.

A few weeks here in Scotland and I am, at last, able to eat again. I'd lost my appetite completely, my head filled with horrors I won't name, and the burden of my guilt for all the men who died at my hand, and those who are still at the Front whom I left behind. You wouldn't recognise the scrawny man I've become. But I am slowly regaining my strength.

The doctors have been kind, but sometimes I wonder at their absurd treatments. They think a little golf and the occasional walk around the grounds will help. Hypnosis is another favourite of theirs. I don't see how playing at sports or falling into a trance will empty the gruesome memories from my head. I'm too thick skulled for such simple measures. Yet I suppose it's worth a try.

I am also commissioned to write as much as possible. Every battle, every terrible thing I can recall, I outline in a journal. The doctor discusses my notes with me. You've never seen a grown man cry so much (though I do most of it when the doctor has gone). I didn't know I had so many tears. It's a ghastly business, but somehow, I think it helps to get it down on paper.

It's the shame that is the most difficult to overcome. You see, the reason I fell into this oblivion is because of something that happened back in March. We had just finished the morning hate (this is what we call "stand to," or waking an hour before dawn to guard against an enemy raid of men sporting bayonets. A despicable thing). We had scarcely finished a quick breakfast when a grenade landed in the trench. It took a flash—just a flash, the shortest inkling of a second, yet the longest moment in my memory—to decide what to do. My commanding officer and several of my men sat nearby. If I threw myself over the grenade, they would be saved. It was the honourable thing to do. But I hesitated, and scrambled to my feet—too late. The blast killed all five men, blew a few rotting sandbags to hell, and all descended into chaos. I was spared; sprayed with shrapnel and lost my hearing for a few hours, suffered an excruciating pain and ringing in my ears, but I was spared.

I live, but my commander—and friends—are gone. Had we not lost our commander due to my hesitation, we wouldn't have had to march again so soon to join the battalions in Verdun. Thousands and thousands went down, Evie. All because of that tiny moment of hesitation months earlier.

I have felt like nothing but a coward ever since. I failed, utterly, in my position as leader of my men. I didn't mention it to you before because I couldn't. The shame goes beyond anything I can describe. It's their faces that haunt me at night, the screams I hear as the phantom gas swirls around them. And now I've left them behind again, in the hell they call Verdun, facing all that terror every day. What sort of leader cracks into a thousand shards like brittle glass and abandons his men? The guilt strangles me sometimes.

I've thought often about you and your journals, how you used to carry them around. Now I understand that we can express ourselves on paper in a way we can't out loud. Which reminds me—how are your columns coming along? Well, I hope.

The pressed daisies I enclose are from my daily walk around the lake. Their sunshine makes me think of you.

Ever yours,

Tom

P.S. Visitors are allowed, but I'll need permission, and I would rather you didn't ask your Uncle to look in on me. We aren't well acquainted, and I can't put on any false cheer these days. I am able to leave the grounds most days as well, venture into town or around the lake. I would dearly like to see you.

From Evie to Thomas

7th September, 1916

Richmond, England

Dear Thomas,

Thank you for writing when I know it must be so hard for you to tell me what you are going through. Your words mean so much to me.

While I can never fully understand the horrors you have witnessed, I refuse to shy away from the truth. I saw the film *The Battle of the Somme* last week. I am ashamed to admit I'd been putting it off, afraid to see the brutal reality for myself. I found it terribly upsetting—everyone left the picture house with reddened eyes and without speaking a word—but I am glad to have seen it, and to understand a little better what you face out there.

While the film and your descriptions distress me, it serves no purpose to pretend it isn't the truth. Do not blame yourself for what happened. Never blame yourself, Tom. This is nobody's fault but those who brought this war upon us. The blame lies all with them. And for all that I am saddened to hear of the loss of your commander and fellow men, at least that moment of hesitation spared *you*, Tom. And for that, I would wish you a lifetime of hesitation. That extra second is sometimes all we need to make the right decision, even if it doesn't feel like that at the time. God must play his part in these matters. It was his will that you survived.

We heard of the most dreadful casualties at Verdun and the Somme, although reports in the papers back in July were of nothing but remarkable victories, and terrific bombardments and vigorous attacks on the enemy. I am terrified to know that you were among them. So many didn't come back. While I am desperately sorry to hear of your suffering, I am also—selfishly—full of relief to know that you survived the worst of it and are away from the firing line for a while.

Try not to resist the doctors' treatments. They really do know best. And please try to eat. I cannot begin to imagine you as "scrawny." That chubby young fellow who used to pinch whatever he could from Cook's larder—scrawny? That strong hearty fellow whose laughter filled a room and made the chandeliers shake—scrawny? I don't believe it. Eat, Thomas, please. You really must. For me, if not for yourself. If you will not eat, then neither will I, and you know how desperately bony I am at the best of times. And if they cannot clear you to return to the Front, if this is the end of your war, then so be it. You have done your bit. You have done far more than your bit.

I am glad to hear that you have rediscovered the joys of writing—you've had plenty of practice, after all. The bundle of letters from you is now so thick I can no longer keep them beneath my pillow. (Perhaps I didn't tell you that I ever did.) I, on the other hand, cannot seem to write a decent word. My columns drip out of me agonisingly slowly. It is like walking through wet sand. My words trudge across the page *thud thud thud.* I seem to have lost all sense of joy in the process, which is why I am writing this letter to you rather than finishing the dreaded half-written piece I am due to send off to Hopper tomorrow morning. Procrastination is a terrible companion. Truly. He gives me a headache.

Thank you for the beautiful daisies. They made me smile—as did the thought of you picking them by the lake. To know that you saw them and thought of me—well. It is in the simplest things we find the greatest treasures sometimes, is it not. You will be pleased to hear that I have added their pretty little sunshine faces to my flower press. In return, I have enclosed a violet, picked and pressed in the spring. It was the first of the season. It brought me such cheer and hope to see it while I awaited word from you. I do hope it will bring you the same cheer and hope now.

I have also enclosed another sketch. A chiffchaff. Isn't he a darling little thing? We have them in the garden and they sing such a sweet song. I sketched this handsome fellow while he warbled away to his sweetheart on the fence post. I do hope his amours were rewarded.

Do take care, Thomas. I joke to try and cheer you, but you know I worry so very much.

Evie

XX

P.S. Do let me know about visiting. If you can get permission I can be on the train tomorrow.

From Evie to Alice

10th September, 1916

Richmond, England

Dearest Alice,

How are you? No word for a while now and, of course, I think the worst. Can you tell me where you are? Will you get any leave? I find myself in urgent need of an Alice hug and the sound of your laughter. I used the last of the soap today that you gave me as a gift last Christmas. I wept as the last of it dissolved into suds in my hands. Everything reduces me to tears these days.

What do you know of the condition of emotional weakness? Thomas is recovering from it in a hospital for officers in Edinburgh. He seems terribly glum. Says he is stick-thin and undergoes treatments of hypnosis. I am rather alarmed by it all. Perhaps you can reassure me. I'm hoping to arrange for one of my Scottish cousins to look in on him. Actually, Alice, I rather hope I might find some excuse to visit them so that I can look in on him myself.

I mentioned it to Hopper (who is rather unsympathetic to Tom's condition). He says Thomas needs only the care and treatment the doctors can provide and strongly believes that my visiting will cause him distress and remind him too much of home and make it much harder for him to focus on his recovery and returning to the Front. Do you agree?

I hardly think Hopper is in much of a position to offer an opinion on the effects of war, since he fights only from a desk and can have no idea what Tom is going through. I find myself becoming rather tired of Hopper's company. He drinks too much brandy and becomes loose tongued and speaks unkindly of the staff at the LDT. I cannot even repeat the things he says about Jack Davies.

Please write soon. Make me laugh. Cheer me up. Make me smile. Remind me of happier times. I recently saw the film *The Battle of the Somme* and find myself unable to stop seeing the images in my mind.

I miss you terribly.

Evie

X

From Alice to Evie

17th September, 1916

Somewhere in France

Dearest Evie,

Never fear, *mon amie,* I am alive and well! I've been working at a field hospital at the Front in ▉▉▉▉. It's been nonstop. Absolutely bone wearing. It's a real slaughter here; more so than any of the other battles I've tended, but I go in every day with a bright, rouged smile, whispering comforting words, making light of something when I can. It's difficult, but there's enough of a grim attitude to go around and frankly, someone needs to cheer us on to a victory.

Also, I think I've found my new calling. It started with singing lullabies and songs from home to sweeten the boys, until one afternoon, a nurse from New Orleans heard me singing. She taught me a few tunes; jazz she calls them. Apparently they're all the rage in the dance halls in her hometown. It's a new kind of music, not yet popular, she said, but lucky for me, I'm at the forefront of invention. We've managed to enlist a bugle player to join the foray as well. Our merry-making is brief and infrequent, unfortunately, but as welcome as rain in the desert.

As for your Tom, <u>go to him</u>! From all that I have seen here, what the men need most when they are suffering is to feel a woman's love, feel cared for, to know that their sacrifice means something. Hypnosis and the like is all very well, but he needs tenderness and a reason to hope for the future. You'll show him that in volume, won't you, dear?

I miss you, too!

Alice

P.S. Yes, those are my lips on the paper. Sending you kisses!

P.P.S. I don't think I'll be able to take leave until after this mess at the ■■■■ ends. They need every spare set of hands. I'll let you know as soon as I'm able.

From Thomas to Evie

19th September, 1916

Edinburgh, Scotland

Dear Evie,

Thank you for your kind words, and as for visiting, I can't think of a single thing in this world that would make me happier, dear girl. I'm as alone as one can be, except for the good doctor. I've lost too many friends, my family. I feel adrift sometimes, more alone than I ever imagined possible. Your face might anchor me back to this world. I'll speak to the staff at once about the protocol—if you're able, and it pleases you to come all this way.

I've done as you've instructed and accepted the treatments. Can't say that I believe in them all that much, but I've noticed the nightmares seem to be abating some. Whether or not they're related, I have no idea. Either way, it helps talking to people who understand what I've seen. The doctor says I have a reasonably mild case of war neuroses. Something to be grateful for, I suppose. Some have it so bad they've been sent off to the lunatic asylum.

I've posted your chiffchaff over my bed. I'll think about that bird with its little song, wooing a paramour. That's a happy thought and I could use more of them.

Send word when you can visit. I'll do my best to keep my hopes up that it will be soon.

Ever yours,
Tom

Telegram from Evie to Tom

21 SEPTEMBER 1916

TO: LT. THOMAS HARDING % CRAIGLOCKHART WAR
HOSPITAL, EDINBURGH
SENT: 11:23 / RECEIVED: 12:14

WILL BE WITH YOU FRIDAY. TRAIN DEPARTS TOMORROW
MORNING. WILL STAY WITH COUSINS IN LEITH.
TERRIBLY ANXIOUS TO SEE YOU. P.S. MR. CHIFFCHAFF
IS UNITED WITH HIS LADY LOVE. E.

From Evie to Alice

28th September, 1916

Leith, Scotland

My dearest Alice,

I was so very glad to hear from you. You make me smile with
your endless positivity. You are perhaps the only person I know
who could possibly find reason to smile during such awfulness.
You are a tonic. A pure tonic. What is this "jazz" music? It
sounds awful! I'm afraid I'll hardly know you when you come
home. Do you think life will ever be the same again? I don't
know how we will ever forget these years.

So, to news from England, or rather Scotland.

I went to him, Alice, and now I don't know how I shall ever be parted from him again.

We met in the hospital gardens—a more beautiful place you couldn't wish to see. He was dozing on a bench when I arrived, a blanket over his knees and the afternoon sun on his face. So peaceful, and yet he is so tormented by his dreams. The smile that lit his face when he saw me—oh, Alice. We didn't speak a word. He simply held my hand as I sat beside him and it felt like the most natural thing in the world to feel the beat of his pulse beneath my fingertips.

He is so terribly thin. So physically broken and haunted by what he has seen and done. The doctors tell him he will make a full recovery, which is wonderful news, and yet my heart breaks to hear it because when he recovers he will return to France, and I will be without him again and I don't know how I can bear it.

I've been here a week now and hope to be able to stay in Scotland until he is fully recovered, if Mama (and the post-mistress) can spare me. I'm staying with my aunt and uncle in Leith. Their driver takes me to the hospital where my cousin, Angela, is a nurse. She has been a tremendous help in making arrangements for Tom and I to see each other. We meet at the bench beneath an oak tree and talk while the birds serenade us from the branches above.

He improves a little each day, but he tires easily and must go for treatment regularly so my visits are brief.

You will, no doubt, wish to know if there has been any exchange of love between us. I am anxious to know whether he ever received the Christmas letter I belatedly sent to him, but I cannot bear to ask. He has enough troubling him without my adding to his emotional struggles. It seems to me that I have known Tom all my life, and yet I haven't known him at all until these long hard years of war. You thought me madly infatuated when I first declared my love for him (I know you did, although you never said as much), but something has changed and I know now with a certainty I have rarely felt about anything, that I love him with the deepest affection possible.

I love Tom Harding!

I cannot tell him so I share my secret with the waves. They carry my love away on the turn of the tide, and wash it back to shore the next day along with the driftwood and pretty shells that I collect during my long walks, each perfect shell a reminder to me to be patient, to remember that nature will work its magic and produce something beautiful in the end.

All I want is for him to recover. To get better. To become the old Tom once again. We were frivolous and childlike when we met in London last year. Now there is a quiet understanding between us. A closeness we hadn't known before. That gives me the greatest comfort of all.

As part of his treatment, he is encouraged to write things down: memories, anxieties, etc. He has taken to writing me a little note to take home with me after each visit. Really, I do not know how my heart won't burst.

Stay safe, darling girl. Keep those red lips smiling and singing your jolly jazz songs. I can think of nobody better to put on a show to cheer the troops. You always were an impossible show-off!

    With much love,

    Evie

    XX

P.S. Go easy on the bugle player. I fully expect to hear that his lips have strayed from his instrument and have found a new tune to play upon your scarlet smilers!

From Thomas to Evie

1st October, 1916

Edinburgh, Scotland

Dear Evie,

    I enjoyed our tea and game of cards yesterday, even though you're quite the cheat. I'd forgotten how good you are! Will would have had none of it. As much of a jokester as he could be, he was such a sore loser, especially to his little sister.

    Your friendship means so much to me, Miss Elliott. I hope you know that. I look forward to your visit tomorrow.

    Yours,

    Tom

From Thomas to Evie

5th October, 1916

Edinburgh, Scotland

Dearest Evie,

I don't know what to say except I apologise. My episodes don't usually happen during the day, but to hear booming thunder . . . I hope you aren't hurt. My instincts took over and I had to keep you safe. The shaking in my hands subsided about an hour after you left. The doctor says I need to hear these sounds more often, to dull my sensibilities to them. He's considering moving me to another wing of the hospital, closer to the noise of town.

If you'd like to skip your visits for a while, I understand completely.

Yours,
Tom

From Thomas to Mr. Charles Abshire

10th October, 1916

Edinburgh, Scotland

Dear Charles,

I have enclosed all the paperwork you required with necessary signatures. I think it best Hopper continues to run the paper for now, as we discussed. Jack Davies will have to play nice with him a while longer. I'll remind him to mind his p's and q's. On another note, I can't believe our Miss Wren is generating so much fan mail. We may consider opening a permanent column to highlight female voices after the war. Something challenging and interesting, not: "How to Bake a Proper Christmas Goose" or "The Best Knitting Needles." Evie would be bored silly by such a column.

I hope you're well, Charles. Home feels like a distant memory, but I hope it will soon become a reality.

Sincerely,

Thomas

From Evie to her mother

15th October, 1916

Leith, Scotland

Dear Mama,

A few lines to let you know that Scotland is astonishingly beautiful in the autumn and that all is well.

Tom continues to improve at a rate of knots—much to the surprise of the doctors here who find him something of a medical marvel. They say he will be well enough to return to France soon. I suppose I should be happy for his recovery, but I am desperately saddened to think of him going back. I find myself looking for excuses for him to stay while he is ever eager to return, and get back to his men. I know I must admire his loyalty, but still.

I will send word when dates are settled and to let you know of my expected arrival home. Uncle Boris and Aunt Isobel send their regards. They have been incredibly generous letting me stay and giving me the use of their motorcar and driver to take me here and there. You would like it here very much, with the exception of the stiff breezes which play havoc with hats and hairstyles and make it almost impossible to walk upright at times. We must come back on a holiday when we are at peace again.

Will always loved it here, didn't he? I think of him often as I know you do, too. I saw a young man on crutches yesterday playing with his little girl on the beach and I thought what a wonderful father Will would have been. I miss him dreadfully. I wish we spoke about him more often. Perhaps we can try when I return? Look through old photographs and laugh at his childhood escapades? We must do whatever we can to keep his memory alive. We owe him that much, at least.

Your ever-loving daughter,
Evelyn

From Thomas to Evie

1st November, 1916

Edinburgh, Scotland

Dear Evie,

As difficult as it was, I cherished our talk today. Remembering Will, how much has changed . . . Your tears, somehow, made me feel less alone. I don't know how to thank you for listening to my terrible stories. You have a heart of gold.

Sometimes I can hardly believe that you're here. My dearest, closest friend has elected to stay in Scotland, far from her own home—for me. I can't imagine how I'll ever settle the score.

Ever yours,

Tom

From Evie to Jack Davies

3rd November, 1916

Leith, Scotland

Dear Mr. Davies,

Please find enclosed my latest column. As you know, I have been visiting relatives in Scotland these past weeks, and have also been to Craiglockhart War Hospital to visit Tom Harding, who improves with great speed. I am moved to write about the condition of war neuroses which I see here, in abundance. I know it may be risky for the paper to print my thoughts (since they are not always expressed with the timidity one might expect of a woman), but I believe your readers need to know more about this "condition"—not least so that they may help their loved ones by understanding it a little better.

You might send word to let me know your thoughts?

I expect to return to London soon and perhaps we could meet for lunch to discuss the future of the column. I may not be a trained journalist, but I feel increasingly compelled to tell the truth of the things I encounter.

Also, I hear rumours of a Women's Army Auxiliary Corps being established. Perhaps I can find some way to get myself over to France after all, as we discussed.

Yours sincerely,

Evie

A WOMAN'S WAR

by our special correspondent in London,
Genevieve Wren

"To sleep, perchance to dream . . ."

And so it goes on. Month, week, day, hour, minute, second . . . time drags interminably on and still the battles rage and still our men fall faster than winter snowflakes.

No year of this war has been the same. With each new battle, it seems we must relearn what war means. Each offensive brings dangers beyond the familiar rifle and bayonet our men were trained to use. Now they face poison gas, powerful shells, all manner of disease . . . weapons for which there was no training. Weapons which—in some cases—didn't even exist two years ago.

And yet, amid all the gunfire and the rumble of shelling that those who live on the south coast can hear, carried on the wind all the way from France, there is another weapon our men must confront, a weapon as deadly as any other: despair.

For the past month, I have been an occasional visitor to Craiglockhart War Hospital, in Scotland. It is an impressive military hospital for officers who go there to recover from the trauma of battle. And yet, if you were to visit—as I have—you could be forgiven for thinking these men were nothing but frauds. They walk on both legs without the use of crutches. They swing both arms by their sides. They have no need for face masks to hide their injuries. These men suffer in an entirely different way. They suffer in their minds. The horrors they have seen and the endless sounds they have endured night after night stay with them, so that they can no longer function as normal men. Some have lost the power of speech, such is the extent to their distress.

Here, at the hospital, it is called "war neuroses." Those who suffer from the condition are referred to as "lacking moral fibre." There is a sense among those in the highest levels of command that these men are weak minded. Not real men, if you will.

These patients are something of an oddity to the doctors, who treat them not with medicine, but with hypnosis and hot baths and the occasional round of golf. While I am no medical expert and cannot fully explain the symptoms, what I do know is that this is not an affliction that can be treated with a bandage and good bedside manner. This goes far beyond the reaches of normal medical knowledge. Just as our men were not trained to deal with the new weaponry they face at the Front, so our doctors are not trained to deal with this new "disease."

So, what can we do? As mothers and wives, sisters and friends, how can we help the men who don't return to us with broken limbs, but who return to us with broken minds? Perhaps we can do nothing other than to listen when they are able to talk, to hold their hand when it cannot stop shaking, to understand that the sound of a passing train or a distant rumble of thunder may be nothing more than an everyday occurrence to us, but for them is a reminder of everything they fear and takes them back to the trenches in an instant.

This war may be a battle of many things, but it is also a battle of endurance. None of us were prepared for it to last so long. None of us were equipped with the skills needed to cope. And yet cope we do. Somehow we find a way.

So please continue to send your letters, your words of pride and love and encouragement, and ask those you love to tell you what they see and hear—not only when they are awake, but in the silent hours of their dreams. Let them know that, whatever happens, to you they will never be lacking in anything. Let them know that, to the people who matter the most, they will always be the best kind of hero.

Until next time—courage!

Genevieve

From Alice to Evie

5th November, 1916

Somewhere in France

Dear Evie,

I'm returning your letter at last. Sorry to have taken so long. The horrific battle I mentioned has raged for months and I've been on my feet day and night, exhausted beyond anything you can imagine. Scan the news reports for the most devastating battles and that's where I am, in the thick of things. It appears to be winding down, thanks be to the great potato in the sky. I don't think any of us can last much longer at this pace.

As for your Tom, you see? You did the right thing, going to him. Poor man. It sounds like he was really shaken. Could you hint at your confessional Christmas letter? (What on earth did you tell him, darling? I hope you didn't hold back.) Perhaps you can get at it that way. I can't imagine he would broach the subject himself, even if he has read it, especially in his present condition. Just remember he asked you to visit him—in Scotland, no less. How could that not be love? Dash it, Evie, perhaps you should just tell him. What if he returns to the Front and doesn't know? Could you bear the agony? Could I?

Sending hugs to you both. Say a little prayer that I'll be moving on soon. I feel my good cheer slipping and that won't do, not for me.

Alice

XX

From Thomas to Evie

20th November, 1916

Edinburgh, Scotland

Dear Evie,

Cards again tomorrow, or a walk in the garden? Don't forget your umbrella this time. My scarf is still soaked through and will make for poor cover.

Yours,
Tom

From Evie to Alice

20th November, 1916

Leith, Scotland

Dearest girl,

You don't sound yourself at all, no mention of music, or men. It must be awful for you out there, but think of all those you have nursed back to health with your pretty smile and that sparkle in your peepers. You are a marvel and I have nothing but the greatest admiration for you.

I've tried, several times, to talk to Tom about my Christmas letter, but I can never find the right words, or moment.

He seems so fragile still. I just can't bear to burden him with expectations of love, on top of everything else. You, more than anyone, know it isn't in my nature to be patient, but with this I must be. Perhaps he will remember better when he recovers. He is a little muddled at times, and reacts to the slightest of bangs or loud noises. War has turned my brave-hearted lion into a kitten. It wouldn't be fair to smother him with my own selfish needs. Not now, at least.

Come home soon. I miss you terribly.

Evie

XX

P.S. Have you heard anything about the Women's Army Auxiliary Corps? I am making plans for adventures overseas. I'll be on the first train to Dover if I get a whiff of a chance.

From Thomas to Charles Abshire

22nd November, 1916

Edinburgh, Scotland

Dear Charles,

I'm sending a quick note to thank you for the cigs and scotch, and also your concern. I fear I'll never be free of the heavy load I now carry, but I am on solid ground again. That has to be enough for the time being. I wish I were returning to

London, victory behind me, but I've been told I'm to return to the Front in a few weeks.

Keep me abreast of news about Davies and Hopper. I'm grateful for your constructive influence on them.

Wishing you well,

Thomas

From Alice to Evie

1st December, 1916

Somewhere in France

Dear Evie,

I'll be home on leave in three days! It will be a short visit, but long enough to go for a drive and eat some Christmas goodies. Something to revive my waning spirits. Yes, even I am succumbing to the melancholy coating everything. It's desperate here and no one can endure this at such length without being affected. I'm desperately sad you won't be home while I am, but I wouldn't dream of asking you to part from Tom. I daresay he needs you far more than I do.

Kisses,

Alice

From Thomas to Evie

18th December, 1916

Edinburgh, Scotland

Dear Evie,

How wonderful to celebrate Christmas with you, even a quiet one, a week early. That little tavern in town was perfectly cosy. Roast chicken and potatoes, a tot of brandy by the fire. For just a few hours it felt like we were living in another time. The time before it all.

I'll remember it always; the first real laugh I've had in ages, the way the firelight lit your face. If only I could bottle you up and take you with me when I return to the Front.

Ever yours,
Tom

From Evie to Thomas

20th December, 1916

Leith, Scotland

My dearest Thomas,

How unbearable to endure another goodbye. We seem to dance around each other like autumn leaves, forever twisting and twirling about until a gust of wind sends us skittering in different directions. How I wish we could be still for a while, that the winds of war would end and let us settle.

It will be bittersweet to wave you off tomorrow: so glad to see you well again and so sad to watch you leave. How typical of you to show such fortitude when others would have gladly run back to their mothers' apron strings. You'll be on the train when you read this, hurtling south again towards the camps on the South Downs and on, across the Channel towards France. Your men will be so encouraged to see you again. Don't think of it as returning to war. Think of it as returning to good friends.

I'm writing this in one of the lovely little harbour cafés where I've spent many hours these past weeks. The vastness of the sea reminds me how big the world is, and how little of it I have seen. When the war is over, I want to travel as far as I can so that I know what you were all fighting for—what we are trying to save. Do you remember me mentioning Lillias Campbell Davidson's little travel book? I found it in Papa's library and shared a few lines with you on appropriate dress for cycling tours: ". . . have your gown made neatly and plainly of flannel without loose ends or drapery to catch in your [bicycle]; dark woollen stockings in winter, and cotton in summer; shoes, never boots . . ." I have the book with me now. I was so full of enthusiasm when I first read those lines, but it seems to have all been knocked out of me since. I mustn't let war do that to me, must I? One must always have adventure in life, or the promise of it, at least.

Was there something you wished to tell me when we parted yesterday? There was a moment when you hesitated and I felt sure you had something terribly important to say. Perhaps I am imagining things? If not, and there were things left unsaid, perhaps they could be more easily expressed in a letter. "I'll call for pen and ink and write my mind."

And now the proprietor is closing up, so I must end and seal this. Tomorrow I'll leave the rugged landscape of Scotland and return to the starched perfection of Poplars. I can't say I'm relishing the prospect. I rather feel as though a piece of the Highlands has settled in my heart. I hope to return in the spring, circumstances permitting.

For you, a goodbye gift. An oystercatcher. I drew him during one of my long walks along the mudflats when I was waiting to visit you. He was so patient, breaking open his oysters against the rocks. I imagined him finding a pearl to treasure. With a little patience we might all find something to cherish. Do you think?

Happy Christmas, Thomas.

With much affection,

Evie

XX

From Thomas to Evie

24th December, 1916

Somewhere in France

Dear Evie,

I'm settled in again, as much as one *can* be settled here. It's odd how, with only a few days back, it feels as if I never left. This war is seared onto the very fabric of my being.

A few of the men looked at me funny when I returned, but only one made a comment about my time in "that" hospital. If I weren't a Lieut., I would have pounded Private Johnson's face for his snide remarks. But the last thing we need is to fight amongst ourselves. Instead, I cut him sharply with a few choice remarks. He was too stupid to understand my rebuttal but plenty of the others got it. That was satisfying enough.

Now to a more peaceful thought. I'm placed under the care of a nurse here on request of my doctor in Edinburgh—Rose Blythe is her name. She's a kind soul, bright and breezy, and has a natural empathy about her. I suspect you'd like her a great deal. She is instructed to watch me for any signs of regression. I would have despised such nannying not so long ago, but I must say I'm rather glad of her company. Many more of my friends and comrades were lost in the battle that raged in my absence. Without Rose I find myself alone all too often.

Thank you for your letter, which kept me company on the long journey back here. I'll picture you in that harbour café. It sounds like heaven. My world has grown smaller, not larger unfortunately, but that will change for me, too, I hope. When the war is over, I'd like to spend a good long while at home, knock the business back into shape and then, perhaps, a spot of travelling. A visit to America or the Mayan villages in Guatemala. Maybe somewhere in the West Indies.

In your letter, you asked what we are fighting for, what we are trying to save. My dear girl, we're trying to save you. And every woman, child, relative, and friend that mean something in this world. Protect our home and what is ours, defend our interests, our way of life. At least that's why I'm here. The other "honourable" nonsense is the talk of a naive man who hasn't spent time in battle, or perhaps the few I've met who are true warmongers. I was one of those naive soldiers before, as was our dear Will.

But I am here to save *you*—just as you have saved me. I'm not sure I can properly express my gratitude for your lengthy visit. That's what I was trying to say when we parted. How deeply I care for you. You have been the greatest friend a fellow can ask for, and I am so thankful.

Ever yours,
Tom

From Evie to Alice

25th December, 1916

Richmond, England

Darling Alice,

A very belated Happy Christmas to you. You must think me very remiss to have forgotten you, but you see, I haven't! My Christmas wishes to you, although belated, are heartfelt.

Alice, I have discovered something very troubling and I have to tell you because there is nobody else I can. When I returned from Scotland, I pressed Mama to talk about Will. He feels so absent and I feel dreadfully sad that we don't share our memories or look at photographs of him more often. I asked Mama if I could see the personal effects that were returned to her after his death. She became very flustered and took to her bed with one of her headaches. It is not the first time she has avoided the subject.

Alice, I'm afraid I did something awful. While Mama was in town earlier today, I looked through her writing desk, hoping to find some of Will's things, and I discovered a packet of letters. They were written between Will and his French nurse, Amandine. I don't wish to betray his confidence until I can confirm the implications of the sentiments exchanged, but suffice to say I am rocked to the core. There is also a letter from Will to Mama, to be read in the event of his death and expressing his last wishes. He gives an address in France where Amandine can be contacted.

Mama has never mentioned this. I can only presume she found it all too shocking to accept. I don't know how to confront her about it because then she will know I was rummaging through her things like some sort of awful vagabond. If I do mention it, she will only forbid me from interfering, and I feel that I must.

I plan to write to Amandine this afternoon to try to make some sense of things. I only hope I am doing the right thing.

Happy Christmas, darling.

Evie

XX

From Evie to Amandine Morel

29th December, 1916

Poplars, Richmond, London SW, England

Dear Mademoiselle Morel,

My name is Evelyn Elliott and I am the sister of Will Elliott, whom I believe you knew briefly while working as a nurse at the Front before his sad passing. I recently came across some of Will's personal effects which were returned to my mother after his death.

Mademoiselle Morel, I write to you now because I need to know if the things I read in Will's letters are true. If so, I would very much like to offer you my assistance, and my sincere apologies on Will's behalf for not getting in touch sooner.

Perhaps you could write to me at the above address. It is very forward of me to ask, but if you would be kind enough to write, and perhaps to allow me to visit you in Paris at some stage when the war is over, I feel I would be doing my duty to Will as a sister, and to you as his very dear friend—and more.

I look forward to hearing from you.

Yours sincerely,

Evelyn Elliott

Paris

21st December, 1968

The gardenias lend the most wonderful scent to the room. Margaret remarks on them as she refreshes the vase with water, removes any browned petals, and breathes in the velvety perfume of the blooms.

"Hothouse flowers," I say. "The privilege of the wealthy." It is an extravagance I have indulged in every Christmas. An extravagance she took such pleasure from.

Margaret laughs and tends to the flowers as she tends to me: gently, respectfully, and with good humour. She cannot know of the memories the flowers conjure.

I am as patient as I can bear to be while she turns her attention to me. It bothers me that I must lie here, all needles and tubes. It bothers me that I cannot see Paris as I would like to: the cafés, the gardens, a hearty serving of Burgundy beef; strolling with her arm in arm along the tree-lined boulevards; sipping a café crème or savouring the aniseed tang of a pastis beneath the red-and-white-striped awnings of the cafés in Montmartre. I'd almost forgotten how much I love it here, almost forgotten how much I love life. But this time—my last—I must be content to observe Paris from my apartment, while my tired body limps on and I get ever closer to my final days. Margaret talks about returning to Paris in the spring. I tell her it is beautiful, and encourage her to come back.

"We'll both come back, Mr. Harding!"

My smile conceals the fact that I know I will not see the beauty of a Parisian spring again.

Through the tall French doors of the apartment bedroom here in the sixth arrondissement, I can look out over the rooftops towards the famous tower, watching it fade as the night envelops it. I think of how she longed to see it, the look of childish excitement on her face when it first came into view. Somehow it feels right that everything should come full circle—here again, amidst the souls of so many friends, the soul of my former life.

They tell me I suffer from a cancer of the lungs. It seems ironic to me that I have survived two wars and several shattered bones. I even evaded the terrible Spanish Flu epidemic that tore through the clearing stations at the end of the war, and then through Europe, and very nearly tore my world apart. And yet it is my ability to breathe—the most natural thing in the world for a man to do—that will take me in the end.

I grumble as Margaret administers various medication. I am not a good patient and yet she does her best to keep things cheerful. "I'll be finished soon, and then you can continue on with reading your letters."

I turn my eyes away from her, back to the window. I don't want to be inside. I want to be sipping *vin chaud* in the Lilac Garden of *La Closerie des Lilas*. I want, so much, to be the vibrant young man I once was. I wonder, did I ever truly appreciate my good health and my ability to breathe without a struggle? The arrogance of youth takes everything for granted. Everything, that is, until you find yourself at war, pushing your bayonet into the enemy's chest before he pushes his into yours.

At the sound of the telephone, Margaret rushes from the

room. I prop myself up so I can see the people of Paris below. They rush about, scurrying home to be out of the biting wind. Margaret's voice drifts through the hall and I close my eyes, straining to make out her conversation. She gives little away. I hear only the name, "Delphine," and a melodic stream of passable French.

When she returns, she sets a tea tray on the table beside me. "You need to eat something. It's been hours, Tom. And don't try to hide your food in the bin again." She fixes me with a glare.

"What did she say?" I ask, ignoring the fresh pastries and tea.

"Everything has been arranged as planned." She smiles then. "Delphine is happy you had a comfortable journey and is looking forward to seeing you tomorrow." She fusses with the curtain, pulling it so the folds hang straight. "You must be looking forward to seeing her," she adds.

Delphine, the gift that none of us expected to discover.

"I am, Margaret. Very much."

She notices the letter I have in my hand. The final precious letter—the one I promised to read here, in Paris. The one I will read at the end.

"You always said she wrote such beautiful letters. You must be longing to know what it says," Margaret remarks.

I rub my fingertips across the sealed envelope; across her elegant handwriting. "I waited a long time for so many of her letters, Margaret. I can wait a little longer now."

Margaret plumps my pillows and says she will check on me in a while. She pulls the door closed behind her, leaving me alone with my thoughts and the scent of the gardenias that take me back to the first time I went home on leave and she wore a gardenia in her hair. She had beautiful hair, like ebony silk. It seems ludicrous to me now that I never noticed it before those autumn days we spent together. It was as if I noticed everything about Evie for the first time that week.

I pick up the next bundle of letters, neatly labelled "1917," and let her words take me back there . . .

PART FOUR

1917

"He simply felt that if he could carry away
the vision of the spot of earth she walked on,
and the way the sky and sea enclosed it, the
rest of the world might seem less empty."
—*Edith Wharton*, The Age of Innocence

From Thomas to Evie

1st January, 1917

Somewhere in France

Dear Evie,

Happy New Year, old girl! I hope you enjoyed your Christmas feast and your mother's party. I thought of you often, envisioning you dancing and entertaining the guests. I presume Hopper was there, making a nuisance of himself. You mentioned your mother was planning to invite him.

I find myself in reasonably good spirits. I think, perhaps, 1917 will bring good things and I'll get home for good. At the very least, I plan to apply for leave again in a few months.

Speaking of leave, you wouldn't believe what some of the men are doing. I caught Sergeant James chewing cordite pulled from his rifle bullets to give himself a fever. Shortly after, the nurse gave him a few days off to recover. I was furious! But what kind of man would I be to rat out anyone who needs to get away from it all for a while. I'd be seen as the enemy and we have plenty of those as is. One learns to turn a blind eye.

Could you send some books? I'm desperate for new reading material. The long hours between action means too much time to ruminate on things and I'd rather lose myself in good literature. Many of us swap books and Nurse Rose has given me a few, but we can't carry too many at a time, or our packs become too heavy. I've read *Prester John* by John Buchan several times, and a couple of Nat Gould's horse racing novels. I'd like to read more of Gould and something by your William Blake or Palgrave. Perhaps H. G. Wells?

Did I tell you about *The Wipers Times*? It's a satirical newspaper, written by the soldiers. Two men found an old printing press and started it up from the Belgian town of Ypres. News from the trenches, if you will. It is darkly humorous and quite often lampoons those in command. You would laugh at the section called "Cupid's Corner," an advice page for those with "difficulties relating to 'affaires de cœur.'" I read a poem called "Moaning Minnie" that stuck with me (a Moaning Minnie is a German mortar, or sort of cannon/gun), and chuckled a little at the derision, but while the magazine is an amusing diversion, it isn't a literary meal, if you know what I mean. I need a few books with heft and look forward to what you send.

I'm glad you're back to your drawings. We don't see much wildlife as you might imagine, and your birds remind me of home. I hope you're well, Miss Evelyn Elliott. I think of you often.

Ever yours,
Lieutenant Thomas Harding

From Evie to Alice

20th January, 1917

Richmond, England

Dear girl,

No news from you for a while? I hope all is well? I have several things to tell you:

1. Hopper became rather amorous beside the fountain in Trafalgar Square on New Year's Eve. He kissed me, Alice—and I'm afraid I kissed him back. It was a perfectly pleasant kiss in the way that kisses are, but it was not the type to send a girl weak at the knees and, well, the truth is that when I closed my eyes I could only see Tom and rather wished it were his lips on mine.

2. I have been bedridden with an upset tummy the last two weeks so have been able to avoid Hopper since. He sent flowers and wished me a speedy recovery. Mama is already planning her wedding outfit. I sent a thank-you note and explained that I felt rather embarrassed about the whole event. More flowers arrived in response. What am I to do?

3. I wrote to Amandine Morel, but have yet to get any reply. Should I write again, do you think, or wait a little longer? I am terribly anxious to hear from her. Mama knows nothing about my attempt to contact her.

4. Thomas tells me he has a new nurse attending to him. Rose is her name. I have a feeling she is to become a thorn in my side. She "comforts" him and lends him reading material. I am green with envy—not least because I know how "comforting" you have been to the poor buggers in your care and I cannot stop thinking about rouged lips and jazz tunes.

You see, I am in a terrible tizz and need your wise counsel immediately. How I wish I was out there with you, rather than here enjoying the crackle of the fire alone. I have nobody to share these little pleasures with. Everybody I love is over there.

I long to hear from you.

Your friend,

Evie

XX

From Evie to Thomas

25th January, 1917

Richmond, England

Dearest Tom,

A very Happy New Year to you! I'm so sorry not to have written before now. I have been laid up with an upset tummy and rather thought I was going to die I felt so wretched, but I rallied and feel quite myself again. In fact, I feel better than ever, but I suppose that is always the way when one has been bed-bound for weeks.

Of course, Mama blames my illness on my late night New Year's Eve revels. I found myself in Trafalgar Square with friends and a rather unsavoury bunch of revellers (long story). Perhaps I shouldn't have paddled in the fountain after all. I almost think Mama was sorry to see me recover, denying her the opportunity of saying "I told you so" when I perished from overexertion.

Anyway, here I am, very much alive and with another year sweeping ahead. What will it bring, I wonder? What surprises lie in store?

What better medicine than to see an envelope with your writing. It has become something of a habit, you see. Like eating and sleeping and breathing in and out, your letters and my replies, written at the desk in Will's room—it is what life has become. I'm afraid I am rather hopelessly dependent on your words.

It is shocking to hear what the men will do to be sent home—Alice also writes of the Blighty wounds: cordite poisoning, bullet wounds to a hand stuck above the parapet, men shooting themselves in the foot. Only a desperate man could do such a thing. I can't say I blame them, and I am glad to learn that neither do you.

I am heartened to know that you are finding time to read again. Thank goodness for Nurse Rose and her travelling library. I hope she is proving useful in your continued recovery. (Be careful, Tom. It would be dreadful to hear that you had died of a broken heart after everything.) For such a scholarly young man you haven't mentioned your books very much in recent months. You were always such a keen reader—head always stuck in a book. There were many summers when I tried to catch your attention by turning cartwheels or some such antics, and yet you never noticed me. Far too busy following the adventures of Huckleberry Finn.

I took great delight in raiding Papa's library and have enclosed three volumes. One each of Blake, Palgrave, and Kipling. I hope their wonderful prose will prove to be more enriching than your satirist newspaper. I am currently enjoying a spirited read by a new lady novelist. You wouldn't know of her, but I will show it to you when you return.

As for my little birds, I am happy they bring you joy. I miss their singing during these brutal winter months. We've had weeks of hard frosts and I haven't seen so much as a single robin since I was up and about again, although I throw bread crumbs and break the ice on the water in the bird table to try and entice them. I am eager to bring Rusty the bicycle out of hibernation and take to my postal duties again, but Mama insists I stay indoors until the weather improves. I feel like a caged animal.

Any news from the newspaper? I picked up a copy recently and thought of you. I'm afraid my column has lapsed rather in the wake of my being bedridden. Genevieve is much missed, apparently. Fan letters continue to arrive—mostly of the supportive type, although some are rather nasty and condemn her very existence! Jack Davies says it is good to provoke opinion. The sign of a job well done.

Papa believes the Yanks will join the war soon. They must,

surely. I don't see how the president can avoid it any longer. And it seems likely that Sir Henry Lawson's report will, after all, result in the formation of a Women's Army Auxiliary Corps. They are in dire need of relieving the men in noncombatant roles so that they can serve on the front line and bolster troops. Numbers were decimated during those bloody battles last summer. They have no choice but to turn to the women and allow us to do our bit. I'll be the first in line to volunteer for a position in France if it goes ahead.

Write soon.

With affection,

Evie

P.S. I do not have a bird ready to send, but I promise to send one next time. Perhaps an owl? Such wise old things. I hear one hooting mournfully in the woods when I can't sleep at night. Sadly, nobody ever replies to him.

From Alice to Evie

8th February, 1917

Somewhere in France

Dear Evie,

Greetings, my love. You've been rather busy haven't you, gallivanting in fountains, kissing handsome men, and digging into family secrets! How I wish I were there with you. Do tell all about this secret letter you discovered. Of course you should pursue it—if you are certain no one will be hurt terribly in the process. Sometimes secrets are best kept buried. You will know how best to handle it. You always were the wise and sensible one.

Are you still writing your column? The friend I know would have caused a stir at the newspaper by now, or marched her way to the top of their payroll, woman or not. I would very much like to read your pieces. Would you enclose a clipping or two in your next letter?

You'll be pleased (perhaps unsurprised) to know I've met a lovely doctor named Peter. He's from a rather wealthy family in London—the Lancasters. Do you know them? He felt the pull, as so many of us have, to offer our services where they might be best used, so here he is, saving lives. Dreamy, really.

This brings me to your Thomas. If you won't tell him how you feel and you're certain he doesn't love you, I'm afraid you must move on. Suffering unrequited love is the worst. You're far too pretty and clever for that. Besides, it seems you have a perfectly suitable gentleman banging at the door. We can no longer be choosy in matters of love. There will be no men left at all if this war goes on much longer. Thomas has had his chances. If Hopper persists in kissing you, I say kiss him back.

Alice

X

From Evie to Alice

13th February, 1917

Richmond, England

Dear sweet Alice,

Thomas writes and tells me he cares for me—as a friend. Caring for someone is not the same as loving them, is it? He doesn't love me. I grow more and more certain of it every day. I've dropped plenty of hints and there have been so many opportunities for him to tell me his true feelings, and yet he has taken none. Whether he ever read my Christmas letter or not, I suspect it doesn't matter now.

This is a love of one half. The worst kind of love. This "friendship" of ours will never become anything more than that, I'm sure. I care for Tom dearly, but without any indication that he feels the same it is becoming increasingly hard to maintain any hope. Perhaps it is just a symptom of war, bringing out fanciful notions of romance. I grow weary of it all; weary of the battle raging in my heart. Shall I give it up entirely? Tell me what to do, Alice. I am incapable of rational thought.

And—as you so rightly point out—there is John Hopper, waiting patiently in the wings, always taking me to lunch, constantly charming Mama and Papa, forever settling those copper eyes of his on mine as if there is something he wishes to tell me. He may not set my heart aflame, but he has good prospects and I am, after all, a woman in need of a husband. Perhaps he wouldn't make such a bad compromise after all?

As for the secret, I still haven't had a reply from Amandine and find myself imagining the worst. Paris suffered that awful influenza epidemic last year. Maybe she's dead? I can't explain it. It's as though Will is forcing me to remember her. I know nothing about her, and yet she is in my thoughts continually.

Awful news from here. Some of the NCF supporters—women—were arrested on charges of plotting to murder the Prime Minister. It is all over the papers. Whatever next?

Please forgive me for being so despondent. You know how I struggle in the wintertime. I'll be much improved by the time we see the first blossoms of spring.

Thinking of you always.

Evie

XX

P.S. I do know of the Lancasters. Terribly nice family. Nothing bad to say about them and if I remember Peter at all, then I believe you may have met your match, and I could not be happier for you.

From Thomas to Evie

14th February, 1917

Somewhere in France

Dear Evie,

I'm sorry to hear you were ill, though dancing in a fountain with Hopper (he wrote recently and mentioned your having spent time together) would give me an upset stomach as well. Perhaps you should rethink your company? I'm teasing, of course, but I hate to think of you miserable and in bed. Not my fierce little Evie.

I've had a little fun this evening for a change—I've just returned to my bunk after a show with Elsie Griffin. She sang a few tunes, but my favourite was "Danny Boy." Judging by the cheering after, I'd say it was everyone's favourite. The woman has the voice of an angel.

Lately I've listened to live poetry, and I've seen a few "plays" (smaller and somewhat poor versions of the originals, but so much appreciated these days). Many entertainers have trudged out to France, and there seem to be more and more on the way. God love them for risking their lives to raise our spirits. It has really helped. My tremors have lessened considerably, though I thank Nurse Rose for that, largely. She's all positivity and light, that woman. Full of heart. Not as clever as you, though.

I'm in a reserve trench for a while for a respite from the Front, thankfully. I've had tasks to accomplish, a lot of paperwork and such, but it's been a relief resting and reading the books you sent. Thank you for those. I've been greedy with them— read two already. My mind is starved for something beyond life and death and destruction.

I dreamed about Will last night. I don't wish to upset you, but if he were still alive, things would be different, somehow. I just know it. Your brother knew how to laugh at anything, even the grim. Sometimes I feel his presence so acutely, it startles me to remember he's not here. I miss my father, too, but it's different, you know? We never got along and I was used to his absence, sad as it is to admit.

Happy Valentine's Day. If I were there, I'd take you to Carlisle's for chocolates and sugared cherries, maybe dancing afterward. I hope the stationery I've enclosed is a suitable substitute, though I suspect Hopper is spoiling you silly and that writing paper will be a poor substitute for the attentions of dashing chaps who spoil you with champagne and dinners.

If writing to me has become a habit, I'm glad for it. Hopefully it isn't one you wish to shake.

With affection,

Tom

P.S. The Women's Army Auxiliary Corps would put you in the line of danger. I must admit, I'm not fond of the idea of you joining.

From Evie to Alice

15th February, 1917

Richmond, England

Dear Alice,

Help! Hopper proposed! Yesterday, on Valentine's Day. He has spoken to Papa and everything. I'm so confused, Alice. My head says accept him. My heart says don't.

Mama is furious with me for not accepting immediately. She considers it unbecoming for a woman to play games with a gentleman's heart and says I should snap him up before someone else does.

I'm writing this from my bed, where I'm pretending to have a migraine. Well, it began as pretence but my head really throbs now.

What am I to do?

Evie

From Evie to Thomas

3rd March, 1917

Richmond, England

Dear Thomas,

I'm sorry for not writing in a while. I'm really not myself at the moment.

Thank you for your last letter and the lovely stationery. How on earth did you find such a thing? I can hardly bear to write on it, the paper is so pretty. Your words had me imagining lazy hours lost at Carlisle's. You are a brute for putting such thoughts into my head when there is no way I can shush them. I'm not sure which was the more appealing: the sugared cherries or the dancing.

That you have time to think of me at all—a friend so far away—is a wonder, considering all the troop entertainments you write about, and the additional distractions provided by Nurse Rose. You say we would get along, but I'm afraid I would be rather a disappointment and would only cloud her "bright and breezy" nature. I'm also grown horribly gangly and thin.

I have no appetite. Or perhaps I'm just starved of the things every young woman needs in order to thrive.

I was comforted to hear that you dreamt of Will. We have been so long without him now, yet I sometimes forget, and I look for him in the apple orchard or the stables. It is important to share our memories of him, don't you think? Actually, I wanted to ask you something. What do you remember of the French nurse he was sweet on? Amandine Morel. Do you recall any of the circumstances in which she returned to France? I remember you wrote about her taking ill and returning to her mother in Paris, but I can't recall if there were any more details about the nature of her illness. You'll most likely think me silly to ask, but I've been thinking of her a lot recently.

I'm glad to hear you're enjoying the books. I've taken the liberty of enclosing Jules Verne this time, Will's favourite.

With affection,

Evelyn

From Alice to Evie

6th March, 1917

Somewhere in France

Dear Evie,

Well, well. Hopper finally did it. I'm not at all surprised, I must say. How did he ask? Was it terribly romantic? For some reason I imagine him being stiff and formal, brandy in the Drawing Room and a cough to clear the throat. Did he declare his love for you?

Darling, I know you are confused but you have said it yourself that Tom Harding is blind when it comes to matters of love. He sees friendship with his best friend's sister, yes. Adoration and love? Perhaps not. Perhaps never. After all, he didn't respond to that Christmas letter you sent, spilling the contents of your heart, did he? I fear your Tom may have his head firmly in the sand when it comes to matters of romance.

Whatever you decide, don't toss your future away on a whim. And don't let your mother sway you too much. You aren't the type to do things just because of appearances, my courageous, clever friend. Remember it is your choice and I know you'll make the right one.

Bisous,
Alice

From Evie to Alice

15th March, 1917

Richmond, England

Dearest Alice,

Thank you for your words. You are right. I cannot forever wait for Tom Harding without any assurance that he is worth waiting for, and yet I can't bring myself to accept Hopper either. Which is why what I am about to tell you comes at the perfect time.

I am going to France. I am a fully enrolled member of the newly formed Women's Army Auxiliary Corps (WAAC). It has all happened in such a rush. I wrote to the Labour Exchange to enquire about enrollment and received a very prompt reply (fortunately I got to the post before Mama. She would have been far too interested in the contents of the long envelope bearing the stamp OHMS). I had to report to the Board of Examiners for various examinations and passed them all with flying colours.

Oh, Alice. I'm terrifically excited. At last I am to have some purpose in this war. A proper part to play. I even have my own uniform (being tall I only needed to take it to the tailor to make a slight adjustment to the greatcoat, whereas some of the women look as if they have shrunk, their skirts and coats hang off them so dreadfully).

Embarkation orders came through last night. I am to depart from Victoria Station on the Continental Boat Train to Folkestone and from there we sail to Boulogne and once in France, on to our HQ on the Western Front in Rouen. I leave at the end of the month. A matter of days now. I haven't told anyone, only you. Mama will fuss and Papa will attempt to drill me to death. I know it will be dreadfully upsetting for them— especially Mama—but it really is the only way, and kinder to not put them through the misery of worry and spare us all the inevitable arguments and bad feelings. Far better to just leave and explain everything in a note, don't you think?

I considered telling Hopper in confidence but I'm afraid he will tell Mama or—worse still—try to dissuade me, so I've decided against it and will write to him. Explanations are so much easier when one has time to construct them properly. Perhaps my going to France (running away?) is an answer to Hopper's proposal in itself. I feel so sure of this opportunity. If I go to France and live a little, perhaps I will be more ready to settle into a life of marriage when I return?

Desperate times call for desperate measures and I am proud to know that whatever role I'm given will allow some fellow to join the men in battle. I'm hopeful for a position as a clerk or a telephone operator. It turns out that my little stint at the post office here might prove to have been very useful after all.

I will write more when I can. For now, *Au revoir!*

Your friend,

Evie

X

P.S. I received a sniping letter from a woman who finds my column in rather bad taste. I must admit that I smiled as I read her words. Goodness, she gave me a good telling off. It is important to stir the soul, is it not, and I am glad my words galvanised her to write to me. Journalism isn't about sugarcoating everything to make it more palatable. I know some who fall easily into the trap of propaganda—but I refuse to do so. In fact, I hope my time in France will provide plenty more fuel for me to throw onto the flames. I would happily read sackfuls of outrage if my words of truth can reach people.

From Evie to Thomas

15th March, 1917

Richmond, England

Dearest Thomas,

A few lines to tell you that I am to come to France as a member of the WAAC. I depart at the end of the month. There is no point trying to deter me. It is done. Paperwork signed. Uniform commissioned. I am to spend the rest of this war (however long that might be) amongst it all. There are, after all, only so many badly knitted socks a Tommy can expect to endure. My skills are much better served in other duties. I'm hoping to work on the telephone lines, or as a clerk.

Don't worry. I won't be binding my chest and cutting my hair and rushing to the trenches with a bayonet. I know where the dangers lie and I will be keeping as far away from them as possible, yet I find myself feverish with excitement and trepidation. Finally, I will see this war for myself and play my part rather than watching interminably from the sidelines.

My parents know nothing about it. I plan to leave a note which they will find on the morning of my departure. By the time Collins takes it up to Mama on her breakfast tray, I will be on the boat train to Folkestone. I will face the consequences when I return.

Please think of me and send me good luck in your prayers. I will send word when I arrive. Who knows—we might yet see each other beneath those starry French skies you have written about so often. I would very much like to see you, Thomas. Even with the sound of shells pounding in my ears it would be worth it to see that silly smile of yours.

I have enclosed three more novels and a book of British Garden Birds. I thought you might like to see how accurate (or otherwise) my sketches are.

Don't worry about me. I am but a migrating bird, Thomas. I will leave England's familiar hedgerows for a little while, but I know they will be waiting for me, more beautiful than ever, when I return.

With all good wishes.

Your friend,

Evie

X

Telegram from Thomas to Evie

17TH MARCH 1917

TO: EVELYN ELLIOTT, POPLARS, RICHMOND, LONDON SW
SENT: 10:14 / RECEIVED: 11:54

YOU ARE AS STUBBORN AS A MULE. CAN'T DISSUADE
YOU BUT NOT HAPPY ABOUT THIS. RECONSIDER? IF NOT,
PLEASE BE CAREFUL. TOM.

From Thomas to Evie

20th March, 1917

Somewhere in France

Evie,

When I read your letter, I was furious. I tried to be level-headed, but I wound up throwing a private's helmet clear into no man's land. It was shot up immediately, of course, and he had to get a new one. I don't want you here amid the gloom and gore. It isn't the place for someone like you and won't be good for you. It isn't good for anyone. For some reason, I feel I need to protect you and I can't abide you destroying that pure goodness inside you, or seeing something horrible to test your spirit. What if something were to happen to you? I don't think I could stand it, Evie. We talked about this at length in Edinburgh, yet you insist on putting yourself in harm's way.

Please say you'll make it a short stay and for God's sake, be wary of the men. They haven't been around a real woman in months, and even years, some of them. Keep your wits about you. If you came to any harm at the hand of one of our own I can assure you I would see red, and couldn't be held accountable for my actions.

Tom

From Evie to Tom

25th March, 1917

Richmond, England

Dear Thomas,

Your letter disappoints me. That you believe a woman has no place in this war, that you believe I cannot handle the gloom and the gore leaves me furious. I had expected more, from you of all people.

This is the opportunity I've been waiting for. I imagined— hoped—you would be happy to see me stretch my wings and broaden my view of a war I have seen only through your eyes these past two years. Do all men believe that women are incapable? Must I return to the knitting of comforts and bide my time like a good girl?

You say you would protect me. Keep me safe. Would you rather I were confined to a safe dull existence where I grow old knowing nothing but tea at four and dinner at eight, or would you rather I live a little dangerously and thrive? If you wish to protect me from something, then protect me from the monotony of life as a privileged young woman awaiting the confines of married life. I cannot think of anything more certain to drive me to an early grave.

In any event, it's decided. I am going to France and that is all. Perhaps my words are best kept for others from now on. I would hate to think of you tossing another helmet into no man's land on my behalf.

We have written often of birds, you and me. How strange then, to rediscover—just yesterday—these words from Miss

Brontë's *Jane Eyre*: "I am no bird; and no net ensnares me: I am a free human being with an independent will."

I will leave it at that.

Evelyn

From Evie to Alice

30th March, 1917

Richmond, England

My dear Alice,

I ship out tomorrow. I am all butterflies and nervous excitement. I hope I am doing the right thing. I'm sure I am, although I could hardly bear to look Mama and Papa in the eye over dinner this evening.

Tom, meanwhile, wrote to express his frustration with me. He seems to think France unsuitable. He says it isn't the place for "someone like me," by which I presume he means a woman of my position. Honestly, Alice, I believe he would truss me up and place me in a cage for safekeeping. I wish I'd never mentioned the WAAC to him because his words of caution nag at me like a fretful parent and I only want to feel confident and assured.

In any event, I will sail tomorrow whether Thomas Harding supports me, or not.

Stay safe, darling.

Much love,

Evie

X

P.S. You can write to me at the address given on the inside flap of the envelope.

From Evie to her mother

30th March, 1917

Dearest Mama,

This war has changed all of us in many ways, and I hope you will—one day—be able to forgive me for what I am about to do.

I have left for France. I enrolled with the WAAC and passed the various tests and examinations. I will be based at the Western Front, close to Rouen, under the supervision of Helen Gwynne-Vaughan. I expect to be assigned as a clerk or telephone operator. More men are desperately needed at the Front. My taking one of the auxiliary roles will free up one more man to take up arms. When you multiply that by the thousands of women volunteering, we can make a real difference.

I had to do my duty. That is all.

I have informed John, and promised to give him my answer when I return.

Mama, I know you think often about Will and I must ask you to consider what he would have said about this if he were alive. He would have supported me in this decision, I know he would, even if he did worry for my safety. I must ask you and Papa to support me in the same way. Will was incredibly honourable and brave. I'm going to France in his memory as much as for my own desire.

When he was alive, Will always said if there was anything he could do for me, I had only to ask. I never extended the same invitation to him, and now I can only regret that. If there had been anything he had asked of me before his death—or after, in a letter perhaps—I would have done it, no matter how difficult or unexpected. I hope I would have found the courage to honour his request. Wouldn't we owe him that, Mama, to honour any last request Will made of us, and not hide it away along with his medals and cricket things and childhood toys? We all have our secrets, but some are not ours to keep in the first place.

I hope you will give me your blessing now, and pray for me.

I will write when I arrive in France and will send word as often as I can.

Ever your loving daughter,

Evelyn

X

From Evie to John Hopper

30th March, 1917

Richmond, England

Dear John,

Please try not to be angry when you read this, but I have left for France.

I am enrolled with the WAAC and will be based at the Western Front, close to Rouen, under the supervision of Helen

Gwynne-Vaughan. I expect to be assigned as a clerk or telephone operator. Finally, I have the chance to do my bit and for that I am immensely grateful and proud.

I know you will be disappointed by the sudden nature of my departure, especially since you haven't yet had an answer from me, and for that I am sorry. I do not wish to play games with you, but I also feel certain that assisting in the war effort is something I must do. More than anything, I believe that if I am to find the right answer to your question of marriage, I will find it in France. For that alone, I hope I have your support and understanding.

Jack Davies is already aware of this. I will know more when I arrive in France and am assigned my new duties there. I will continue to send my column to you in the first instance, as has become our arrangement of late.

I will send word as often as I can.

Yours,
Evelyn

From Evie to her mother

4th April, 1917

Rouen, France

Dearest Mama,

A few lines to let you know that I am safely arrived in France. We hear the shelling and gunfire in the distance, but I am in no danger, I assure you.

We are all in good spirits, happy to do our bit at last (even if some of the men were rather scathing about our ability to do any of their jobs at all).

Send my regards to Papa and to all at the house.

I will write again soon,

Your loving daughter,

Evelyn

X

From Evie to Thomas

7th April, 1917

Rouen, France

Dear Thomas,

I suspect you are still cross with me for being here, but in case you should wish to write again I wanted to let you know that I have arrived in France, and to pass on an address where you can contact me.

The journey was rather arduous (not helped by heavy seas), but I am happy to be here. I am based in the town of Rouen and appointed as a telephonist. This, I am glad about. Some of the women have been assigned to wait on the officers. Others have been given roles as cemetery gardeners. Given these alternatives, I am thankful for my position in the military telephone exchange.

We are staying in a dreadful little hostel in a camp behind the lines. The bathroom arrangements are rather undesirable, but I refuse to complain. This is, after all, what I wanted. To be amongst it all—even if that does mean taking a bath in a makeshift shed accessed through a coal cellar. I hope the image makes you laugh. Who would have thought I would see the day?

I feel quite safe here, although we hear the shelling and gunfire in the distance, which is unsettling to say the least. Those who have been here longer assure me I will get used to it. They say they don't hear it anymore, although I can't believe that to be true.

If you are still angry with me, then I suppose I will have to accept it, although I will be bitterly disappointed. If not, please write. Even a few lines to share your state of mind and good health? I also still wish to hear what you remember of Amandine Morel, Will's French nurse. I can't explain why at the moment, but anything you remember about the circumstances in which she left her post as nurse would be gratefully received.

I will write more when I have the chance. What news from the Front? Can you tell me where you are? Good news that America has declared war on Germany. I wonder when the first American troops will arrive.

Your friend,

Evie

From Alice to Evie

8th April, 1917

Somewhere in France

Dear Evie,

You're in France! I'm torn between being afraid for your safety and thrilled that you made it here at last. I know it was what you dearly hoped for and that you will be pleased to play your part now. So much is happening here, so much drudgery and despair, that I need a reason to be glad. You've done it!

I'm in the town of Clouette at the moment, and will likely be here another couple of weeks. I'll ask the head nurse, see how I might secure a transfer to be near you. It was clever of you to join up now. It will give you proper time to consider Hopper's proposal.

Doctor Peter has been moved to another location, but he writes to me almost every day. I never knew a man who had so much to say, but our letters go on for pages sometimes. Unabashedly, I wait for the post, hold my letters tightly against my chest, and squirrel them away until I can pore over his elegant hand in private. He is the only man I've ever met who thrills me; I'm in awe of his brilliant mind and his passion. He's so noble, so determined. Plus he's handsome as a prince. Who knew one man possessed so many qualities? Oh, there I go, gushing about him. I think I am in love. *Love,* I say! And not the foolish infatuations I have felt before. Now I quite understand the difference.

I am sorry you and Tom are falling out. Are you certain he wasn't simply being protective of an old friend? Surely he doesn't think you can't handle things in France just because you're a woman. It doesn't sound like Tom. But listen, dearest. Can you feel the way this war is changing you, even in your short time here? Imagine what Tom has seen and done, all he has lost in the last two years. Can you blame him for wanting you safely at home? I want you safe, too! I understand why you need to be here as I do, but I can't help but want you far from harm, as selfish as that is. It's out of love, you see? Perhaps you misread Tom's feelings. It sounds like he doesn't know his own. Some men need proper encouragement, (which is why I left a little note in Doctor Peter's notebook).

Just a little advice before I close—you mustn't become too serious while here. One can't survive the rigours of war if one doesn't catch some air from time to time, if you know what I mean. Find a way to bring yourself some cheer. And make friends with any soldiers you might meet. They need encouragement so desperately now. They don't care what circles we come from these days. That's the only beauty in all of this bloodshed. The ranks and classes of yesterday are falling away like dead leaves. Now, we're all in this together.

I am so proud of you.

Affection, kisses, love.

Alice

From Thomas to Evie

15th April, 1917

Somewhere in France

Dear Evie,

Please accept my apology for yelling at you. A gentleman shouldn't send an angry telegram to a lady, and certainly not from the battlefields of war.

Of course I don't believe your womanhood makes you incapable of handling this, nor of proper reporting or writing excellent articles. Somehow you assumed I thought you aren't strong enough to be here. You're one of the strongest people I know. Have I ever treated you as an inferior? You know how cracking smart my mother was, how much I admired her gumption. I see the same qualities in you. Selfishly, I fear for your safety and want you protected at home, even if it means you might suffocate from boredom and regret. At least then, I won't lose you. I have lost too much to the Germans already.

To answer your questions about Amandine Morel, yes, of course I remember her. She's the only girl I have ever seen Will fall hard for in all our years as friends. She was beautiful, but also had a great sense of humour. She kept your brother on his toes. I don't know anything about the circumstances of her leaving, however. Our battalion had marched on and the two wrote a few weeks of feverish letters before Will was killed. I sent word of his death to her at the field hospital where she was based but was told she had fallen ill and returned to her home in Paris. Has she been in touch? Is she looking for him now?

I hope you find what you are seeking here in France. If it is inspiration you're after, and malaise you'd like to banish, there's plenty here to help you with both. I look forward to hearing how you are getting on. I hope you will continue to write to this ridiculous cad, despite his unintended insults to you.

Ever yours,

Tom

From Thomas to John Hopper

28th April, 1917

Somewhere in France

Dear John,

I have reviewed the latest documents from Abshire and I am impressed by the paper's numbers. Abshire has been copying the most important information for me and forwarding it on since Father's death. Well done. I will admit I am miserly with praise, but perhaps we can put the past behind us. The world is at war so family should stick together, shouldn't we?

I like your idea of adding another war column from a male perspective to partner with Evie Elliott's, though I would caution you not to give it more play than hers. She has worked very hard to be recognised as a proper journalist, and she deserves all the accolades. She writes every few days to keep me abreast of all news from her new appointment at the switchboard in Rouen.

I hope all is well in London. Beware the zeppelins and stay safe.

Sincerely,

Lieutenant Thomas Harding

From Evie to John Hopper

5th May, 1917

Rouen, France

Dear John,

A few lines to let you know that all is well here and to enclose my latest column. I must warn you that it does not make for pretty reading, so I will understand if you and Jack feel inclined to edit it heavily, or indeed if you cannot print it at all, although I believe you are not ones to shy away from the truth.

I am appalled and incensed by what I have seen here. The War Office is doing a remarkable job of portraying this war as nothing more than a jolly foray into the French countryside. The men are desperate. It is like another world entirely, a world of unimaginable suffering and fear and loss. Not one of gallantry and chests bursting with pride as they would have us believe. Not a single man would come here willingly if he knew the truth. No human being should have to live this way. Ever.

I hear the Germans are now bombing England with airplanes rather than zeps. Dear God, what next? Perhaps I am safer here in France after all. Lloyd George will have his work cut out for him. I do not envy the man taking office amid such uncertainty.

I must close but will write again soon.

Yours,

Evelyn

A WOMAN'S WAR

by our special correspondent in France,
Genevieve Wren

"The View from the Front"

For so long, I have imagined this war. I have seen it in my dreams, in my nightmares. I have pictured it through the eyes of family and friends close to the action. Mostly, I have read about it through the reports printed in our newspapers.

Now, after years of wishing to do something more useful than knitting, I am here, amongst it all. I hardly recognise it as the same world I have known for twenty-three years.

Nothing I ever imagined could have prepared me for the bleak reality of war, and certainly nothing I have read in the newspapers resembles what I see here with my own eyes.

We have been done a great disservice by those who

claim to bring us the news. In bold typeface marching across the newsstands they tell us of "Great Victories" and "Terrific Advances." They would have us believe this war is nothing but boys playing a game. We read of bravery and fallen heroes and learn of the loss of a loved one, another dignified end to life, described in the neat handwriting of a general, safe in his bunker while he sips the best French brandy available.

They deceive us. Conceal and fabricate.

There is no such thing as a dignified end. Not here. When our men fall, they fall hard. They fall into thick mud where the corpses of hundreds of horses lay rotting beside them. What dignity is there in that? What dignity is there in any of this?

There is no glory to be found here. Only fear and suffering. Grown men weep for their mothers and beg for a swift end. The men live each day as if it were their last, and that is no way to live at all.

So what can we do, apart from ignore the newspapers who shy away from the truth?

We can encourage our men not to spare us the gory details. Of course, the censors will do their best to strike out their words of brutal honesty, but let us read between the lines. Let them tell us, if they can. Let them talk of the bloodiest battles, be it in letters or poetry or face-to-face during their home leave. Let them cry like babes in our arms, knowing that they must return to it.

Those who cannot endure it, we call deserters. Shoot them by firing squad. Call them cowards.

But they are just human beings—you and me—who simply cannot suffer this hell any longer. The real cowards are those back in England, in charge of the printing presses. The real cowards cover up the truth and shy away from the reality of this "war to end all wars" before sinking into their warm beds. *They* are the ones who deserve our scorn. *They* are the ones who should bow their heads in shame.

Let us demand the truth. And let us pray for a swift end to this war.

Until next time—courage!

Genevieve

From John Hopper to Evie

16th May, 1917

London, England

My dear Evelyn,

On a personal note, it is wonderful to hear from you. On a professional note, I encouraged Jack Davies to run your article, all of the gory details included. I am so glad I did as it sparked a real fervour among your fans and a complete uproar among the other newspapers.

This morning when I arrived at the office, I met a crowd of conscientious objectors outside the door. They want to submit an anonymous article supporting your claims and denouncing the war. I cannot abet potential prisoners, of course, so I turned them away. Shortly thereafter, the police arrived, questioning me and the other staff. Davies was furious, but I reminded him of our duty to make a profit for the newspaper.

Regardless, I think what you're doing is important. The more abhorrent aspects of war should be made public. Citizens deserve to know the truth. I know you agree, so I urge you to submit another piece immediately.

In other news, I find myself wondering if the woman whom I admire beyond all others will ever accept my proposal. I do hope you will decide soon, Evelyn. A man in my position cannot wait forever.

Yours,
John

From Charles Abshire to Thomas

18th May, 1917

London, England

Dear Thomas,

I write to inform you of unsettling news. Our war columns have elicited a flood of response. Letters come from supporters and naysayers, and more unsettling, policemen, lawyers, and councilmen. The *London Herald* has also received this sort of attention, and they employ two female columnists. I'm not entirely sure what to do about it. Your cousin seems to think it is a grand thing. He is further spurring on our columnists and it is putting the paper at risk in the form of serious reprimands with potentially very expensive consequences, or worse—closure.

Thomas, I value my time being a part of this family, and pride myself on having run the financial aspect of your father's business for so many years, but I cannot abide making a mockery of the paper. I will not stay to see its ruin. I care too deeply for you and your father, as well as my future. Take care to watch John Hopper.

I am glad to hear you are well. I look forward to seeing you walk over the threshold for good.

Best wishes,

Charles

From Evie to John Hopper

25th May, 1917

Rouen, France

Dear John,

Thank you for your letter. I am astonished to hear of such a furore caused by my words. I am sorry it led to you being in rather hot water with the constabulary. This is, however, what we wanted, is it not? You and Davies have certainly encouraged my honesty, and to not shy away from the truth.

Already, I have seen so many things here that I wish to write about—things I believe readers need to know. I find it difficult to limit my observations to the number of words permitted by the space allocated to my column, so I am only too happy to write as often as I can. Far too much has been concealed from the British public. The truth must be known before thousands more men lose their lives in such senseless battles as those we saw last year at the Somme and Verdun.

I find myself particularly moved by the soldiers' cemeteries, many of which are in Rouen, which is close to a number of hospitals. Some of the women in the WAAC have been given the task of maintaining the cemetery gardens. Do people back home even know that such a job is carried out here—by women—and no doubt replicated across France and Belgium? To see such well-tended gardens—and the peace they bring— amid such atrocities is really very sobering. Perhaps I will write a short piece about it. Something a little gentler might appease some of the diehards who are causing a bit of a stink for you.

I will send another piece on as soon as possible.

As for my answer, I hope you can wait on it a little longer? You have been a great help in my journalistic endeavours, and I've enjoyed our luncheons and dinners and many conversations. The thing is, I am too distracted here to think about marriage. The future seems so intangible when every day may be the last. If you do not feel able to wait for an answer, then of course I understand.

Yours in truth,

Evelyn

From Evie to her mother

15th June, 1917

Rouen, France

Dearest Mama,

A few lines to thank you for your letter and to assure you that I am safe and well in France and quite settled in my work here. I understand that you were angry with me for leaving as I did, but I am encouraged to hear that you support—and admire—my decision now. Your concern for my welfare is entirely understandable, especially since you have already lost one child. I do not intend to deprive you of another. Who would cause you all this anxiety then?

We await the arrival of US troops. Many believe the war is nearly at an end, yet I hardly dare let myself believe it. I see so much suffering, Mama, and it humbles me. We led such comfortable privileged lives before all this. Nothing will ever be the same, will it? I hope not. We must be changed by this, or what on earth is it all for.

John Hopper writes and urges me to give him an answer. He tells me he admires me but I wonder, is admiration enough? Am I naive to wish for fervent declarations of love? One can admire a painting or a dress—not the woman you love with all your heart. I sometimes wonder whether Hopper sees me as something else to add to his prized collection of Egyptian artifacts. You and Papa have always been so madly in love. I want that passion too. Would you deprive me of the chance of it by pushing me into a marriage I cannot be sure of?

Thomas writes as often as he can. He has become such a good friend to me these past years, just as he was to Will in the many years before. Mama, I know this will make you cross but I cannot shake thoughts of Will nor the matter I referred to in my previous letter. In your reply, you said you have done nothing but protect the interests of the family and that you urge me to do the same and leave well enough alone, but I cannot. I know that Will asked for your help, and I beg you to honour his request.

Please send my love to Papa. I will write again soon.

Your ever-loving daughter,

Evelyn

X

From Evie to Thomas

25th June, 1917

Rouen, France

Dear Thomas,

Did you forget about your old friend, Evie? A month has passed without word from you and I can only imagine you find yourself smothered beneath the care and attentions of Nurse Rose and incapable of reaching for your pencil. It is strange, but now that I am in France—closer to you—I have never felt further away. When I was in Richmond, I felt a connection to you across all the miles. Now, I feel that I have become a chore; a niggle at your conscience. Something you must do, rather than something you cannot do soon enough.

It would ease my mind to know that you are, at the very least, in good health. If your heart is no longer in mind of our exchanges, please let me know and I will bother Alice with my musings and ponderings, and not you. Perhaps the young Irish soldier I met recently would appreciate my bird sketches instead. I must say, the Irish have an unusual charm. Really, I wouldn't be at all surprised to find myself travelling to Tipperary, despite it being such a long way.

In other news, I am now operating the telephone lines. My rusty schoolgirl French is much improved and all those tedious lessons with Madame Hélène have, at last, been put to some practical use.

Perhaps you will write to me again. If not, then I cannot be sorry for the exchanges we have had these past years. You have kept my mind from dissolving entirely into a deep well of grief and despair. You, Thomas Harding, have kept me alive with your words and the promise of your return. It would break my heart to think you had given up on me now.

And thank you for the few lines regarding Amandine Morel. To hear—again—how devoted Will was to her (and she to him) makes me more determined than ever to find her. I will explain all another time.

Yours in hope and friendship.

Evie

From Evie to John Hopper

30th June, 1917

Rouen, France

Dear John,

No word from you for a while, so I hope all is well in London and at the paper. I have enclosed my latest piece.

Perhaps you could write to let me know if it runs and, if so, what the reaction is. I don't wish to cause difficulty for the LDT. You know how friendly I am with Tom Harding. The last thing I want is for my ambitions as a journalist to affect his ambitions to succeed his father and see his legacy flourish.

I am sure between yourself and Jack Davies you will do the best for all involved.

With fondness,

Evelyn

A WOMAN'S WAR

by our special correspondent in France,
Genevieve Wren

"No Job Too Small"

I sit beside a young soldier whose life slips further away with each word I write. To see row upon row of beds in this makeshift field hospital is like looking at the end of the world. Not two minutes ago a young boy—just turned fifteen—lost his fight to survive. He had lied about his age, so desperate to be a man, so desperate to enlist and join the fight. He was a boy with so much to live for, yet he said he wanted to make his mam proud. What a waste, what dreadful futility.

When you see, up close, the brutal reality of war, it is hard to believe that anything you do—one small person—will ever make a bit of difference.

But it does.

Like so many other women, I am doing my bit here with the WAAC. I dress in uniform. I follow orders. I sleep in a dilapidated dormitory that any decent gardener would refuse to grow his tomatoes in. It is far from the comforts of home, and the continual distant sound of shelling is a stark reminder of what is happening not so very far away. At times, I wonder what on earth I am doing here, or how life brought me here at all. My role is only one tiny cog in a very large military machine, but it is a role once filled by a man. By taking up his work, he has been able to join the fight. When released in volumes, those additional men are of great importance. But we must never forget our own importance, too.

Never feel your role is insignificant. Never feel your small contribution cannot make a difference. It can. And it does.

I will continue to do my part here in France, and as I

do, I will fight this war with the only weapons permitted to me: my pencil, my paper, and my words.

Until next time—courage!

Genevieve

From John to Evie

5th July, 1917

London, England

Dearest Evelyn,

I couldn't wait to hear from you so I had to write to tell you the latest column created a sensation—again!

A pack of angry readers stood outside our doors the morning after the paper went out. By mid-afternoon, it had turned into a horde. They picketed outside, chanting about dismissing the column and "this woman" who wrote it. Others demanded we do something about ending the war (as if it is in our hands). We could not print fast enough to keep up with the demand. The police arrived, yet again, and broke up the disturbance. The downside is, after the incident, I suffered a belligerent "request" from the War Office to cease. They said if we do not comply, the paper will be shut down.

Still, I would like to run a few more of your columns and then we will pull it, or perhaps shift its focus entirely. For now, though, hold off on the next few months to let some of the fervour pass. We'll aim for an autumn return for Genevieve Wren.

I have been in contact with Tom Harding. He tells me you two still exchange letters at quite a pace. How lucky he is. I will continue to watch the post for word from you.

Evelyn, I know that marriage may feel like an impossible thing to think about right now, but I cannot tell you how happy you would make me if you would only write with a "Yes." I can offer you a very comfortable life, a life in which you need never work again. Imagine the fun you and that friend of yours (Annie?) will have, lunching and shopping to your heart's content. What other man can offer you such prospects? What other man deserves the beautiful Evelyn Elliott on his arm? I can certainly think of none.

Be safe over there. You are greatly missed.

Yours, with affection.

John

Telegram from Thomas to Evie

12TH JULY 1917

TO: EVELYN ELLIOTT, ROUEN, FRANCE
SENT: 18:33 / RECEIVED: 19:52

INJURED IN BATTLE. NOT TOO SERIOUS. OPERATION ON RIGHT HAND MEANS NO LETTERS FOR NOW. I WILL SEND TELEGRAM OR WRITE WHEN HAND HEALS. AFFECTION. T.

From Evie to Alice

11th September, 1917

Rouen, France

Dearest Alice,

What news? I hear of dreadful casualties in the area where you are and cannot stop thinking of you working in such awful conditions. I hope you are bearing up.

So much is happening now I can hardly keep up with the intelligence coming down the wires. The girls in the exchange here really feel that things are moving towards a conclusion and that victory will soon be ours. I hope and pray for it with all my heart.

John presses me for an answer still, and Tom suffered an injury to his right hand. He says he cannot write for a while, which is probably just as well. Sometimes I haven't the energy to write to either of them.

I often find myself thinking about Will. I somehow feel closer to him here, knowing a little of what he experienced. I wonder what he would say if he could see me. His little sister, among it all. I remember he once teased me about being smitten with Tom Harding. I laughed at the notion—Tom Harding! But he was right, wasn't he. Perhaps it has always been Tom. The thing is, Alice, when I see a few lines from Tom, my heart devours every single word. When I read letters from John, I feel suffocated.

Yesterday, I started thinking about that silly notion we all had to spend Christmas in Paris. It seems impossible now, doesn't it, and yet I have more reason than ever to want to go. I need to find someone, you see, who, if I have things straight, will be most precious to me. But more on that when I see you. It isn't the thing for letters.

Please write soon.

Much love,

Evie

X

From Evie to her mother

3rd October, 1917

Rouen, France

Dear Mama,

A short note to tell you that I am well and still enjoying my work here on the switchboard. We relay dozens of messages per hour. It's exhausting, but the time passes quickly and I sleep well at night.

I am quite out of any danger, although we hear the distant pounding of shells and the rat-a-tat-a of gunfire. It has become so familiar to me that I often don't hear it at all. I wouldn't wonder that I will find the tranquillity of life back at home rather unusual. I'll have to ask Cook to walk around the house banging on her copper pans to make things feel ordinary.

I hope you and Papa are in good health. It looks unlikely that I will be home for Christmas. It will be rather quiet around the table this year.

Your loving daughter,

Evelyn

X

From John to Evie

10th November, 1917

London, England

Dear Evelyn,

I have not heard from you in three months, and I am worried. Please let me know that you are all right. I assume you are caught up in the action there?

If you are willing, I would like to run your column again next month. The fervour has abated some, yet demand is still high. Everyone asks when Genevieve Wren will write something new. Now is the time to strike.

I still have hopes for a spring wedding. Your mother has started to look for a dressmaker. Let's not leave things until the last minute, all right? I hope you will not disappoint me.

Sincerely,

John

From Thomas to Evie

1st December, 1917

Somewhere in France

Dear Evie,

Forgive my awful script. This is the first time I've committed to writing a letter since my hand healed. I thought for certain they would send me home, but they found plenty for me to do in the reserves. I have to say, I am glad of it. This feels more like home than anywhere else now. Here, with my men, my brothers in arms. They are all the family a fellow could ever wish for. What is there in London for me anyway?

Charles has filled me in on business at the *London Daily Times*. It appears Hopper's reports vary quite a lot from his. We're facing threats from the War Office now. I'm sick over it, but there's not much I can do from here, other than make threats I can't really enforce. I suppose I'll ride it out, just as I do this damnable war. When I get home, there will be a reckoning of sorts, you can count on that.

It's getting to be that time of year when my thoughts turn to Christmas. Let's close our eyes and pretend we're at a party, shall we? My journalist would note every detail, I'm sure, so I'll do my best to paint a picture for you. Here goes.

The ballroom shimmers in tinsel, red ribbon, and heavy boughs of garland. Though grief clogs the air and dampens the festivities at the beginning of the evening, the somber ambiance dissipates as drinks flow and music pours through the room. Somehow, the spirit of Christmas and firelight and familiar faces bring the town together. For a few hours the restlessness subsides and the anguish within us retreats.

At the banquet, we feast on duck and pheasant, and celery à la parmesan. And all the puddings! Christmas pudding with brandy sauce, currant pudding with almond sauce, sugared chestnuts. We drink mulled wine and beer, and gin. We grow as fat as kings.

At the end of the night, you and I sit outdoors and share a smoke on the lawn, quietly looking in the direction of France and planning to spend another Christmas there soon.

Will you join me in my reverie?

Your friend,

T

From Evie to John

20th December, 1917

Rouen, France

Dear John,

A few lines to wish you a Happy Christmas. I hope you find someone to dance with in the fountain in my absence. I can hardly remember the girl I was a year ago. Life could not be more different, nor my heart more troubled.

It is snowing here and everything looks rather beautiful. Impossible to believe the world knows such horror among such a peaceful scene. Give my love to your mother.

With all best wishes,

Evelyn

From Evie to Tom

20th December, 1917

Rouen, France

My dear Tom,

Another Christmas approaches and another year of letters between us slips away. There must be enough to fill a book by now.

Talking of which, please accept a small gift from me. A small volume of W. B. Yeats poetry. It was left by one of the officers and I can think of nobody who would get greater pleasure from it. "And a softness came from the starlight and filled me full to the bone." His words are so delicious, I could eat them.

Happy Christmas, Tom. I caught a snowflake on my tongue this morning and made a wish for you.

Always your friend,

E

X

Paris

22nd December, 1968

With some difficulty, I settle into a chair at the café across the street from the apartment. Lamplight glows against the windowpanes, gleams against the rows of glasses dangling above the bar, and spills over the dark wood panelling. It's as cosy as I remember, and yet it's not the same without her—not as bright, not as warm, not as it should be.

Margaret sits several tables away and lights a cigarette before opening a copy of the day's news. I'm grateful for her discretion, for giving me this rare moment of privacy, free of tubes and attendance and procedures. In truth, I shouldn't have come. Upon waking, I felt my frailty in every bone, and in the wretched pain in my lungs. Had my eyes not betrayed my dismay at the prospect of skipping my rendezvous with Delphine (and had it not been Christmas), I am sure Margaret would have insisted I stay in bed.

"Tom! You made it!"

Delphine's cheerful voice rings out behind me like church bells on Christmas morning, brightening my heart with its wonderful Gallic melody. I struggle to stand and greet her, but give up and sink back into my chair.

"Please don't get up," she says as she pulls her chair a little closer.

"I'm not entirely sure I can," I reply, a wry smile passing my lips as I look into her eyes. Just the same as her aunt's.

She kisses each of my cheeks in the French way and covers my hands with hers, squeezing briefly. "It is so wonderful to see you, Tom!"

"And you, my dear!" It really is. She is awash with life and vitality. A scent of violets floats about her shoulders, reminding me of violet-scented letters.

"The year was much too long, Tom! I'm so pleased you came. Christmas wouldn't be the same without you and . . ."

The name slips away, drifting among the cigarette smoke that winds towards the ceiling from the tables beside us. I manage a weak smile, but it feels foreign, stiff, like muscles gone unused for too long.

We exchange stories, catch up on things, remember. When we fall silent, I watch Delphine polish off a generous slice of tarte tatin and regret the loss of my sense of taste. Nothing tastes the same since she departed.

"You haven't touched yours, Tom." Delphine motions to my slice of uneaten tarte.

I don't bother to bore her with tales of taste buds and a gut that doesn't work properly, the constant ache in my chest. Like Margaret, she might counsel me on how to prolong this life that, quite simply, doesn't need any more living. Not much more, anyway. Just enough.

"I wanted to give you this." I push a small package across the table. It is wrapped in gold foiled paper.

Delphine smiles, lighting a familiar pair of blue eyes. The very same blue, passed down from generation to generation. Her own daughters inherited them, too.

She rips the paper away and gasps as she opens the little box inside. "Oh, it's beautiful!" She fastens the gold chain around her neck, running her fingers across the small bird charm that nestles against her throat.

"A wren," I say. "It belonged to my mother. It became rather a favourite of your aunt's."

Tears glisten in Delphine's eyes. "I will treasure it. Thank you."

I smile again, shift in my seat, and reach for another packet on the chair beside me. "I thought you might like these, too. Some books that belonged to your father. A few letters and photographs as well. They are rather old and battered now, I'm afraid. Much like myself."

She laughs and touches my hand affectionately. "You are not old and battered. You are wonderful, and fascinating."

She is so like her aunt, it breaks my heart to look at her, to hear her charmingly positive view of life. But I take comfort from knowing that our memories will live on through Delphine and her family. I take comfort that we found her, that we connected the strands of the family.

I've kept the most important letter separate to those inside the packet.

"This is a letter written by your father. I found it in the pocket of his greatcoat after he passed away." I pause to cough into my napkin, then continue with shaky breath. "The enemy's bullets found Will before he ever had a chance to send it. It was returned to his mother, along with his personal effects."

Delphine takes the letter gently, turns the fragile paper over in her hands, and begins to read.

Unsent Letter from Will to Amandine

7th May, 1915

My dear Amandine,

We are to have a baby? I am reeling in shock, but so happy to know it, just the same. I have always longed to be a father. Thank you for telling me, though there is little I can do to help right now, stuck here at war, beyond sending you a portion of my wage. I'll arrange it straightaway. If the war ends soon (I imagine it must), then who knows what the future might hold for us. No one has captured my affections as you have and I will, of course, do the honourable thing by you and our child.

If anything should happen to me, please write to my mother, Carol Elliott in England. Tell her about the baby. I will prepare a letter to her also, so she will be informed of my wishes should I not be able to tell her in person. She will help you in whatever way she can, I am sure of it. Her address is Poplars, Richmond, London SW.

I wish you very well, Amandine. The times we spent together were reckless and passionate, but I don't regret a single moment. To know that a new life blooms in your belly gives me the greatest reason to survive this war. It gives me glorious hope.

With all fond wishes and love,
Lieutenant Will Elliott

My eyes prick with tears at the sight of Will's familiar script, and my heart grows heavy at the thought of all he missed by never knowing his daughter.

"Thank you," Delphine says, her voice laden with emotion. "I will treasure this always."

We sit in comfortable silence awhile, immersed in our thoughts.

Our time together is too brief—shortened by my discomfort, which I cannot conceal for too long. Delphine promises to visit at the apartment and Margaret takes me home where she settles me beside the fire.

I snooze for a while, lulled by the warmth. I dream a little. As always, she is there.

When I wake, I take up the final bundle of letters.

How much there was left to say. How much was very nearly left unsaid . . .

PART FIVE

1918

*"I love you not only for what you are, but
for what I am when I am with you."*
—*Elizabeth Barrett Browning*

From Evie to her mother

2nd January, 1918

Rouen, France

Dear Mama,

Wishing you a Happy New Year. Thank you for the linen and hand cream, which both brought me enormous—and much needed—comfort.

I hope you managed to have a pleasant Christmas, despite everything. I will admit it felt rather strange to be away from home. I had a little smile to myself when I remembered the first Christmas we were at war and the fox got into the farmer's pens and stole the best geese. We were almost goose-less and thought it the greatest imposition. I would have a year of empty dinner plates just to sit again at the dining table with everyone back together.

We made the best of things here, as one does. The weather has not been kind. Hard frosts and bitterly low temperatures. I can hardly remember what it is like to feel warm.

Now to the topic of John Hopper. Did you see him over Christmas? His letters are never very lengthy or descriptive. His last (sent some weeks before Christmas) spoke of a spring wedding, which he informs me you are busy organising a dressmaker for. I am furious with him for presuming to know my mind, and am not best pleased with you for permitting him to run away with it. I sincerely hope he hasn't told people I have accepted? As for dressmakers. Really Mama. You know very well I have not yet made up my mind as to the matter of marrying Hopper at all, in the spring or otherwise. I know I have delayed longer than is reasonable, but these are extraordinary circumstances and they do not lend themselves to the ordinary way of things. How can I even think of a wedding with all that I see and hear every day? In any event, I have always wanted a winter wedding, as you well know. Snow sprinkling the lawns and the scent of cinnamon and cloves in the air. But enough of that for now.

What news from home? I hear scant reports across the telephone wires about incidents on the home front. I do worry about you being so close to London. At times like this I wish we lived in some remote part of the Yorkshire Dales or somewhere the Germans couldn't find us.

With fondness,

Evie

From Thomas to Evie

4th January, 1918

Somewhere in France

Dear Evie,

Here we are again—a new year, and another year of war. I won't deliberate on that thought much. There's no point. All we can do is hope this will end soon. The Americans have been a Godsend. Supplies keep rolling in, and we have enough troops at last to give the front line a proper rotation to the reserve trenches.

Have you heard about the tanks? They're another "innovation to weaponry," or so we're calling them. Really, they're just armoured vehicles made of metal—a sideways rhomboid on wheels—and the wheels are covered with large bands that grip the soil. Massive guns that resemble cannons are attached to either side of the thing. The Mark IV, we call them. Not the most efficient of weapons as they're slow and cumbersome, but they're far more destructive now than when they first entered the war a year ago. I watched one malfunction in the middle of battle, but the men inside were protected. An incredible concept. Metal boxes on wheels: a better way to kill more. A pretty filthy concept at its base.

Meanwhile, things appear to be a mess at Fleet Street. The LDT, while flourishing in terms of circulation, continues to be the centre of scandal. I keep reminding myself to trust my cousin, but I find it more and more difficult. Have you heard anything from him directly? I would appreciate any information.

Thank you for the Yeats poetry. I'm consuming it like a starving man, and can't wait to get back to my books at home. I hope you like the belated Christmas gift I've enclosed. I thought I'd never part with it, but somehow, this Christmas I knew it was time. The necklace belonged to my mother. She was a birder, too, you see, so the little golden wren charm was perfect for her. At least my father thought so. When my parents divorced, she gave it to me. I've carried it ever since, but I think it's time it graced a pretty, slender neck and there is only one I can think of.

If you turn it over, you'll see I had it engraved.

Yours,

Tom

From Evie to Thomas

10th January, 1918

Rouen, France

My dear Thomas,

Happy New Year. How can it be 1918? How on earth has this war been going on so long?

The necklace is so beautiful and I'm afraid you brought a tear to my eye with the lovely sentiment you had engraved on it. *May you soar.* Gosh, I will treasure it, Tom, with all my heart. Thank you. I am touched to know it was your mother's as I know how very close you were to her and how terribly you miss her.

I often wish I could look back over all the letters you have written to me, but of course they are in my writing desk at home, tied up with a red ribbon, and I am here, far away from them. I remember the very first letter you sent, full of such hope and naivety, and so terribly formal. It was always Lieutenant Thomas Harding this and that and the other. Now, it is simply Tom. Better, I think.

I hope you have tossed all my letters to you into a fire, or that they've became lost in the mud somewhere. I'd be rather embarrassed to read them again. I do, however, hope that you kept some of my little sketches. They started as something to pass the time, but now I feel there is far more to those little birds.

It cheered me greatly to read your wonderfully descriptive account of Mama's Christmas party. We will make a writer of you yet, dear boy! I could almost taste the wine and the currant pudding. I read your words several times, as if by reading I could satisfy my longing for such delicacies. But they only made my stomach growl in despair and, I hate to admit it, I went to bed that night in a terrific sulk. You would have laughed to see the scowl on my face.

We did our best here to make merry, but the odd nip of *vin rouge,* no mistletoe, and very little in the way of music made it all rather tedious. Christmas Day feels much like any other here, doesn't it. One day becomes another, and another, and still we are at war. And yet I still find my dreams wandering the streets of Paris. Sometimes, our foolish little plan to go there is the only thing that keeps me believing in better times to come. When I close my eyes I can smell the coffee and the freshly baked croissants. I can hear the melody of an accordion player beside the river. I can see the top of the Eiffel Tower piercing the clouds above our heads. This is very silly of me, I know, when Paris isn't the city it once was. War raids, influenza, and rationing have swept across our lovely city just as they have across the rest of northern France. Perhaps Paris will not be the city of my dreams after all.

I'm very sorry to learn of trouble at the newspaper. I know it cannot help to have all that to worry about when you are still in recovery. I think you should be proud of your little paper, hammering it out with the big hitters, causing headlines all of its own. I'm sure John will have things in hand and no doubt things are not quite as bad as they seem from your dugout. I suspect it is the distance that troubles you as much as anything—not being there to take matters into your own hands. Never fear, your time will come.

Everything will seem brighter when the war ends. We will step out of these pages of words and worries and act as normal civilians, living normal lives again, looking to the future and all that it holds.

Write soon.

Evie

X

Letter from Evie to Alice

5th February, 1918

Rouen, France

Dear Alice,

How are you? All goes well here. I have been promoted to a senior rank. I'm immensely fond of the girls and very proud of the work we do here.

With the promotion, I feel unable to abandon my post so

I have relinquished my home leave and let someone else take their turn in my place. It's odd, but I feel uneasy when I think of returning home. I would far rather be here, even with all the discomfort and dangers. I can only dread the things waiting for me when I go back: Mama will sulk with me for leaving the way I did, and Hopper will march me down the aisle without so much as a "How do you do."

I don't have much else to tell you, so I will close for now. It is bitterly cold today and my hands long to be back inside my mittens. I hope you and your doctor are still corresponding. Tom sent me the most beautiful necklace as a Christmas gift. The man is infuriating.

Kisses to you,

Evie

X

Letter from Evie to her mother

20th May, 1918

Rouen, France

Dear Mama,

My apologies for not writing in a long while. Things have been very hectic here and I often find myself too tired to write.

I heard about the dreadful bombing raid in London over-night and pray that nobody we know was killed or injured. Please send word as soon as possible.

My heart is heavy when I think of the war at home; it's unimaginable, even after seeing the zeppelins creep through our skies.

We suffered a heavy bombardment and many losses at the British camps and hospitals in Etaples. I am very worried for Alice who was stationed there recently. I haven't heard from her in a while so I'm not sure if she has moved elsewhere.

I long for the day this will all be over, when we might sleep soundly again without such worries.

Your ever-loving daughter,

Evelyn

X

From Alice to Evie

22nd May, 1918

Somewhere in France

Dear Evie,

I have been injured in the bombardment at Etaples—nothing too awful, but enough to be sent back to a hospital near the coast to recover fully. I leave in the morning.

More soon, but there's no need to worry, darling. I'm well enough and all is intact. Be safe.

Alice

X

From Alice to Evie

30th May, 1918

Brighton, England

Dear Evie,

I'm in Brighton, safe and sound. They're forcing me to take a few weeks' leave of absence, but really, it isn't anything to fuss over. I was hit with shrapnel in the cheek and my torso in several places, all fairly minor wounds. I'm recovering well. Mother insists I retire from my volunteering, of course. She didn't want me in France in the first place. I don't know how to explain to her just how desperately I want the war to end, yet that I must be there somehow. Here, I feel like a ghost, like I'm living some paler existence. What a strange reality to be faced with.

Doctor Peter has sent me letter after letter, and lots of little gifts. Oh, Evie, he says he has a question he would like to ask, but he insists things must be done in the proper order. What other question could it be! I adore him. I can't believe I'm saying this, but perhaps I am the marrying kind after all!

We've had more bombings in London. Mother is terrified. She has heard the distant rumble of destruction and seen the sky light up with what could only be explosions. Over one hundred buildings damaged in one night.

Before I left Etaples, typhoid and influenza were ripping

through camp. Please take care and be vigilant. It's very serious, this round.

   Bisous,
   Alice

P.S. Any news of your Tom? And what of Hopper? Did he reply to your note?

From Evie to Alice

15th June, 1918

Rouen, France

Darling Alice,

How are you? I was worried sick about you and much relieved to know that you are back in England to recover. I sensed it, you know. My heart told me you were in difficulty and here I am, entirely helpless to do anything other than put pen to paper as usual. I understand completely about your wanting to be back here, but rest up, please. Promise me? You have to get better or your Doctor Peter will never be able to ask you his question! I could not be happier for you. Marriage will suit you very well, I am certain of it. The doctor's wife! Mrs. Peter Lancaster. How wonderful. I will be your bridesmaid and you will wear Chantilly lace and have a posy of orange blossom.

I wish I had news to cheer you up and make you laugh (although perhaps laughter causes you pain with your injuries?). Anyway, I have none. Life is uncommonly bleak here. More heavy losses every day.

In a rather curious turn of events, the latest rotation of nurses brings a friend of Tom's my way. Do you remember he was placed under the care of a Rose Blythe when he returned from Craiglockhart? I often thought he was sweet on her. She is now stationed at a field hospital close to our little dormitory here. I could hardly believe it when I saw her name badge. She tells me Tom never stopped talking about me. That it was Evie this and Evie that. She presumed I was his wife until he set her straight! Actually, she is very nice. Older than I'd imagined and (dare I say) not quite as pretty as I'd imagined either. I hate to admit it, but I'm terribly relieved.

I long to walk with you along Richmond Hill and gaze over the meadows towards London. I can hear skylarks singing and a warm breeze tugs at the curls about your cheeks. You are telling me some silly story or other about your time in finishing school in Switzerland and how you never could master the art of graceful skiing. I link my arm through yours and rest my head on your shoulder and we reminisce and laugh and I admire the wedding band on your finger.

Not long now. I can feel it.

Take care my darling girl.

Evie

X

Letter from John Hopper to Tom

17th June, 1918

London, England

Dear Thomas,

I received your advice on the columns. Not to worry, I have everything in hand here. Don't worry about the reports you have received about silly interfering women getting themselves a stint at Holloway for trying to promote their pacifist agenda. Violet Tillard and her NCF busybodies have no business meddling in current affairs, and they aren't bothering us here at the LDT at all. They should stick to knitting and leave the important things to us men. Honestly, they should have given that Tillard woman longer than a sixty-day sentence, in my opinion.

As for Charles Abshire, he is an interminable bore and a worrying Mother Hen. In your shoes, I would show him to the door in a hurry.

Remember, cousin, I built a fortune using my own talents. There is no need to ceaselessly doubt me. I am lucky in business. It appears I am lucky in love as well, for I am planning a spring wedding with Miss Evelyn Elliott. Her mother is beside herself with joy, though I'm sure you knew all, given how often the two of you exchange letters. I hope you join us in our happiness.

I will forward on any news from the paper.

Sincerely,

John Hopper

From Evie to John

19th June, 1918

Rouen, France

Dear John,

I have enclosed a new column. I hear worrying news about publications being raided and closed down, and journalists being placed on trial and imprisoned, yet I feel I must continue to write the truth. I do not, however, want to put Tom Harding's newspaper at risk so I trust you will deal with this accordingly.

I leave it in your hands, John, and hope you find my words suitable to print, without being too seditious or liable to cause any further dissent.

Evelyn

A WOMAN'S WAR

by our special correspondent in France,
Genevieve Wren

"A Light in the Dark"

If you lie awake at night, know that you are not alone. Hundreds—thousands—of restless minds fill those dark hours. It is the worst time. The silence. The space to think.

I wake often at night, my bed rocked by the pounding of distant shells and I wonder: Whose lives did that

one take? What agony did they know in their final moments? What agony will their loved ones know for the
rest of their days when the telegram boy knocks at
the door and delivers that fateful news? It is an unimaginable grief, worsened somehow by knowing their
bodies will not be returned to us and must ever be
lost to the scarred French countryside, worsened by
the fact that we are so far away and unable to imagine the place where our loved ones fell. Not in their
homes, nor their beds, nor the fields they played in as
children. Not in a place we have ever known.

Bravo then, to those who have tried to tell us and
show us with brush and pen and camera lens so that
we might know better where our loved ones fought.
Bravo to the men and women doing what they felt
was their moral duty, putting their lives in danger every day so that they could bring truth to us at home.
Their truths give us some answers to the questions
that plague us: How? Where? Why? What do our loved
ones face?

And what became of those brave front line reporters? They too, like our fallen men, have been silenced.
They too have become prisoners of war; prisoners of
truth. Hunted down. Locked up. Their words hushed
by those who have the power to determine what we
know and what we do not; what we might believe and
what we might not.

This is a war of choices, made by the powerful few
in control. On the battlefield, in the bunkers, in the

offices of those who wield a weapon as great as any howitzer—they decide, and we must bear the consequences, but we do not have to bear them in silent rage.

It makes one wonder what our men—our brave heroes—are fighting for at all. What freedoms do we really have? Freedom of thought? Freedom of principles? Freedom of speech?

I urge you, then, to keep talking. Keep demanding the truth. If we owe our men anything, it is to seek the truth of the war in which they fought, and to remember them.

Above all, we must always remember them.

Until next time—courage!

Genevieve

Telegram from Thomas to Evie

1ST JULY 1918

TO: EVELYN ELLIOTT, ROUEN, FRANCE
SENT: 10:23 / RECEIVED: 11:46

ENGAGED TO HOPPER? YOU HID THAT WELL. THE PAPER IN DIRE TROUBLE AFTER YOUR COLUMNS. DID YOU TWO PLAN THAT ALSO? DISGUST AND FURY DO NOT COVER IT. TOM.

Telegram from Evie to John

1ST JULY 1918

TO: JOHN HOPPER, LDT, 18 FLEET STREET, LONDON EC
SENT: 12:39 / RECEIVED: 14:01

COLUMN MUST CEASE IMMEDIATELY. DO NOT PRINT
LATEST. WHAT HAVE YOU TOLD TOM? A WEDDING?
FURIOUS. EVELYN

Telegram from Evie to Tom

1ST JULY 1918

TO: LT. THOMAS HARDING, AMIENS, FRANCE, 10TH
RIFLES.
SENT: 12:50 / RECEIVED: 14:22

DID NOT ACCEPT JOHN'S PROPOSAL. LETTER TO FOLLOW
TO EXPLAIN. EVIE

Telegram from John to Evie

5TH JULY 1918

TO: EVELYN ELLIOTT, WAAC, SIGNALLERS (TELEPHONES)
DIVISION, BASE HILL, ROUEN, FRANCE
SENT: 9:30 / RECEIVED: 10:04

LATEST COLUMN GONE TO PRINT. ON NEWSSTANDS
TOMORROW. HUNKER IN FOR MORE OUTCRY BUT GLORY
TOO. HARDING FUSSES TOO MUCH. JOHN.

Letter from Evie to John

6th July, 1918

Rouen, France

John,

How could you? How could you tell Thomas we were engaged to be married? He feels cheated and let down by a friend.

I cannot forgive you for this, John, and I certainly cannot marry a man who believes he can decide my future, never mind disregard my friendships. I once told you I believed I would find my answer to your proposal in France, and indeed I have.

My answer is no.

I should have told you a year ago and spared everyone this awful misery.

To that end, I will liaise directly with Jack Davies with regard to future columns. I'm quite sure he has no plans to marry me without my consent.

Evelyn

Letter from Thomas to Evie

15th July, 1918

Somewhere in France

Evie,

I have attempted to control my ire, to cool off, but it hasn't helped. Damn it, Evie! I poured my heart out to you these last terrible years. About everything. My confusion, my struggles, my despair. You know about my father, about me—all there is! How could you betray me? I have supported you in every way possible, in all of your dreams. I cheered as you pursued your desires, as you pursued your love of writing. Yet you use it against me in the cruellest possible way.

Now, all is lost. The paper, our friendship, my family. All is lost, because Hopper skulked around behind my back—with my dearest friend, with one of the precious few people I care about in this world. I may have been unsure about my place at the LDT and Father's wishes, but I would never let the paper fall into ruin and disgrace. You have done that for me, haven't you? You and that lying sack-of-excuses for a man. I should have known better than to ever trust him.

I am disgusted.

Marry him, Evie. You deserve each other. Run off together and enjoy your prestige and estates and perfect lives. Let the war take me. It's where I belong now, on this battlefield among my men who fight with a courage you will never see in that spineless fiancé of yours.

My life may be small compared to your glorious John Hopper of fortune and looks and charm, but I live it with a passion he will never understand. I will make my father proud, and my countrymen, and I will never lower myself out of fear. Did you ever ask your future husband why he isn't at the Front? Perhaps you should. The answer isn't what he, no doubt, led you to believe.

I wish you well. Even in my rage, I hope you never burn with anger and disappointment as I do now. I am sorry it has come to this.

Goodbye, Evelyn.

Tom

From Evie to Alice

28th July, 1918

Rouen, France

Darling Alice,

Dreadful, dreadful news. Thomas got wind of Hopper's proposal and thinks I have accepted. I am absolutely <u>furious</u> with

John. What right does he have to presume my acceptance and spread word that we are to be married? How could he do such a thing?

Tom sent the most awful telegram, followed by a letter so full of anger my body aches with a physical pain to even think of it, and I'm afraid it gets worse. The LDT is being closed down temporarily because my articles caused such a stir. Tom believes that me and Hopper planned it together to bring about his downfall. He writes like a madman, Alice. I have never known him so angry. What am I to do? I'm utterly devastated at the thought of hurting Tom and losing his trust. And though his accusations seem absurd in a way, I'm struggling with guilt that I didn't end it with Hopper when I had the chance. The moment he kissed me in that fountain, I knew—deep down—that there was no hope of love for us. I wish I'd told Tom about the proposal, rather than pretending it had never happened. And I wish I had declined John immediately.

I think about my latest column and want to shake myself. Why was I so hell-bent on telling "the truth"? What does it matter in the end? We are still at war. Thousands of men are dying every day. My words make no difference at all. All they have achieved is to destroy the only true thing I have ever known. My pen might as well be a knife, stabbing me in the heart with its so-called truths and misplaced principles.

What an awful mess I've made of everything. You know how Tom is. He's as stubborn as I am. He won't forgive me easily. I feel so desperately alone and my heart aches as if it has been physically bruised, while the rest of the world seems doused in laudanum, dull and lifeless.

What on earth am I to do?

Yours in despair,

Evie

X

Official notice from the War Office to
Lieutenant Thomas Harding

30th July, 1918

London, England

Dear Sir,

We have issued two notices of warning to your establishment the *London Daily Times* at 18 Fleet Street regarding the incendiary nature of your column titled "*A Woman's War.*" In a heedless manner, the paper has continued to print both unethical as well as offensive libel about the war to the detriment of our militia and the Crown. Too much is at stake for us to ignore this blatant disregard for the law. At this time, the *London Daily Times* press will be closed until further notice, or until all proprietary rights have been relinquished to the government, effective immediately.

Sincerely,

Admiral Michael Jenkins ℅ War Office, Whitehall

From Alice to Evie

1st August, 1918

Brighton, England

Dear Evie,

Try not to fret, my love! Men are easy to anger, quick to forget, and your Tom has loved you his whole life. I see that now more than ever, just by his reaction. He will get over this and the paper will survive—as will your friendship. You protected your interests and there's nothing wrong with that. He would do the same. Besides, how were you to know Hopper would *lie* about your engagement? Really, is he so desperate? I'm glad you never gave him an answer, the toad. He doesn't deserve you.

In time, Tom will understand this. Let him cool off, as you said, and then write to him. I think it is time the words you very much need to say are finally spoken. Until then, perhaps you could apply for a period of leave. Imagine if we could meet and have that walk together? This will blow over before you know it. Trust me. It will.

I am thinking of you.

Alice

X

From Evie to Thomas

3rd August, 1918

Rouen, France

My dear Thomas,

You haven't written so I can only presume you are still furious with me. You *have* to believe me when I tell you that I did *not* accept John's proposal. I am outraged he should lie to you about it, and to me. The snake. Yes, he proposed, but I had not given him an answer. I didn't mention it to you because what was there to say when I had not settled on a reply?

This is all so infuriating I could scream. If only I could talk to you in person. If only I could look you in the eye and explain. I am sure then you would understand. Do you forget all our years of friendship so easily? It has to count for something, Tom, surely.

As for the columns, I thought you believed in speaking the truth? I thought you believed in <u>me</u>. None of us wanted this war, but it has given me a voice, a sense of purpose I never had before. In a way, we are all puppets, playing a part in a play without script or direction. We ad lib. Make choices under the glare of the spotlight. Make a mad dash for it—isn't that what you once said? Irrational, ill-thought-out, silly, hotheaded choices. You have done the same. Do you forget your skirmishes? Your irrational rush to protect a friend, endangering your own life in the process? Far more heroic than writing a piece for a Fleet Street rag, perhaps, but in the heat of the moment we are all war-crazed.

I am desperately sorry if I have hurt you, or your livelihood, in any way. To hurt you means I hurt myself, and please know the absolute agony I feel as I try to structure my thoughts into some semblance of sense and order. You—more than anyone I have ever known—know where my heart and my morals lie. I only wanted to do my best, to help others, to have something my own that made me proud. I'd rather hoped you would be proud of me, too. I am changed, Tom. We all are. Would you have that spirited girl placed back in the pretty parlours of her home to idle away the day with embroidery silks and polite luncheons? Or are you happy to have known a girl with ambition beyond her station?

I was not raised to crumple into folds of silk at the slightest obstacle or a show of anger from a man. My father would be ashamed of me if I did. Dear Will would be sickened. I come from a family with backbone and I will not—even for you— give in to the easy path.

With or without your blessing and your friendship, I am not Little Evie anymore and I will continue to do what I am doing.

With or without your friendship, I will find a way.

Evie

From Evie to Thomas

20th August, 1918

Rouen, France

Dear Thomas,

It's been nearly a month. Please, rage at me. Shout and scream at me. Express your anger in words. Anything but this. *Anything* but this terrible silence.

I can do nothing on earth to change what has happened, but I *can* try to determine what happens next. To that end, I shall swallow my stubborn pride and tell you something I should have told you a very long time ago.

My life has been only made better by knowing you all these years. You have been my constant companion through childhood, through the confusion of teenage years and now, into adulthood and a war neither of us was prepared for. One way or another you have always been there, Tom. With me. For me. To live the rest of my days without your friendship—how few or how many they might be—will be to live my life in a shadow. To know what life might have been, had I spoken the things I feel in my heart right now, will be my greatest sorrow.

I cannot stop thinking that as suddenly as it started, this war may end. It may end tomorrow, as may any of our lives. If this were the last chance we had to say something to each other, would we choose to remain silent? Would we turn our heads and walk away?

I cannot.

If these are the last words I ever write to you, I have to share a secret I've been holding for some time. I'm in love with you. With every beat of my heart and every breath that I draw, I love you, Thomas Harding.

I love you, and always have, and always will. Tom and Evie. Wasn't it always the way of things? I wish it were still. If you would only forgive me.

There is nothing more I can say. If you cannot bring yourself to reply, then please know that I will respect your decision but I will never hear a silence with greater clarity, nor feel it with greater agony.

Always,

Evie

X

Letter from Sophie Morel to Evie

1st October, 1918

127 Rue Chanterelle, Paris, France

Dear Miss Elliott,

Thank you for your many letters. Please accept my apologies for not replying sooner. I was not sure how to respond—or, indeed, whether I wanted to. It has been a difficult decision, but I hope, by writing to you I do what *ma chère* Amandine would have wished.

I am Amandine Morel's mother. My beautiful daughter died during childbirth. She was so young and had so much joie de vivre, so much to live for. I miss her with every breath I draw. Amandine's baby—a daughter, Delphine—survived against all odds and is now in my care. She is all I have in the world and is most precious to me.

Your letters, although a great surprise, offer me some consolation. I am happy to learn that my daughter loved so fine a man as your brother William. Amandine spoke of him often, and loved him. She feared her "condition" would bring shame upon our family, but she believed William would do the honourable thing and marry her when the war was over. That she was robbed of the chance to know such happiness breaks my heart.

I was not sure whether to reply to you, Miss Elliott. Delphine and I live happily together, and I could not see why she should need the complication of English relations in her quiet, simple life. However, I recently discovered a packet of letters which Amandine brought back with her from the Front. All are from your brother, William. He wrote with great affection. He was an honourable man, and your letters assure me that you wish to be as honourable in his stead.

I have enclosed one of the letters. I felt you should like to see it. I hope it is agreeable to you that I keep the others—and Will's photograph—so that I might show them to Delphine when she is old enough.

In such times like these, we must cherish those things for which we are most grateful. Having seen the photograph of your brother, I can now see the resemblance very clearly. Delphine has his eyes. I have enclosed a photograph of her so you may see for yourself.

I wish you well, Miss Elliott, and hope that we shall see victory in the new year.

Perhaps we may meet one day, when circumstances allow.

Avec tout affection,

Sophie Morel

From Evie to her mother

5th October, 1918

Rouen, France

Dear Mama,

Do not be alarmed but a bad strain of influenza has arrived at our camp and we are placed under strict quarantine. The nurses tell me it is the Spanish Flu that has already rampaged across half of Europe. But I am well.

Still, should anything happen to me, I beg you to write to Sophie Morel at 127 Rue Chanterelle, Paris, France and make arrangements to visit her as soon as you can. Sophie is the mother of Amandine Morel, and as such, is the grandmother of Amandine and Will's child—Delphine. I have enclosed a letter here that Sophie sent to me. It is from Amandine to Will. I ask you to promise me this, Mama. If it is the last thing I ask of you as your daughter, I beg you to honour my wishes, and Will's.

I will send word when I know more about the situation here.

Your ever-loving daughter,

Evelyn

X

Enclosed letter from Amandine Morel to Will Elliott

1st May, 1915

127 Rue Chanterelle, Paris, France

Mon cher Will,

I hope you are well and that these few lines find you safe. As you will see from the address, I have returned to Paris.

I know this will come as a shock, but I am pregnant, Will, and there is no doubt the child is yours. There is no place for a pregnant nurse at the Front so I secured dismissal and returned to Paris to stay with my mother.

Ours was only a brief romance but I sometimes feel I know you better than I have known any man. We threw ourselves into passion, did we not? I will never forget how you held me, so tenderly, or how you whispered to me of love. I did not dare to whisper it in reply, but I cherish our time together.

I do not expect marriage. I understand the differences between us make anything more than our brief romance impossible, but I had to share the news of our child. A child born from love is the most wonderful product of war. Our futures lie in this child's hands. Should I write again when the baby is born? If you do not wish to know more, please tell me and I will not contact you again. I understand this is difficult for you in your position.

Paris is changed, and the journey was arduous. Soldiers questioned me at every town. I hardly recognise the city of my birth. Refugees line the streets, desperate for a loaf of bread. I am happy and full of gratitude to be away from the worst of it, here on the outskirts.

I must tell you, *mon cher* William, *je suis amoureuse de toi.* I am in love with you. How quiet my days are without you. Your songs and good humour gave me more pleasure than I can say.

I wish you well, *mon amour,* and pray for your safety.

Amandine

Letter from Charles Abshire to Thomas

7th October, 1918

London, England

Dear fellow,

I am forwarding a letter, addressed to you, that appears to have been lost in the mail. It was written by Miss Evelyn Elliott during December 1915 and recently made its way back to her home in Richmond. Her mother brought it to the office here as she wasn't sure how to get it to you.

It boggles the mind to think about the circuitous route it has taken to finally reach you, but it finds its home at last.

I hope you are well, dear boy. There's talk the war is drawing to a close at last. We are all cautiously optimistic here.

Godspeed.

Charles Abshire

Unsent letter from Evie to Thomas

25th December, 1915

Richmond, England

Happy Christmas, my dear Thomas,

I am sitting here beside the fire, warming my toes, and I find myself imagining you are here beside me, warming yours. I have worried about your toes ever since you wrote to me about them last year. So here we are, sitting together in my imagination on Christmas Day and it is the most natural thing in the world. You and me and a belly full of roast goose! What could be more perfect?

There is something I must tell you, Thomas, although it scares me to do so. Nevertheless, I don't know what else to do other than to write it all down because what good are our emotions and feelings locked away inside us? They must be seen and heard, felt and known.

The thing is, I am in love with you, Tom. Madly and stupidly. Perhaps I always have been. Perhaps, if I'd looked closer, paid more attention, I would have recognised the signs sooner. It took a war and hundreds of miles to make me see how very dear you are to me, Thomas Harding. You've always been there, haven't you? Always. Except now, when I long for you to be here with all my heart, you are not.

Do I dare to believe that you might love me in return? You haven't given me any reason to think it, so I must content myself with imagining it is so. I can see a future stretch out before us, like paint in water, swirling and dancing. Might we have children? Happiness? Companionship into old age? I imagine we have a little apartment in Paris where we like to spend our summers and Christmases. We can see the Eiffel Tower from the balcony. Perhaps you will ask me to marry you at the very top. I will, of course, say yes!

You see why I like to write, don't you. I can weave a story from the thinnest of fabrics. I can weave a story when there isn't even one to tell. At least, not yet.

So, now you know.

I love you, Tom Harding. I love you, I love you, I love you.

Last night, I looked at the stars and I thought of you doing the same.

Come, gentle night, come, loving, black-brow'd night,
Give me my Romeo; and, when I shall die,
Take him and cut him out in little stars,
And he will make the face of heaven so fine
That all the world will be in love with night
And pay no worship to the garish sun.

Now that I have finally found the courage to write these words, I do not know if I have the courage to post them to you. I cannot bear to think that my feelings will come as an unwelcome surprise. I hate to think of you reading this with alarm, uncertain as to what to do next. I can almost hear you: "Evie Elliott—in love with *me*?"

I have to be brave, and believe that you will read my words and feel only joy to know that my heart belongs to you.

Dearest, it snowed a little just now. I sat at the window and watched the flakes tumble from the sky. I opened the window and let the flakes land on the paper. They—and my heart—are my Christmas gift to you.

Happy Christmas, my love.

Always,

Evie

XXX

Telegram from Nurse Rose to Thomas

12TH OCTOBER 1918

TO: LT. THOMAS HARDING, 10TH RIFLES, AMIENS, FRANCE

SENT: 14:47 / RECEIVED: 15:33

EVIE ELLIOTT GRAVELY ILL. SHE ASKS FOR YOU. PLEASE COME SOONEST. ROSE BLYTHE

From Rose Blythe to Thomas

12th October 1918

Base Hill, Rouen, France

Dear Thomas,

Please see enclosed a short note from Evelyn. I am with her here. She is very sick, Tom. She insisted I take down her words and send them to you.
Sincerely,
Rose Blythe

Dictated letter from Evie to Thomas

Tom,

I am very sick, and I'm afraid. This disease weakens me with every hour that passes. I love you. I love you so much, my darling. E

Telegram from Nurse Rose to Evie's mother

12TH OCTOBER 1918

TO: CAROL ELLIOTT, POPLARS, RICHMOND, LONDON SW
SENT: 09:23 / RECEIVED: 10:45

YOUR DAUGHTER EVELYN VERY ILL. PRAY FOR HER. I
AM WITH HER NIGHT AND DAY. NURSE ROSE BLYTHE.

Telegram from Thomas to Evie

12TH OCTOBER 1918

TO: EVELYN ELLIOTT, WAAC, ROUEN, FRANCE, % ROSE
BLYTHE.
SENT: 10:55 / RECEIVED: 11:15

SECURED EMERGENCY LEAVE. I AM A FOOL. I AM
COMING, MY DARLING! WAIT FOR ME! PLEASE, GOD. YOU
HAVE MY HEART. TOM.

From Rose Blythe to Alice Cuthbert

13th October, 1918

Rouen, France

Dear Miss Cuthbert,

I am with a dear friend of yours, Evelyn Elliott. I am sorry to tell you that Miss Elliott has fallen gravely ill with the Spanish Flu. She is feverish and struggling to hold on but she begged me to send word to you to tell you she loves you dearly and that she wishes you the happiest of lives with your doctor.

I am so sorry to have to send these words to you. The disease is rampant here, as I believe it is throughout much of Europe. That so many survived the years of war only to be struck down at the last by a strain of influenza is especially cruel.

I will stay with Miss Elliott until the end, and hope you will join me in praying for her.

Sincerely,
Rose Blythe

From Thomas to Rose Blythe

13th October, 1918

Rose,

They won't let me in. I begged your colleague to bring this note to you. Can you speak to your superior or someone on my behalf? I've scaled the fence around the back, but was caught. I desperately need your help. Please, Rose. I must see her. I beg you.

Tom

From Rose Blythe to Thomas

13th October, 1918

No, Tom. It isn't safe. You must say your goodbyes another way. I am so sorry.

Rose

From Thomas to Evie

13th October, 1918

My darling girl,

I am a mess of tears and regret, of utter devastation. I tried to see you but was prohibited by the quarantine. I raged at the blockade like a madman—three men had to hold me back. I don't care if I contract the disease. God in heaven, Evelyn Maria Constance Elliott, I am nothing without you. Nothing!

Your last letter broke my heart and what a stubborn idiotic fool I was not to reply to you instantly. My stupid pride wouldn't allow it.

Damn it, Evie. All this time I didn't realise, I swear I didn't know. Yet it is so clear to me now. And then Abshire forwarded a letter from you, written at Christmas 1915. It was lost these last years and recently returned to you in Richmond. That it made its way to me now is a miracle. The stubborn wall inside me melted away, and emotions that were trapped behind it have poured forth, unrelentingly.

My darling Evie. I have loved you since the first time you threw rocks at the pigeons on my lawn, pigtails flying. I loved you when you beat me at cards, and raced me on horseback, and read poetry by candlelight while your brother and I listened on, mesmerised by the cadence of your voice. And now I love the woman you have become—full of laughter and hope, yearning to make her mark on the world.

When Hopper said you were to marry him, I felt as if a black curtain had fallen and the only cord tethering me to this wretched, God-forsaken earth was gone. Like a fool, I believed him, and now I may lose you. My bull-headed behaviour may have cost me everything. I should have known you could never love a man like Hopper. You are too pure of heart, too intelligent for him. Too beautiful. Will you ever forgive me? After all that Shakespeare I was nothing but a foolish Romeo.

This war has changed me. *You* have changed me—opened my eyes to the beauty left in the world, to the hope that pulses deeply inside us, come what may. You've opened my eyes to the honour in bringing truth to others, and sharing who we are for some greater purpose. Most of all, you have shown me how to love.

Fight, my darling! Please, Evie, you have to fight with all

your strength. I fought as you commanded, now it is your turn. Fight! I don't know how to go on without you. Give us a chance to take flight, my love, like your soaring birds. I will be here, waiting for you on the other side.

With all my heart,
Tom

November 11, 1918 at 11:00 A.M.

Armistice Day

"At eleven o'clock this morning came to an end
the cruellest and most terrible War that has ever
scourged mankind. I hope we may say that thus,
this fateful morning, came to an end all wars."
—Prime Minister David Lloyd George

Paris

24th December, 1968

Christmas Eve.

It was always her favourite day of the season. She loved the anticipation—the promise of things to come—of what might be.

I think of us that second Christmas after the war ended. Christmas 1919. Together at the top of the Eiffel Tower, just as Evie had always dreamed we would be. Of course, she had always imagined Will and Alice would be with us. Will, we remembered as we looked at the stars glittering back against the Seine. Alice, we wished good luck for the impending birth of her first child.

Evie said it was perfect at the top of the tower that evening with the snow falling around us, although I complained bitterly of the cold. She only laughed and took me for *vin chaud* to warm me. It wasn't the wine that warmed me though. It was being with her, watching her, loving her.

That was when I asked her to be my wife. She said yes before I'd hardly got the words out. "Yes! Yes! Yes!"

I cross the bedroom to look out of the window, see the tower again. With each step, I wince. My joints protest, my lungs rasp against their disease, and my will has all but drained from my body. There's no enjoyment now of the little things to which I looked forward always. A pile of crisp newspapers, fresh from the press; the way the sun streaks the horizon with fire before it slumps to bed; the chatter of songbirds while I savour my first cup of tea in the morning. It has all dulled. I want to join *her*, forever, the way it should be.

I feast my eyes on the skyline, absorbing it one last time before I close the bedroom door and pull the crinkled envelope from my pocket.

Moving to the mirror, I peer into it and study the lines of my face—a road map of happiness and pain with only one destination remaining. With a steady hand, I pull on my British Army uniform jacket, musty from disuse but somehow as familiar as my own skin. Once each button is clasped, I don my cap. For a moment, I see a vivid stream of memories, the clatter of war I once worked so hard to suppress. When they fade, there is one image left.

Evie.

Her eyes are filled with mirth, her mouth upturned in a mischievous smile. "Of course I will marry you, Lieutenant Thomas Archibald Harding!"

My heart lurches as I sit on the edge of the bed and clutch her final letter to my chest.

Hands trembling, I open the envelope as carefully as I can and unfold the pages. A faint scent of violet infuses the air around me. It is as if she has walked into the room and settled on the bed beside me. I hear her voice as I read her words, feel her ever nearer.

1st November, 1968

My darling Tom,

How can I ever write these words—my last to you? How can I ever truly tell you what my life has been because of you?

And yet write these words, I must. My time draws closer.

We fell in love through our words, didn't we? In the harshest and darkest of times, we found the brightest, most beautiful thing of all. We found love. We found each other, and for that I will forever be grateful.

I will never forget the touch of your hand when I came out of my fever. Yours was the first face I saw when I opened my eyes. Yours were the first words I heard. Only Tom Harding could have fought so stubbornly to get through the quarantine lines. And we have dear Rose Blythe to thank for that. You always said the two of us would get on, and I am glad to have called her my friend over the years since.

When I woke and saw you by my bedside, I knew we would never be parted again—and we never have been. Which is why I know you will feel the pain of our separation so acutely. But please know this, my love. I will always walk beside you. I will always be there—watching you, loving you, missing you, waiting for you, and when your time comes, don't be afraid. I am not. I am ready for the next life and the great adventures we will have together there, for all eternity.

I hope you did as I wished and took this letter to Paris to read. Our last Christmas together there was one of the happiest, wasn't it? What little we knew then of the challenges the New Year would bring. I am glad we didn't know it was to be our last. We would have looked at things rather differently then. We would have doubted and questioned every moment—was it happy enough, was it perfect enough—rather than simply enjoying the moment for what it was. And you have given me such wonderful moments, Tom. You have given me the best and happiest life I could ever have wished for.

We are but birds in flight, you and me. Let us catch the thermals together now, and soar.

Merry Christmas, my darling.

Forever yours,

Evie.

XXX

"Merry Christmas, Evie." My words are a whisper, joining the echoes of laughter and love as the most precious memories of my life dance like snowflakes around me in the room, and the gentle melody of a Christmas carol drifts up from the street below . . .

"Silent night, Holy night, All is calm, All is bright . . ."

I rest my eyes. Just for a moment.

All is calm.

All is bright.

All is as it should be.

Epilogue

From Delphine to Will Harding, editor
of the London Daily Times

February, 1969

Paris

Dear Will,

I hope you are doing well and that you are all finding small ways to cope since your father passed away. I miss him dearly, as I am sure you do, too. Even the Paris apartment feels sad, if that makes sense to you.

It was a lovely funeral, wasn't it. Richmond illuminated by a perfect winter sun, just as Tom would have wanted, and with plenty of Shakespeare and good literature to see him off. It gives me great comfort to know that he will rest in peace now beside your mother. Tom and Evie, together again. After all those years of separation during the war, how incredible to know they were never parted again. Even at the very end, they were only apart for a matter of weeks. Theirs was a very special sort of love. A model for us all, I daresay.

While your father was in Paris over Christmas, he brought with him a packet of letters—an impressive volume of correspondence between your parents and their friends during the Great War. I had no idea they had written so fervently. Did you? He gave instructions to Margaret for them to be left in my care.

Having read them, I felt I should do more than lock them away in a dusty attic somewhere, and I wondered if the newspaper might be interested in publishing them as an historical series. With your mother having written her column for the paper during wartime, and the reins having being passed down to you from your father, the LDT seems like the right place for their exchanges to be shared. It really does make for a fascinating insight into the war. Some of the more personal sentiments we can, of course, leave out, although I find them wonderfully romantic. Much like your parents!

I look forward to hearing from you with your thoughts.

Perhaps you and the family could visit when the weather improves? Much as I love Christmastime here, I do look forward to the blooming of the chestnut trees on the Champs-Élysées. After all, who can deny the beauty of Paris in the spring?

With all best wishes,

Delphine

THE END

Acknowledgments

Though writing can be a lonely process, no book is complete without the help of many. It really is a huge team effort and we are so grateful to everyone involved in making *Last Christmas in Paris* so special, especially our wonderful editor, Lucia Macro, who shared our excitement and belief in this book from the very beginning, and took a huge leap of faith in letting us tackle this—seemingly impossible—project!

Huge thanks to the team at William Morrow: our publisher Liate Stehlik, Molly Waxman, Jennifer Hart, Michelle Podberezniak, Carolyn Coons, and everyone involved in cover design, interior design, copyediting, and production.

To our terrifically talented agent, Michelle Brower, who connected the two of us several years ago, and who said YES to this idea without a moment's hesitation. Thank you for your wisdom and passion, and for first suggesting the idea for Tom's "Paris" scenes, which made this book so much more. In fact, you make all of our projects so much more.

Thank you, also, to our tireless rights agent, Chelsey Heller, for bringing our words to readers around the world.

Huge thanks to early readers, especially Hazel's sister, Helen

Plaskitt, and Heather's good friend and fellow author, Kris Waldherr. Additional thanks to Brien Brown for helping with a few important historical details. And as always, huge thanks to our families and friends, for their continued support and belief in us.

About the authors

About the book

Insights,
Interviews
& More . . .

Meet Hazel Gaynor

Deasy Photographic

HAZEL GAYNOR is the *New York Times* and *USA Today* bestselling author of *A Memory of Violets* and *The Girl Who Came Home*, for which she received the 2015 Romantic Novelists' Association Historical Romantic Novel of the Year award. Her third novel, *The Girl from The Savoy*, was an *Irish Times* and *Globe & Mail* (Canada) bestseller, and was shortlisted for the 2016 Bord Gáis Energy Irish Book Awards Popular Fiction Book of the Year.

Hazel was selected by *Library Journal* as one of Ten Big Breakout Authors for 2015, and her work has been translated into several languages.

Originally from Yorkshire, England, Hazel now lives in Ireland. ❧

Meet Heather Webb

Angie Parkinson

HEATHER WEBB taught high school for a decade before following the Muse to fiction. Her historical novels *Becoming Josephine, Rodin's Lover,* and *Fall of Poppies* have received national starred reviews, and in 2015, *Rodin's Lover* was chosen as a Goodreads Top Pick. To date, her books have been translated to many languages worldwide. When not writing, Heather flexes her foodie skills, geeks out on pop culture and history, or looks for excuses to head to the other side of the world. She is a member of the Historical Novel Society and lives in New England with her family, and one feisty rabbit. ∾

Reading Group Questions

1. Women's roles changed dramatically through the course of WWI. What are your thoughts about Evie's place in the war, at home, and in France? Which factors came into play to cause these changes?

2. How did WWI affect societal structures and values? Are the effects still felt today?

3. Newspapers were the main source of information for the public in WWI. How do you feel about the War Office encouraging positive messages through propaganda while also suppressing the worst details of the war from the Front?

4. Thomas blamed himself for the decimation of his troops in 1916. Do you believe he—or any officer leading a battalion—is responsible for the loss of human life?

5. There was much controversy surrounding shell shock and war neurosis, during this time. Soldiers were initially made to believe they were weak or "lacking moral fibre." What are your thoughts about this, especially in terms of how we treat PTSD today?

6. Letters were of vital importance during WWI as they were the only means of communication between loved ones. What were your emotional reactions when reading these letters?

7. Do you still write letters? Would you like to see a return to traditional letter-writing?

8. Do you think Will's mother was right to conceal the truth about his child from the rest of the family? What do you suppose were her motives?

9. Christmas is a time for family and reflection. What are your favorite family Christmas traditions?

10. Evie, Will, Thomas, and Alice plan to spend Christmas in Paris. Where would you love to spend Christmas, if not at home? ∽

A Love Letter to Letters
A note from Hazel and Heather

When we began this book, we didn't have the faintest idea what the process of co-writing would be like, but we were excited to tackle this new adventure. We're so glad we did. Here's the story of how *Last Christmas in Paris* came to be.

We first "met" in 2013 after being introduced online by our mutual agent, Michelle Brower, who had a sneaky feeling these two history nerds would get along. She was absolutely right. We hit it off instantly and for the next couple of years we supported each other through our journeys in publishing. In early 2015, Heather approached Hazel about writing a short story for an anthology she was working on which would focus on the events surrounding Armistice Day in WWI. That anthology became *Fall of Poppies: Stories of Love and the Great War*, a moving tribute to those lost and left behind in war. As the anthology was nearing completion, we both felt there was an awful lot more to say about this world-changing event. We had another story we wanted to tell.

Towards the end of 2015 the idea to co-write a historical novel began to take shape through a series of "What if . . . ?" e-mails. The final concept for a novel, written through all four years of the Great War, emerged from a frenzied Facebook messenger exchange one afternoon and *Last Christmas in Paris* was born. Letters were such a critical part of the war—the only way loved ones could keep in touch—so it felt right that this book would be an epistolary novel. What better way to tunnel into the hearts and minds of our dear Evie and Thomas?

At the outbreak of war in 1914, it was famously declared that it would be over by Christmas. This was what brought us to the idea of a group of friends making plans for the Christmas of 1914, which become horribly interrupted. Four Christmases would come and go before the war was over and the soldiers returned home. Since Paris was under threat of occupation by the Germans in the earliest stages of the war, it seemed this iconic city of romance would be the perfect place for Thomas and Evie to long to visit. And of course we both love Paris, too!

Once the topic was settled, we had to decide how we would accomplish this! But how do two writers, living in different time zones, in different continents, write a book together? It sounds difficult, if not impossible, but far from being either, we absolutely loved the whole experience.

The book was written through a literal exchange of letters of our own. Hazel would wake up in Ireland first thing, pen a letter from one of her characters, and excitedly wait for a reply. Several hours later, Heather would wake in the U.S.—ecstatic—to ▶

find mail in her inbox. She would respond in kind, sending her characters' words over the e-waves. The process felt so organic; the story flowed, and in no time, we had a first draft! Editing, on the other hand, became an operation of military precision. We used comment bubbles and colored fonts to carefully track our changes, and somehow, it just worked.

Of course, having a writing partner demands a lot of trust and commitment. We navigated the pressures of juggling our individual writing projects, and the demands of kids and family life along the way as well. Often, one of us would contact the other to explain a delay because the kids were sick, or the heating was broken, or some other crisis got in the way. Skype chats and Google Hangouts became weekly pow-wows to flesh out plot snags and character arcs.

But at last, we met! When *Fall of Poppies* released in March 2016, Hazel traveled to the U.S. as part of the book tour. Our first face-to-face meeting was in a hotel room in Connecticut (amid much squealing), and after several days of trains, car rides, events, cocktails, and laughs, we became the best of friends.

Writing this novel has made us both long for a return to the handwritten word. It is only because of the permanency of the letters written during the war that we are able to understand so fully its impact on those who lived through it. Shortly after beginning, Hazel was given a packet of letters written from her great-grandmother to her son, Jack, during WWII. The letters were returned, addressed "To Mother" after Jack went missing in action. He was never found and the family still don't know what happened to him. To have this piece of family history is amazing, and to see the outpouring of emotion and the little snippets of daily life at that time is truly something to be treasured.

Writing can often be a lonely process, so it was wonderful to share that process with someone else. This book was a challenge in so many ways, but a complete joy in so many others. And the best part? In writing "The End," we not only completed a book, but we also made an incredible friend along the way. ∾

Researching the Great War

Writing about an event as monumental as the Great War was a daunting prospect to say the least, but from the very start, we knew we wanted to portray the event through the eyes of a soldier at the Front, and a woman in England. In addition to writing about trench warfare—a rather well-known topic— we were also keen to explore some of the lesser known aspects of the war, such as the role of the press and propaganda in informing the British public, the importance of the postal service, the roles of women outside of nursing, the burgeoning psychological understanding of shellshock and PTSD, as well as the impact of the Spanish Flu epidemic, which killed more people than the war itself.

Perhaps one of the difficulties when writing about an event such as this is the sheer volume of material available. Where do you start, and where do you end? What do you leave out, and what do you include? There is an extraordinary amount of primary source material about the war, documented in—of course—the thousands and thousands of letters sent to and from the front, as well as in the legacy left behind in the photographs, poetry, and books that were written at the time. To have access to these first-hand accounts was so inspiring and moving and really helped us to get inside the minds of our characters.

Of particular help were Vera Brittain's *Testament of Youth, Letters from a Lost Generation: First World War letters of Vera Brittain and Four Friends*; *Letters from the Trenches* by Bill Lamin; *Letters and News from the Trenches and the Home Front* by Marie Clayton; *The Lengthening War: The Great War Diary of Mabel Goode* by Michael Goode; *The First World War Galleries* by Paul Cornish; and *War in Words* by Corporal Daniel W. Phillips.

The Imperial War Museum in London was also an incredible resource. Heather made a trip in hopes of seeing artifacts first-hand. Reverently, she wound through the museum, reading every plaque, taking extensive photographs and notes, and purchasing more books than her suitcase could carry. She has also visited several memorials in France.

For those left behind at home like Evie, the war was often presented in a different light from what actually took place in the field. For example, on the first day of the Battle of the Somme, there were 60,000 British casualties, yet the press reported the event as "a day of promise" and stated "things were going well for Britain and France." War propaganda became a matter of course in England as government departments attempted to control what the public saw. In fact, letters from the Front went through heavy censorship, making it difficult for anyone to truly know what ▶

was really going on. Often wartime causes this sort of repression of rights and upheaval, but WWI marked the first time in western history that it took place on such a large scale.

Womens' roles changed dramatically during the war as they took on the jobs left vacant by the men. In 1917, the Women's Army Auxiliary Corps (later named Queen Mary's Army Auxiliary Corps) was established to free up men from the administrative and supportive tasks to bolster numbers at the front. More than 57,000 women served in cookery, mechanical, clerical, and miscellaneous roles between January 1917 and the end of the war in November 1918. Evie's desire to write about the war was inspired by the few brave female journalists who did, indeed, get to the Front, most notably Nellie Bly, who reported from the Eastern Front for the New York Evening Journal. Novelist Mary Humphry Ward was also given a VIP "tour" of the Western Front as a guest of the War Office. Her subsequent account of what she witnessed, in the 1916 publication, *England's Effort,* was written at the express request of former U.S. President Roosevelt in order to encourage American involvement in the war.

One of the most poignant—and tragic—points we came across again and again in our research was how much the world hoped the Great War would be "the war to end all wars." History, as we know, tells us differently. In this centenary period, the Great War has returned to the forefront of our minds, and suddenly one hundred years doesn't seem so very long ago. Writing *Last Christmas in Paris* during this unique period of reflection and remembrance made the whole experience particularly poignant, and as historical writers we are very grateful to have been able to write this story now. ❧

Interesting Facts About the Great War

- 38 million soldiers and civilians died worldwide during the WWI conflict.

- French Intelligence read, sorted, and shipped 180,000 letters written by soldiers each week.

- Florence Marie Cass, a telephonist, was one of many female telegraphists and telephonists who received the MBE for displaying "great courage and devotion to duty" during the First World War.

- American writer Edith Wharton toured military hospitals on the Western Front and also visited battlefields like Verdun. Her fundraising for refugees earned her a decoration as Chevalier of the Legion of Honour in 1916.

- One third of the planet's population was infected during the Spanish flu epidemic coming in at roughly 500 million people.

- 140 million socks were delivered to British troops, as well as 50 million pairs of boots.

- 80,000 British women and more than 35,000 American and Canadian women worked as auxiliary nurses, ambulance drivers, cooks, telephone operators, clerks, and other miscellaneous positions during the war.

- To prevent from accruing blisters, soldiers urinated in their boots to soften them. Urine was also a good antiseptic that prevented trench foot.

- More than 95 percent of all soldiers in the trenches contracted lice.

- On the Western Front alone, 250,000 horses died in combat.

- More than 100,000 carrier pigeons were used to relay messages, and managed to reach their targets nine times out of ten. Parrots were kept in the Eiffel Tower to alert soldiers to approaching aircraft. They could spot planes before human lookouts.

- Official war photographers were instructed not to take highly disturbing photographs. The pictures that were considered too bleak were destroyed.

- Soldiers were prohibited from carrying any sort of camera to the front, though some disobeyed and took pictures with a VPK-Vest Pocket Kodak.

- Official British photographer Geoffrey Malins shot a film called *The Battle of the Somme*, which sold 20 million tickets in six weeks in 1916. ∽

Lord Kitchener's Guidance to British Troops

This paper is to be considered by each soldier as confidential, and to be kept in his Active Service Pay Book

You are ordered abroad as a soldier of the King to help our French comrades against the invasion of a common enemy.

You have to perform a task which will need your courage, your energy, your patience.

Remember that the honour of the British Army depends on your individual conduct. It will be your duty not only to set an example of discipline and perfect steadiness under fire but also to maintain the most friendly relations with those whom you are helping in this struggle.

The operations in which you are engaged will, for the most part, take place in a friendly country, and you can do your own country no better service than in showing yourself in France and Belgium in the true character of a British soldier.

Be invariably courteous, considerate and kind. Never do anything likely to injure or destroy property, and always look upon looting as a disgraceful act.

You are sure to meet a welcome and to be trusted; your conduct must justify that welcome and that trust. Your duty cannot be done unless your health is sound. So keep constantly on your guard against any excesses.

In this new experience you may find temptations both in wine and women. You must entirely resist both temptations, and, while treating all women with perfect courtesy, you should avoid any intimacy.

Do your duty bravely.

Fear God.

Honour the King.

Kitchener

Field-Marshal ⟿

A Note from Hazel to Heather

Dear Heather,

Thank you for being such an amazing woman, friend and writing partner. I will never forget the sense of anticipation when I opened our file each morning, eager to see what you'd added while I was sleeping! Your letters made me laugh and cry as our Tom and Evie jumped off the page and became real! I'm so proud of our book and feel so very lucky that I got to write it with you.

Much love, Hazel

x

A Note from Heather to Hazel

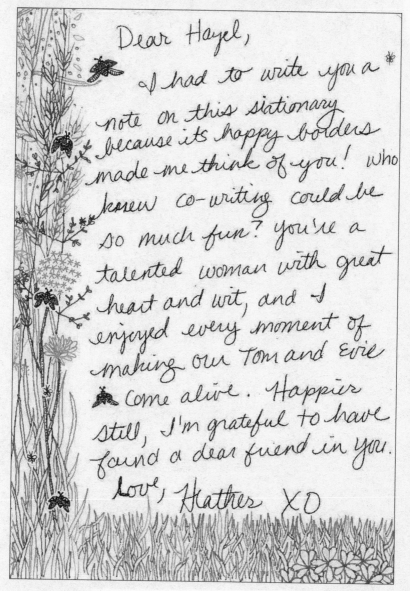

Dear Hazel,
    I had to write you a
note on this stationary
because its happy borders
made me think of you! who
knew co-writing could be
so much fun? you're a
talented woman with great
heart and wit, and I
enjoyed every moment of
making our Tom and Evie
come alive. Happier
still, I'm grateful to have
found a dear friend in you.
    Love, Heather XO

Discover great authors, exclusive offers, and more at hc.com.

WITHDRAWN

31901061060002